The Girlfriend Curse

Valerie Frankel

little
black
dress

Copyright © 2005 Valerie Frankel

Published by arrangement with AVON BOOKS
An imprint of HARPERCOLLINS PUBLISHERS, USA

The right of Valerie Frankel to be identified as the Author of
the Work has been asserted by her in accordance with the
Copyright, Designs and Patents Act 1988.

First published in 2005 by AVON BOOKS
An imprint of HARPERCOLLINS PUBLISHERS, USA

First published in Great Britain in 2008
by LITTLE BLACK DRESS
An imprint of HEADLINE PUBLISHING GROUP

A LITTLE BLACK DRESS paperback

1

ISBN 978 0 7553 4483 3

Typeset in Transit511BT by Avon DataSet Ltd,
Bidford-on-Avon, Warwickshire

Printed and bound in Great Britain by Clays Ltd, St Ives plc

Headline's policy is to use papers that are natural, renewable and
recyclable products and made from wood grown in sustainable forests.
The logging and manufacturing processes are expected to conform to the
environmental regulations of the country of origin.

HEADLINE PUBLISHING GROUP
An Hachette Livre UK Company
338 Euston Road
London NW1 3BH

www.littleblackdressbooks.com
www.headline.co.uk
www.hachettelivre.co.uk

Dedicated to the good people of Manshire, Vermont,
without whom this book could not have been possible.

Acknowledgments

A few shout-outs, in deserved boldface. First, to **Nancy Yost**, who has represented me for seven human years (in agent years, that's fifty-six). Despite this, she is still cheerful, sweet and funny . . . To **Carrie Feron**, who has toiled over four of my books to date. And, unlike some editors in book publishing (or so I hear), she actually edits, making suggestions that always turn into improvements, for which I am eternally grateful . . . To **Selina McLemore**, who is patience and sunshine on the phone whenever I call, and that is rare indeed in New York, and much appreciated by everyone she talks to, I'm sure . . . To **Pamela Spengler-Jaffee** and **Heather Gould**, who squeeze blood from stones daily. And they've got the buff forearms to prove it . . . Also to **Michael Morrison**, the man who says, 'Yes.' **Cokie Roberts** thanked him in her acknowledgments, and she's a woman we can all take example from. So, thanks for everything, Michael!

Peg Silver, thirty-two, could make a man come, but she couldn't make him stay. She'd just spent two hours bemoaning this problem to her friend Nina at dinner, parsing to the syllable what she'd like to say to her most recent ex-boyfriend, if such an unlikely opportunity presented itself.

The night's chosen scenario: Bumping Into Each Other by Chance. Peg would be in a glorious gown, on her way to the Oscars, a nominee for Best Set Design in a Major Motion Picture. As she stepped out of her limousine onto the red carpet, she'd spot Paul in the crowd, looking like he'd just been attacked by dogs. He'd congratulate her, beg her to take him back. She'd be gracious. Briefly pitying. But she had to rush, since her date, Johnny Depp, was waiting, and he was a very possessive man. Besides which, having just won the lottery ('The same day I got the nomination!'), she was flying to the Bahamas for a year as soon as the awards ceremony was over.

Peg smiled to herself as she unlocked her apartment door. She knew, rationally, that spending hours refining tone and nuance in a conversation that would never take place was a waste of time. But, she thought, a girl can dream, can't she? Peg dropped her purse on her bed. The phone rang. She grabbed the receiver.

'Hello?'

'Peg?'

She recognized his voice instantly. It was Paul. He'd Called Out of the Blue. Panicking, Peg clicked the off button, giving herself three seconds to scramble for a good opening line before he called back. Something breezy. Casual. All she could come up with was, 'You bastard, you ruined my life.'

The first time in three months she'd mindlessly answered the phone, the one time the ring hadn't unleashed the flood of Pavlovian pre-traumatic stress syndrome symptoms – tight chest, shaky hands, constricted breathing, skin flush to a capillary-popping red. She felt eerily calm, actually, now that the wait was over. The phone rang again. She took a deep breath.

'Hello?' she said, exhaling sexily.

'Peg, it's Paul. Something's wrong with your phone. I got cut off. And you sound nasal.'

'Paul! What a surprise. How long has it been? A month?' she asked.

'Over three, actually,' he said.

'That long?' she asked, as if marveling at the flight of time.

The morning of the breakup, he'd promised to call her that night. She never called him, not once, which was a show of strength that would fill her with dignity until the day she died. She had buckled a few times, sending him artfully terse and transparently neutral Just Checking In emails. Paul would respond a day later, a week later, with a few sentences – no caps or punctuation – if at all. Lazy, lying bastard. Peg should tell him to go fuck himself. She should make herself proud.

Paul said, 'I need to see you. Tonight.'

It was eight on a Thursday in April, unseasonably hot for springtime in New York City. 'Where's the fire?' she asked, having a pretty good idea where.

'I've been thinking about you constantly,' he said. 'I have things to say, face-to-face. I can't go another night without seeing you.'

This was where she was supposed to say, 'Johnny Depp is a very possessive man.' Instead, she said, 'Can't.'

'You have plans?'

'No.'

'Early day tomorrow?'

'No.'

'Making a show of strength that will fill you with dignity until the day you die?' he asked. He paused, and then said shortly, 'I hope you and your dignity will be very happy together. I'll let you go . . .'

That was it? No more pleading, spilling blood while screaming her name and tearing his shirt? She said, 'Giving up so easy? You've got a lot to learn about groveling.'

He said, 'Please see me. I'm begging. I'm supplicating.– wait, I need to find the thesaurus.'

'Meet me at Chez Chas in twenty minutes,' she said. 'And don't be late.' She'd waited long enough for him already.

Chez Chas was a bistro in the corner storefront of Peg's building on Grand Street in Soho. The restaurant had six tables and a tiny bar. Once featured in *New York* magazine as the smallest three-star restaurant in Manhattan, Chez Chas was, if not an A-list destination, a B+. Peg had never eaten there. They didn't take reservations, and it was impossible to get a table before five o'clock. But the bar – cramped, poorly stocked – usually had a vacancy. Peg had spent many cocktail hours at that bar, with a friend or a Chuck Palahniuk novel. *Fight Club* was a guaranteed male magnet; she met the boyfriend before Paul while reading it.

With a glance in her mirror – she hated her new bangs – Peg ran downstairs to the bistro. She wanted to get one drink in her before Paul showed up. Steady the nerves. The bar was in the rear of the bistro. She had to squeeze between tables, apologizing to diners as she jostled their chairs. She sat on a vacant stool, draping her jean jacket on the one to her left. The bartender was new; the bartender was always new. This month's model was, most definitely, a model. Lean and young, he had a chiseled chin, speckled with stubble, and perfectly chunky bangs.

Peg said to him, 'How do you get your bangs to behave? Hours of private training? Is there a School for Bangs I should know about?'

The bartender nodded, as if he didn't speak English. 'What can I get you?' he asked. No accent. Nor sense of humor.

Peg had had wine at dinner. 'Whiskey sour,' she said.

'Out of sour mix.'

'White Russian.'

'Out of milk.'

'Vodka martini?'

'Out of olives.'

'I'll take it.'

He said, 'As you wish.'

Peg found that oddly comforting. Receiving her cocktail, she checked her watch. Five minutes more. She sipped and examined the couples at dinner. The tables were set up for two. According to Zagat, Chez Chas was 'an ideal date destination.' Six couples had come for a night of French food and romantic ambience. A married couple in the corner (visible rings) talked loudly about an upcoming vacation. Another couple held hands across the table, gazing intensely at each other as if they were in a cult of two. Peg picked up her martini glass and drank her vodka.

They will do it tonight, she thought.

Ordinarily, a happy couple as such, in the shameless adoration of new love, would be too painful to behold. But tonight, Peg surveyed them with hope.

I will do it tonight, she thought.

Fuck caution. What was the point of denying herself? If Paul was sufficiently contrite, if he'd learned his lesson, mea culpaed and beat his chest, why shouldn't she bring him upstairs? Let him demonstrate his contrition by giving her a two-hour tongue bath?

Peg crossed her legs, her eyes drifting from the Moonie couple and settling on another pair. On the surface, they seemed made for each other. Same stylishness quotient, age, ethnic background. Same size head. But the stiff-backed tension and fidgety handling of forks told the very short story of their relationship: a first date that would not lead to a second.

Peg and Paul had had both the glassy-eyed attraction of the Moonies at table two as well as the superficial compatibility of the couple at table three. They'd practically lived together for a year. With centuries of time-honored tradition at her back, Peg wanted to take their relationship forward. To get married, have kids, talk excitedly in restaurants about upcoming vacations, like the couple at table one.

She unfurled her vision of their future on New Year's Day, the morning after their boozy crawl through Tribeca bars toasting to 2005 and each other. Despite the simplicity (the banality) of the idea, Paul was shocked by her suggestion, as if she'd asked him to commit murder for her, not commit to marriage with her. If that was what she truly wanted, he wouldn't stand in her way. She stood in his, begging him not to desert her on New Year's Day. Paul waited until the crack of dawn on January 2.

His call tonight, his 'I've got things to say, face-to-face' could mean only one thing: He'd changed his mind about marriage. Otherwise, why bother meeting at all?

'Another round?' asked the bartender. 'Same thing, or something different this time?'

Peg was stumped for an answer.

The door opened, street noise filtering into the room. Peg turned and saw Paul Tester framed in the doorway. He looked the same. Tall, confident, sloppy smile. Her months of loneliness, self-blame and anger instantly forgotten, Peg smiled as he made his way to her; each polished 'forgive me' as he squeezed between the tables seemed directed at her, not the diners. When he finally got to the bar, he put both arms around her waist and lifted her off of her stool in an embrace that emptied her lungs.

He said, 'You look gorgeous.'

She was still wearing her jeans and T-shirt from work. Not exactly the height of glamour. But Paul had always admired her low-key style. Little did he know that she agonized over her jeans choices, her T-shirts cost eighty dollars apiece, her skin tone was achieved with three types of foundation and she was forever laboring to add volume in her straight, nearly black hair.

'I like the bangs,' he said.

Peg said, 'I like the suit.' Black, three-button, brand-new.

'Picked it out myself,' he said.

She said, 'I'd like to see it on the floor of my bedroom.'

He frowned and said, 'Can we have a drink first? Catch up?'

He'd been in such a hurry to talk. Now he was stalling? He must be nervous, she thought. A glass of confidence would take care of that. He ordered a martini, and another for her.

He said, 'You must be working a lot.'

Her busiest time of year. 'I'm doing the atrium of the Condé Nast building.' Peg was an interior landscape designer, which was a fancy way to say indoor gardener.

Paul said, 'Bird of Paradise?'

She cringed. 'God, no. All tulips, all the time. Next week, apple branches. How about you?'

'Can't complain,' he said, chin out. Paul was a talent agent at CAA for animals. 'Doing a licensing deal for the winner of the Westminster Dog Show.'

'A poodle?' she asked. Wild guess.

'Mastiff,' he said. 'Stanley of Edinburgh. Oversized tartan collars, doggie coats and scarves.'

The bartender brought their olive-free drinks. Peg sipped quickly. Two minutes had been about enough catching up for her. She was ready to put the misery of the winter behind her.

Paul must have sensed her impatience. 'I want to apologize for the way I treated you when we broke up,' he dove in. 'It's been bothering me for a while. I never wanted to hurt you.'

'I never wanted you to hurt me either,' she said.

He smiled feebly. 'I was an idiot, Peg. You were devoted, loving, supportive. Everything I could have asked for, and more. But you blindsided me with the marriage talk. I was hungover. I couldn't make decisions in that condition. You looked at me like you would hate me if I said no. I couldn't give you the answer you wanted, and it didn't seem fair to string you along.'

She nodded vigorously. 'I told Nina that your dumping me was an act of sacrificial love.'

'What did she say?' he asked.

Peg said, 'She cursed your name and spit on the sidewalk.'

'Oh,' he said.

'You were saying how you broke up with me for my own good,' she prompted. 'How, at the time, marriage was repellent . . .'

'Right,' he said, pausing to drain his glass. 'Marriage *was* repellent then. But now, the idea of sharing a life, making a legal partnership, having children, teaching them values and growing together as a family seems like a grand idea. Otherwise, what are we doing? Killing time? Making money? For what? What's it all about, Peg? I'm not asking you to answer that. But I've been asking myself about this stuff from the moment we broke up. I really missed you that first month.'

'Just the first month?' she asked. For Peg, the earliest days weren't too horrific. She'd been through breakups before. Every woman in her thirties in New York had one or two dozen relationships that, in hindsight, were thought of as learning experiences. But as the weeks without Paul piled up, the loneliness grabbed Peg by the neck. The empty apartment, the zero messages on voice mail, the sexual frustration stretched taut, pushing her dangerously close to the excruciating snap of fortitude, the deadly fusing of insecurity and bitterness. Any woman who'd had her share of learning experiences can attest, the insecure/bitterness combo could suck the soul right out of you.

Paul said, 'You were the best thing that ever happened to me.'

She put her hand on his knee, eyes damp. She said, 'Do go on.'

'You showed me everything I know about how to be caring and supportive. It took a while for me to get it. But I have. For the first time, I'm ready to take the next step.'

Peg said, 'And the next step is?'

He said, 'Marriage, of course.'

He was beaming. His sloppy smile spread across his cheeks like melted butter. Peg said, 'I can't believe this is happening.'

'You've got magical transformative powers, Peg. I couldn't see it up close. I had to get distance.'

'Forest, trees, I understand completely,' said Peg. 'You are so fucking hot.'

She got off her stool and reached for him, lips ready to make up.

He held her back and said, 'There's someone I want you to meet.'

'Someone . . . okay,' she said. Was he referring to the shrink who'd helped him see the light? 'I'll meet anyone you want.'

'I mean now,' he said.

'Now, as in *now*?'

'I'll be right back.' He got up, maneuvered around the tables and dashed out of the restaurant.

What the hell was going on? she wondered, rightfully confused and a bit annoyed that he'd bring another person into the privacy of their reunion. This was a party for two, and Peg had no idea who else Paul would want to invite.

Peg watched the door, baffled. The bartender said, 'Is your friend coming back?'

'I think so.' It wasn't possible that he'd run out on her again, was it?

'He owes me for the drinks.'

Reaching into her pants pocket, Peg found a twenty and put it on the bar. She said, 'Did you hear all that?'

'What?'

'He said he wanted to get married, and then ran out.'

The bartender shrugged. 'Do you want another martini?'

Peg said, 'You are the worst bartender in New York. You're supposed to eavesdrop on people's conversations and then, if asked, be ready to offer intelligent and insightful advice.'

The aspiring model said, 'Do you want another drink or not?'

'I'm good, thanks,' Peg said.

Paul reentered the bar. He was tugging a woman by the wrist. She was in her mid-thirties, wearing a skirt suit plucked off the racks of Strawberry's. Tan hose, white shoes, chunky gold jewelry. Her hair was a blond bubble, blown high and dry. Overdone makeup. Ten pounds overweight.

They pushed their way to the bar. Paul said, 'Peg, this is Bethany Bridge.'

Peg greeted her, looking to Paul for further explanation.

Bethany said, 'So you're the woman who transformed Paul.'

'I am?' asked Peg.

Paul and Bethany laughed merrily at her bafflement. Bethany said, 'You're the one who made him want to get married.'

Paul said, 'I met Bethany two months ago at a trade show.' He turned toward the blonde at his side, flashing her a Moonie smile. Bethany returned it, kissed him on the cheek, then wiped away the smear of orange-red lipstick with her thumb.

Bethany said, 'We've been inseparable ever since. We're going to be married in June. But I insisted that before we plan the wedding, Paul had to thank you for what you've done.'

Paul said, 'Thank you, Peg.'

Peg said, 'You're welcome?'

Bethany said, 'Don't be so modest, Peg. Paul said that if it weren't for you, he'd never have been ready to take the next step.'

'I am ready, Bethany,' he said.

'Oh, baby,' she said.

And then they kissed, open mouths. Drool.

Peg dearly wished their next step was off a cliff. Mustering her dignity (which she'd be proud of until the day she died), Peg said, 'I think I'm going to be sick.' She gathered her jacket and bag and stood to flee.

Bethany put a hand on her shoulder. 'I was hoping you would arrange the bouquets at my wedding. Paul says you're a gifted florist.'

'I'm not a florist,' said Peg. 'I'm an interior landscape designer.'

'But you can do bouquets?'

'I'm on an extended vacation,' said Peg.

'You just said you were working at Condé Nast,' said Paul.

'When my schedule clears, I'm going out of town. For weeks. Maybe months. I'm going to the Bahamas. The thing is,' she said, 'I won the lottery.'

Bethany clapped her hands and said, 'Congratulations!'

'Thanks,' said Peg.

'I'm glad Paul cleared the books with you,' said Bethany.

'If only he'd swept the ashes,' Peg said, giving him a mournful look.

'Swept the ashes?' asked Bethany.

'If only he'd fucked me one more time.'

Bethany's rubbery lips formed a red-rimmed O. Paul laughed nervously and said, 'She's kidding, honey. I told you, Peg has a bizarre sense of humor.'

The future Mrs Paul Tester patted Peg on the shoulder and sang, 'Good luck with the rest of your life!' Then she herded Paul out of the Chez Chas.

The bartender put a fresh martini in front of her, and said, 'On the house.'

Peg said, 'You might have a future in bartending after all.'

Ordinarily, if a man described a woman as 'magical,' 'transformative,' possessing 'powers' that inspired him to marry, said woman would feel blessed.

Peg Silver felt cursed. Cursed with a titanic hangover. After her free cocktail at Chez Chas last night, she had had another and yet another to guarantee instant pass-out when she hauled herself to bed. It was now ten o'clock, and she had a full-frontal-lobe throb. Plus, she was late for work, and late to call in sick. When she groped her way to the bathroom to force down Tylenol, she had to confront the horror in the mirror. Crushing disappointment, humiliation and alcohol had taken their toll, making her ordinarily olive skin as white as paste.

One glance, and she'd seen enough. Peg called work.

Her boss, Rica Costaporta, answered, 'Georgia Designs.'

'Rica, it's Peg' – cough. 'Remember a few years ago, that insane homeless man who threw bricks at random people in Times Square?'

'Upper West Side,' corrected Rica. 'The Times Square guy stuck women with syringes.'

'You're right,' said Peg. 'My point is' – cough – 'I've been struck. As if by a brick. With a cold.' Even in her addled brain, Peg thought she sounded convincingly ill.

'I gathered from the coughing,' said Rica.

'Take pity on me,' said Peg, wishing she could tell Rica the real cause of her pathetic condition.

'Stay home and rest,' said her forgiving boss. 'Speedy recovery.'

Peg hung up, and wondered if a speedy recovery were possible for a hollowness in all four chambers of the heart. She crawled back into bed and slept for another couple of hours, having unsettling dreams about pushing a cart uphill. The cart was loaded with tulips and apple branches. And mastiffs in tartan skirts. With chunky bangs.

Around noon, she called Nina Pelham, thirty-one, confidante and former neighbor. Nina was Peg's day-to-day friend, with evening phone calls, weekly dinners and weekend brunches. The only time in ten years that they'd been on the outs was during the ugly breakup of Nina and Peg's brother, Jack. Peg had discouraged their affair from the beginning, but tolerated it for two months. When Jack pulled the plug, Nina let some of her anger trickle onto Peg. That was five years ago. All had been forgiven – if not forgotten.

Peg and Nina didn't bore each other with the stories about their professional lives. Their exchanges were exclusively of a spiritual nature, as in, 'Dear lord, let this guy be the one,' or 'That man is the devil incarnate,' or 'He's broke, but he fucks like a god.' Nina had been freshly dumped by Gary, her boyfriend of three months. He'd taken her to his sister's wedding at the Palace Hotel, had her sit next to his great-grandmother, asked her to dance with his thirteen-year-old hormonal nephew, and then, minutes after the cake-cutting, Gary ended it because, he said, Nina 'wasn't enjoying his family.'

'God, I beseech you,' Nina had prayed at dinner with Peg last night. 'Smite Gary.'

This afternoon, when Nina answered her work phone (she was the head of publicity at Goldenface Cosmetics), Peg moaned, whimpered and sobbed softly.

Nina said, 'It's either an obscene call from a masochist, or Peg.'

'I am a masochist,' said Peg. 'I attract sadists.'

'This is about Paul?' asked Nina.

'Who else? He Called Out of the Blue—'

'You hate Out of the Blue.'

'He begged me to see him right away,' Peg sniffed. 'So I had a drink with him at Chez Chas. It was a disaster. The emotional equivalent of an entire village of innocents gunned down with assault rifles.'

'But you had a speech,' said Nina. 'You didn't give it to him?'

'Not a word,' said Peg. 'Not a syllable.'

Nina said, 'I can come over after work. I'll bring apricot and almond body scrub.'

Peg said, 'Body scrub can't save me this time.'

'I'll throw in a tube of aloe emollient with crushed pearl.'

Four ounces of the stuff went for $200 retail. 'You are too, too kind,' said Peg, meaning it.

'For this quality care package,' said Nina, 'you'd better be writhing in agony when I get there.'

'Nina, he's engaged,' said Peg, a hitch in her throat. 'He met someone else.'

'God smite!' said Nina. 'I'll be there in three hours.'

*

She took four. But she brought Greek salads and soulvaki along with the body scrub and moisturizer, so Peg couldn't complain. The two women sat on Peg's king-sized mattress to eat. Peg gave Nina the blow-by-blow. Nina was an active listener, nodding, gasping, occasional shrieks of horror, eyes sharp and focused.

'So then, after they told me how much they worshipped each other,' said Peg, pacing now at the foot of the bed, 'they kissed. Right in front of me.' She paused, then asked, 'When Paul and I kissed in public, did we look disgusting?'

Nina asked, 'Disgusting how?'

'Unsavory show of tongue. Errant saliva.'

'No,' said Nina. 'You and Paul were very neat.'

Peg was both relieved and disappointed to hear it. In private, they'd been unsightly. 'When Paul and Bethany kissed, they were the only people in the world,' she said. 'Everyone in the restaurant stared at them. In their private moment, they became public property. And I couldn't help thinking, even while they slurped revoltingly, that they looked sweet. You could feel the love in the room. Palpable waves.'

'That sounds awful,' said Nina.

It was. 'For half a second, I actually felt happy for them,' admitted Peg. 'Then I crashed back to reality and wished them dead.'

'If I saw Gary making out with another woman, I'd do more than wish him dead,' said Nina.

With her belly full and story told, Peg grew instantly sleepy, as if hit by a tranquilizer dart. She lay back on her bed, just missing the detritus of their picnic, and closed her eyes. The comfort of a trusted friend was lulling. She let herself drift.

As if in a tunnel, Peg heard Nina clearing the bed of foil, containers and trash. Through the web of near-unconsciousness, Peg heard the echo of Nina's voice.

'Didn't Bart get engaged, too?' she asked.

That woke Peg up. Bart was her ex before Paul. 'Impossible. He equated marriage with purgatory,' said Peg.

Nina said, 'I could swear I heard that Bart got engaged soon after your spectacular breakup.'

'To whom?'

'Some moronic slut, I'm sure,' said Nina comfortingly. 'And Harry, too. I'm positive about that one, but I kept it from you. For your emotional protection. He married the friend-of-a-friend who brought him to my party. The night you two, you know.'

'The process server?' asked Peg. 'I hope she serves him right.'

'I hate to say this,' said Nina, 'but a pattern seems to be emerging.'

'Wouldn't it be scary if all of my exes got married after dumping me?' Peg asked.

Nina said, 'It couldn't be possible.'

'Not in a million years.'

The women stared at each other for a beat of ten. Nina broke the silence and said, 'Maybe we better make sure. For your psychic well-being.'

'My psyche could use a weekend at Canyon Ranch,' agreed Peg. 'But how to begin? We'd have to track them down, ask them intimate questions. I haven't spoken to some of them in years.'

'How intimate is it to ask someone if and when they got married?' asked Nina. 'It's not like asking if they've had warts removed.'

'True,' said Peg. 'But how would we find them?'

Peg had lost track of her exes, purposefully. Breakups were too demoralizing for her to stay in touch. Usually, she had a no-contact policy. Made a clean break. The sole exception to her policy had been Paul, and look what relaxing her rules had wrought.

Nina said, 'I can find them.'

'This does present an interesting challenge for your networking skills,' said Peg. 'But even you might not be able to pull out this rabbit.'

'Ye of little faith,' said Nina. 'Make a list. Last known address, phone numbers, whatever you've got.'

'You know I don't keep anything. I rip the page out of my address book, delete email history, erase phone numbers from speed dial. I've got nothing.'

Nina nodded. 'Doesn't it say in women's magazines that staying on good terms with your ex is a sign of maturity?'

'Women's magazines also advise you to lick your boyfriend's asshole,' said Peg.

Nina found a pad in Peg's night table and said, 'Just write down whatever you can remember.'

Pen in hand, Peg made a list of her exes, starting with the most recent. She wrote:

1. **Paul Tester.** Status known: the bastard who ruined my life.
2. **Bart Oldman.** Last seen in October 2003, sneaking out of my apartment at 3 A.M. with a garbage bag full of his clothes and a dozen applications for law schools in California. No known address, since he mooched off me for six months before vanishing in the night. Employer at the time: Chez Chas. Waiter.

3. **Harry Slolem.** Last seen in February 2002 at a Valentine's Day party at your house. I gave him a card that said, 'I'm Yours.' He read it and said, 'I'm not.' Last known address: 61st and Second. Employer: Paint It Black Contracting.

4. **Ed Teller.** Last seen in May 2000 outside the Chelsea Cinemas. We saw *Miss Congeniality*. I adored it, and he said, 'I can't commit to a woman who likes Sandra Bullock.' Last known address: Broadway and 26th. Employer: None. Collage artist. Showed a couple of times at the Luna Gallery on Spring Street.

5. **Oleg Caspiroff.** Last seen in September 1999 at his apartment, paying me for landscaping his roof deck. He handed me the check, and thanked me for services. I said, 'I'll come back later for dinner.' He said, '*All* of your services are no longer required.' Last known address: 875 Park Avenue, penthouse. Employer: Harry Wilson Jewelers.

6. **Daniel O'Leery.** Last seen in 1997 (winter? late fall?) at 2 A.M., crying into a shot of tequila while apologizing for his complete inadequacy as a man, an actor, a human being – and a boyfriend. Last known address: First Street and Avenue A. Employer: free-lance voice-over actor for cartoon characters.

Unlucky 7. **Serge Shapiro.** Last seen in April 1996, up to his elbows in fertilizer while we planted beds side by side along the Brooklyn Heights Promenade. He said, to explain his reluctance to marry, 'I love you, Peg. I also love Frosted Flakes. It's just not realistic to think I'll love either one of you forever.' Last known address: Cobble Hill, Brooklyn (forget the street names). Employer: New York City Parks Department.

Nina perused the list. She said, 'Jesus, Oleg. He was gorgeous, rich. I always had a crush on him.'

'This could be your big chance. Imagine the meet-cuteness of it. Girl calls friend's ex to find out if he jilted friend to marry a lesser woman and, upon finding out that he's single and far advanced emotionally, they fall hopelessly in love.'

'Would you have a problem with that?' said Nina.

'Oleg likes to bite,' said Peg. 'Hard.'

'That's a bad thing?' asked Nina.

Every inch a publicist, Nina jump-started her cell phone like a chain saw.

Peg said, 'You're seriously going to do this?'

'Watch me.'

'It'll probably take months.'

'Give me one hour.'

'Peg, you haven't changed a bit,' said Violet Masterson, sixty-seven, Nina's assistant at Goldenface Cosmetics.

'I saw you last Wednesday,' said Peg, leaning a hip on Violet's desk, eyeing the closed door of Nina's office. It was Tuesday evening. Peg had just finished work, and come directly to Nina's Union Square office, as she'd been instructed.

'You need to trim those bangs, dear,' said Violet. The older woman had been with Nina for five years, and an employee at Goldenface since the company was founded. She was a natural for the publicity department. Decades of using Goldenface cosmetics had left Violet with the complexion of a thirty-five-year-old. Violet was the one who hadn't changed a bit. Not since 1960.

Violet turned her barely lined mouth into a smile and said, 'I've been working with the investigator Nina hired. I must say, you've dated some interesting and successful men. I'm sorry none of them worked out.'

Peg said, 'You must have tracked down the wrong bunch of guys.'

'We got the right ones,' said Violet. 'They all spoke very highly of you. They called you pivotal in their lives.'

Pivotal now. 'They weren't pivotal for me,' Peg said.

'Just one after the other, a conga line of bad choices.'

'Maybe the next one will be right,' said Violet, with sugar on it. 'You can go in. They're waiting for you.'

Peg swallowed hard. She held her breath, and pushed open the door to Nina's office, bracing herself for the stench.

From behind her ornate mahogany desk with the hand-carved roses and vines, Nina said, 'Peg, right on time.' She pointed to a buxom redhead with pink cheeks in a plush armchair and said, 'This is Stacy Temple.'

Peg nodded at the woman. To Nina, she gasped, 'Suffocating. Can't breathe. Need air.'

Nina sighed. She got up and cracked a window. Nina was dressed, as usual, in a silk suit, this one the color of pale tangerines. Nina loved silk, and silk adored Nina, clinging to her bust, gliding across the flat landscape of her midsection and streaming down her long legs.

The redhead was just as striking, a Technicolor wonder in shiny Day-Glo pink knee-high boots, an orange denim jacket, a yellow ruffle skirt and a pomegranate vinyl tote in her lap. Peg, in her usual jeans, T-shirt and chocolate brown suede jacket felt like a drab mouse compared to these two peacocks.

Peg took a seat on the windowsill, and inhaled the city air. 'That's better, thanks,' she said.

'I'm so used to it, I forget it's there,' said Nina of the smell. So many of the Goldenface products were scented – rose, sandalwood, jasmine, lavender – and Nina had piles of samples in her closet, on the floor, on her desk. In small doses, the scents were calming and uplifting. Cumulatively, it was nauseating.

The redhead said, 'Shall I start?'

Nina said, 'Stacy runs a company called insearchof. com. For a fee, she can find anything.'

Stacy said, 'Usually things. First-edition books, vintage dresses, estate jewelry. My partner, Oliver Ashfield, does computer searches. I hunt in stores and I have a nationwide network of antique vendors on retainer.'

'And these antique vendors had my ex-boyfriends on a shelf?' asked Peg.

'People searches are done on the Internet. Oliver is highly skilled at information gathering. He can gain access to otherwise secure websites.'

'He's a hacker,' said Peg.

'Intelligence technician,' corrected Stacy.

'Seven men on the list,' said Peg, cutting to the chase. 'How many are married?'

'Six,' said Stacy, consulting her notes on a pink Lucite clipboard. 'Paul Tester is engaged to be married in June.'

'I don't suppose you found out when they got married?' asked Peg.

'On an average, within six months of breaking up with you,' said Stacy.

Peg stopped breathing for a second. 'Six months?'

'Daniel didn't until nine months later. But Oleg married a woman two months after your breakup. The rest were all five, six, seven months later. Regardless of how long it took, they all married the next woman they slept with.'

'I can't believe it,' said Peg, aghast.

'I have a flow chart here,' said Stacy, passing sheets of pink paper to Peg and Nina. 'I created it based on my interviews. Which, by the way, were endless. Every one of these guys would not shut up. They would say one thing, and then repeat it five times as if English were my second language.'

'I agreed to pay a flat fee,' said Nina. 'Not an hourly rate.'

Peg read the page.

One week post-breakup
Glad it's over.
Feeling of pressure gone.

Three weeks
Emotions now level, wonder what went wrong with Peg.

Six weeks
New course of self-reflection.
Thinks of Peg as catalyst.

Seven weeks
Wants to contact Peg, but sticks with her policy of no contact.

Eight weeks
Sees self-sacrifice of not calling a virtue.
Gets into idea of thinking of another's feelings.

Ten weeks
Hooked on new thoughtful nature.
Resolves to be a better person in all areas of life.

Twelve weeks
Serendipitously meets a new woman. Grateful for fresh start.

Fifteen weeks
New relationship going well. Sees it as a shot at redemption.

Twenty weeks
Engaged, happy.

Twenty-five weeks
Married. Content.

| Credits Peg for his changed-man status. | Thinks fondly of Peg. |

The paper shaking in her hand, Peg said, 'This can't be true of all of them.'

Stacy said, 'Bart is less grateful to you than the others. But he still owes you money. He says it's in the mail.'

'My no-contact policy has been my doom,' said Peg. 'If I let them call me, I might be married to one of them now.'

Nina's eyes were still scanning the chart. 'Not necessarily,' she said. 'Look at Paul. You were open to contact with him. And besides, if you got back together with any of them, they'd have been the same jerk who dumped you the first time. Being away from you is what changed them.'

'I guess this makes you the Accident Bridesmaid,' said Stacy.

'I've never been a bridesmaid, not once,' said Peg numbly.

'Then you're the Accidental Catalyst. The Accidental Watershed.'

'The Accidental Train Wreck?' said Peg. 'The Perpetual Girlfriend. The Chronic Girlfriend. I suffer from chronic girlfriend fatigue syndrome.'

'I'll tell you what you are: an excellent friend who deserves better,' said Nina. 'Besides that, you, Peg, are the Ultimate Girlfriend.'

'Ultimate, as in "last." Not ultimate, as in "best," ' said Peg.

'Why not both?' asked Nina.

'The Ultimate Girlfriend,' repeated Stacy. 'I like it. But I'm not married to it.'

'Don't say "married,"' moaned Peg.

'It's not all bad,' said Stacy. 'You've made a huge impact on the lives of seven men, their wives, their kids. If it weren't for you, ten children would not be alive today.'

'Ten children?' asked Peg. 'Not Oleg.'

Stacy consulted her notes. 'Twin girls, age two. Named Diamond and Pearl.'

Peg hopped off the windowsill and paced. If she could have, she'd have run in circles. 'You're right,' said Peg. 'I'm going to think positively about this. I have a dark gift. I'm a miracle cure for lame men. I should start a business. Date me for a year, dump me, never speak to me again, and within six months, you'll meet the woman of your dreams!'

'You'd make a fortune,' said Nina. 'I'd handle the PR.'

Stacy said, 'I thought you might want to talk to a few of these men yourself.' She handed Peg a bound pile of pink paper. Peg flipped through the mini dossier of her exes. Names, addresses, phone numbers, email addresses.

'Excellent idea. You should definitely talk to a few of them. Catharsis. Cleansing.' Nina said, 'At the very least, you can ask them if they have single friends to fix you up with.'

The redhead and Peg walked out of Goldenface together. By the time they got down the elevator and onto the street, it was raining. No surprise in April. It fit Peg's mood. She'd get a taxi, go home, crawl under her covers and never come out.

Stacy said, 'Can I have your card? I might be able to throw some business your way.'

Peg fished in her purse for a Georgia Designs card.

Stacy said, 'I do a lot of wedding searches. Finding antique gowns. Caterers. Florists.'

Anything but that. 'Look, Stacy,' said Peg, turning to face the redhead. 'I'm not a fucking florist, okay? I'm not going to weave roses in someone's chuppah or cut star lilies for her centerpiece. I'm an artist. I paint with organic materials. The day I design a corsage is the day I stick my head in an oven.'

Stacy's brown eyes widened, and then narrowed. Peg stared back at her, defiantly. She'd had enough injury for one day. She didn't need the insult, too. Calling her a florist was the last twig.

'This has been a pretty rough day for you,' said Stacy finally. She smiled at Peg, generously, her heart-shaped face softening with sympathy.

Peg stared into Stacy's eyes, the lashes long as spider legs. It was true: Peg was having a rough day, at the end of a rough decade. Stacy hadn't deserved the attack. Her show of kindness despite Peg's rudeness was rare in New York, rare anywhere. The unexpected sympathy from a stranger knocked something loose in Peg's defenses. She started to cry. Tears weighty and wide, bullet-shaped as they fell, lost in the river of rain on the sidewalk.

Two hours later, Stacy and Peg were drinking their fourth refill of coffee at the Greek diner on Broadway and 18th. Peg continued to snuffle and hiccup, the residual effects of a long, hard sob.

Stacy said, 'I didn't think I'd ever get married, or want to, but then I met Oliver and he loved my antique purse collection. How could I resist?'

Peg said, 'You're married to your business partner?'

'We live in my apartment and work out of his. We're neighbors. That's how we met.'

'It won't happen for me that way,' moaned Peg. 'I'm beginning to believe it won't happen for me ever. I may be one of those women who stays single.'

They were both silenced by that depressing statement.

But only briefly. 'What are you searching for?' asked Stacy suddenly.

'Love. Happiness. Joy.'

'I can't find those on Google,' said Stacy. 'Give me something I can get online or in a store. I'll run an object search for you. Anything. Maybe a toy from childhood? Something nostalgic?'

Peg considered this. What she missed from childhood was a feeling, not an object. The feeling that she fit – perfectly, if not harmoniously – with her parents and brother in their West 86th apartment. Although she'd lived at the Grand Street one-bedroom for ten years, Peg wouldn't call it home. At seven-hundred square feet, the place felt too big for one person, hanging on her like a baggy, itchy sweater. But at the same time, it was suffocating, lacking the sunlight for her to breathe and grow.

'I'm shriveling on the vine here,' said Peg. 'I have been for years.'

'Maybe you're a square,' said Stacy.

'Maybe you're a fashion victim,' countered Peg.

'I'm definitely that,' said Stacy. 'I meant, maybe you're a square peg, Peg. And New York City is a round hole.'

'I could never leave,' said Peg, signaling the waiter for the check.

'I'm thinking of leaving New York,' said Peg. She sat at her parents' Indonesian teak dining-room table. She'd come uptown to West 86th Street for Jack's thirtieth birthday dinner.

Pru Silver, Peg's mom, a real estate lawyer, said, 'Very funny. Eat your chicken.'

Peg dropped her fork on the plate. 'Things aren't working for me here. I'm a square peg. I need a square hole. New York is a round hole,' she explained.

'It's definitely a hole,' said Jack.

'A whole universe of opportunity!' said Otto, Peg's dad, a tax attorney. 'That's so corny. Forgive me.'

'Peg, tell us more about how square you are,' said Jack.

Jack was fifty pounds heavier and six inches taller than Peg. But he'd always be her bratty little brother. Whenever she came uptown to the apartment she grew up in, try as she might to resist, she couldn't ward off the slide of regression. One foot outside the apartment, Peg was an independent thirty-two-year-old woman. One foot inside, she was a petulant, angst-ridden teenager.

Peg said, 'At least I'm not a loser who spends my thirtieth birthday with my parents.'

Jack said, 'It's a small price to pay for free housing.'

Her brother still lived at home. He was one of those New York men. No rent to pay, so he was flush with cash to spend on clothes and shows. No laundry to do, nor dishes to wash, nor meals to prepare, he was rich with time to stay in shape. Therefore, Jack had his pick of girlfriends, who managed to overlook or ignore his living arrangement. Nina, prime example, actually believed that Jack was perpetually on the verge of moving out. He hadn't for eight years.

Pru said, 'Your brother is not a loser,' as she started clearing plates.

Otto, on cue, rose from his chair. 'Your mother's not a waitress, kids,' he said, which he'd been saying since Peg was seven. He followed his wife out of the dining room and into the kitchen, arms laden with plates.

Peg and Jack remained seated. She said, 'I'm not getting out of this chair until someone takes me seriously.'

'Mom,' said Jack. 'Peg's not helping.'

'Where's Stephanie tonight?' she asked him. Stephanie was Jack's latest. She fit his type perfectly: light-years ahead of him, but willing to stoop to his level out of desperation.

'She's waiting in the lobby,' whispered Jack.

'You're making her wait in the lobby?' asked Peg. 'You are truly a pig.'

'If she comes up, we'll never get out of here.'

Jack and Stephanie had been together nearly a year. They met at Citibank corporate headquarters, where they arranged mortgages and home equity loans for the Private Bank clients (net worth in excess of $1,000,000). Stephanie had her own place in Murray Hill, a roomy, sunny studio, close to work, that could be converted into a one-bedroom. She wanted Jack to move in. He was reluctant to ditch the comforts of home.

Peg said, 'Stephanie should have dumped you months ago.'

'She won't,' he said. 'She loves me.'

'I'm buzzing the lobby,' said Pru, who had, apparently, heard every word of this conversation from the kitchen. 'She shouldn't be sitting down there with Carlos. He's flirtatious.'

'Don't,' said Jack, standing up. 'I'm on the way out.'

'But I made cake,' said Pru. 'I'm sure Stephanie would love to have some.'

'Stephanie doesn't eat cake,' said Jack.

'She'll eat *this* cake,' said Pru. 'I don't care how embarrassed you are of us. It's dangerous to leave that girl in the lobby. I'm ashamed of you.'

Otto said, 'Is she afraid of us, Jack? You never bring her home. We respect your privacy. What goes on in your room is your business.'

Peg listened as her family hashed over the logistics of Jack's personal life. As usual, their discussion had nothing to do with her. It was Jack's world, this apartment. They indulged him like the Sultan of Brunei. It'd been this way since Jack was ten, when he fractured both legs in a Little League football game. Peg, then twelve, witnessed the incident. Jack took a hit, went flying and landed funny on the field in Central Park. Pru ran after the kid who did the hit. 'He's an animal! He should be put on a leash or locked up!' she screamed at the tackler's parents, who were horrified by the accident. Otto moaned for his son and himself, saying, 'He inherited my non-athleticism! Why oh why couldn't I have been more coordinated?' The ambulance came.

Jack had to stay in traction for eight weeks. Pru and Otto took care of his every need, and hadn't stopped yet, despite his complete recovery and seamlessly healed bones. Jack, who'd gone to Middlebury, had been a ranked amateur snowboarder in his college years.

Peg got the attention she needed growing up. Certainly not more than she needed. She might have wanted more, but she wisely adjusted her needs to meet the available resources. After a while, she'd adjusted so well that she started to bristle if anyone paid more-than-enough attention to her, especially teachers and pushy female friends. She liked arm's length. A comfortable distance.

Hence, her choice of profession, her one day-to-day friend, her flight from West 86th Street at the earliest opportunity. The day after graduation from NYU, Peg went real estate shopping with Pru. They saw the Grand Street apartment on the second day, and made an offer. Pru represented her in the $100,000 purchase (down payment provided by Otto). This was ten years ago. Peg had reimbursed Otto in full. The apartment was hers. It was Peg's only investment, her only nest egg. She wasn't sure what it was worth now – probably double what she'd paid. Peg often fantasized about selling it and living off the capital gains in some rural setting where she could plant acres and acres of property and nurture her landscaping for decades. Nurture her soul, too.

Peg broke into her family's argument, saying, 'New York has infertile soil.'

'What does that have to do with Stephanie?' asked Pru.

'Mom, listen to me,' said Peg. 'Did you piss off some gypsy, or screw a witch out of an apartment? To your knowledge, has anyone ever cursed you and your children to a life of solitude?'

'I did have a client once from Romania,' said Pru. 'He sounded exactly like Bela Lugosi.'

'How can you feel cursed to a life of solitude when you have a family who loves and supports you?' asked Otto.

'Corny,' said Peg.

'My curse,' said Otto.

'Happy birthday, Jack. I wish you many more years of arrested development.' She air-kissed around, and headed for the front door.

'Send Stephanie up,' said Pru.

'I will,' said Peg.

Otto said, 'You weren't serious before. About leaving New York?'

Peg shook her head. New York was all she'd ever known. Except for family vacations to Europe and the Caribbean, and the occasional weekend in New England, Peg had barely left the island of Manhattan. For good or ill, New York was her home. The idea of moving was a mental exercise, a fantasy.

Peg said, 'I could never leave.'

5

On her knees, Peg clipped an apple branch to the size of a pencil. Her walkie-talkie squawked at her hip. She pushed the talk button. 'The Condé Nast people want azalea topiaries now, in the shape of hourglasses.' It was Rica – her boss at Georgia Designs, named after Georgia O'Keeffe, who painted flowers that looked like vulvas.

Peg said, 'I'm doing apple blossoms.'

Squawk. 'They'll pay double for azalea topiaries by next week.'

'But the waste,' said Peg. Apple branches had to die for this?

Squawk. 'They must think money grows on trees,' said Rica, a woman who wasted nothing, not a bud, nor a blade of grass. 'Aren't we lucky to know better?'

Peg didn't feel lucky. She felt alien. She glanced around at the people in the lobby at Condé Nast – at the perfectly turned-out, immaculately groomed staffers from *Vogue* and *GQ* – they could have been from another planet, where Botox was the food of life. All of the gleaming human hangers had demanding bosses, stretch mortgages, weekend functions, gym memberships, offices to report to every morning. Just like Nina. And Jack. Like ninety per cent of New Yorkers Peg's age.

Peg couldn't relate. She assiduously avoided those trappings. As full of scorn as she was for the nine-to-nine lifestyle, Peg envied the confidence and purpose of these women as they clicked by in their heels. They had an air of being exactly where they wanted to be, latte-carrying members of a liberties union Peg would never belong to. Or want to.

Peg resumed her work on the current arrays, making them beautiful even though they'd be trashed just as the buds started to flower. Peg couldn't help drawing the comparison to the boyfriends who'd thrown her away just as she was hitting her prime, and then replacing her with bubble blonde hourglass-shaped topiaries.

Back in her apartment after work, Peg's eyes and thoughts were drawn to the dossier on the night table. The pink pages screamed 'Read me and weep.' It'd been two days since Stacy Temple handed the hot sheets to Peg. She would read them tonight, by gum. Nothing would stop her. She'd face her fears, and her past.

But first, Peg stripped, re-dressed in running clothes. While lacing her New Balances tight, she asked herself, 'After two days of putting it off, what's one more hour?' She left her apartment, and hit the ground running.

Or jogging, if one wanted to get technical about it. Peg's pace was in the eleven- to twelve-minute mile range. She could do ten when she was desperate for a distraction, like right now (more pain, less brain). Her legs churned relentlessly as she tooled across Canal Street toward the Hudson River Park.

A man ran up behind her. She could hear him breathing before she saw him. He whizzed past her in the New York version of 'eat my dust' (or 'suck my soot').

Usually, Peg didn't care about show-offism. For her, running wasn't a race. It was a *raison*. But today, she felt the blood-rush of disdain, and sent knives with her eyes into Speedy's ass.

Face red, knees aching, muscles crying, Peg pounded along the tulip path, toward Chelsea Piers and the two-mile mark, looking across the Hudson River at New Jersey. She started to loosen up, emotionally, too, as if jogging miles justified her consumption of oxygen, as if physical exertion were the way to pay rent for being alive.

A female jogger ran toward her. She was huffing and puffing, way out of shape. They acknowledged each other as they ran by, not smiling exactly, just a half-second of eye contact. Peg wondered if Huff Puff was freshly out of a relationship. Peg had a tendency to slack off on the thrice-weekly run when in the early stages of a new love. When the relationship ended, she'd be right back out here, burning off her sexual frustration, one step at a time. Peg appreciated the irony of it: She was in excellent shape when she had no one to admire her freakishly overdeveloped calf muscles. Peg admired them herself, standing with her back to a full-length mirror, on her tiptoes to make the muscles pop. She would think, I don't have love, but at least I have these.

A tiny dog now, on a leash, running alongside an older man on Rollerblades. As he rolled by, his eyes locked on the movement under Peg's sports bra. Fact is, no amount of Lycra in the world would keep her size 36Bs in place. She had bounce. And, often, nipple burn. Peg fixed Band-Aids over her nipples for long runs. Peg flashed back to her longest run, two summers ago, on vacation with Bart in the tiny town of Manshire, Vermont (population 2,367). She'd gone thirteen miles, a half-marathon. It took two-and-a-half hours. All that chafing caused the band of her sports bra to cut horizontal, long gashes on the underside of her breasts. When she'd limped back to the B&B, she found Bart on a hammock under a pine tree, a beer resting on his belly.

He'd asked, 'Was it the thrill of victory, or the agony of defeat?'

Peg said, 'The agony of victory.' Along with the sports bra injury, her legs were shot. She was sunburned and dehydrated.

Bart, who avoided exercise like employment, said, 'You need to figure out what you're running from, Peg.'

'I'm not running from anything,' Peg said. 'I think of it as, "What am I running toward?"'

Bart took a slug of beer and replied, 'Toward the hospital for emergency knee surgery.'

How he loved his own jokes, Peg remembered, as she trudged up to the field house at the Chelsea Piers and turned around for the return portion of the run. The way back was always easier. She made that her mantra as she ran. Back home. Back to the dossier. Back to the men of her past, so that she might have a future.

Daniel O'Leery
Married: March 1998
Wife: Millie Walsh, vice president of development at Viacom
Children: Walter (aka Wally), eighteen months
Address/phone: 322 East 19th Street; 212–555–7896
Profession: Voice of Larry the Lemming, Stumpy
              the Weasel and Cyril the Sloth for

animated series *SandStan PottyPants*
on Nickelodeon Network

Peg said to herself, 'A lemming, a weasel and a sloth. Perfect for Daniel.' She sat at her kitchen table, freshly showered, a towel twisted in her hair, the dossier of exes open before her. She read on.

Reason for breaking up with Peg (verbatim): 'When we first started dating, I fell in love with Peg instantly. Her kindness and generosity were irresistible. But she brought out the worst in me. For one thing, she drank too much. I had to keep up with her. Consuming so much alcohol gave me unsettling psychological symptoms. I blamed myself for everything – bad weather, the stock market crash, dishes in the sink, my failure as an actor and a man. I had crying jags about a delayed pizza delivery. It was pathetic.'

Peg said, '*He* had to keep up with *me*?' For every sip of wine she had, he'd thrown back two shots of tequila. She'd never spent as much time in bars before or since her relationship with him. And the dishes in the sink *were* his fault, she thought.

When did you realize the relationship was over? (verbatim): 'After six months, Peg started acting strangely. She'd clean the apartment, pay all the bills. She wore lingerie constantly, and developed a candle fetish. She gave me daily blow jobs; all of it, she said, to make me happy. But the more she did for me, the unhappier I felt. I sank into helplessness and depression. I think my mental paralysis made her feel superior. She was a classic enabler. Peg made it easy for me to be a failure. If I hadn't ended the relationship, she would have ruined me. I didn't want to break up, I had to. And I was miserable about it. I cried for a week after.'

So he told Stacy about the hummers, Peg thought, vaguely embarrassed. Every morning, before she left for work, Peg brought Daniel a cup of coffee and gave him head. And still he dumped her! Apparently, that was *why* he dumped her. She hadn't realized that daily blow jobs were the cause of their undoing. Daniel had clearly had some therapy since she'd known him (to wit, 'mental paralysis,' 'enabler'), but not nearly enough. Soggy bastard. Good riddance. She flipped to another page in the dossier.

Ed Teller
Married: November 2000
Wife: Stacia Oslowski, a ballerina for the ABT
Children: Petra, three; Anya, one
Address/phone: 85 Mercer Street; 212–555–2453

Mere blocks away, thought Peg. A jolt of nerves up her spine, she imagined running into him on Grand Street, how awful that would be. He'd say, 'You haven't changed a bit,' while he stood there with his neat little family. Maybe that wasn't such a flattering line after all. Maybe it was just flat.

Profession: Collage artist, on retainer with the
               Stanislov Gallery, East 57th Street

Reason for breaking up with Peg: 'Peg and I fell in love almost instantly. We had incredible passion. But Peg did not stimulate me intellectually. She didn't understand my art, nor my obsession with it. As a man, I'm driven to make my mark on the world. My art is the way I can leave a trace of my existence behind when I die. Peg didn't care about that, didn't understand me. She tried. Probably harder than most women would have bothered to. But taking her to art shows was like escorting a kindergartner to *Henry V*. And having to explain everything robbed me of enriching experiences. She just didn't get art. Very frustrating.'

True, she thought. But who would 'get' why a piece of canvas pelted with raw egg and coffee grinds with the word 'soap' smeared in lipstick in the corner was worth $10,000? Or why a plastic sculpture of a penis with a big smiley face and false eyelashes was considered 'genius' by *Art Forum* magazine? She and Ed did have volcanic sex. He could go for hours, flipping her around the bed like a pancake. And he was loud. Moaning and grunting with each thrust like a sweaty tennis player.

When did you know the relationship was over?: 'After about six months, Peg attempted to paint in oils, a still life of a magnolia tree. It was ghastly. She wanted to discuss her progress. Get tips from me on style. I was torn between honesty and compassion. I lied to her. Told her it was brilliant. I hated myself for lying, and realized that a life with Peg would always be about compromise. In turn, I started to find her every word repulsive. I had to end it. I still found her attractive. Breaking up was a sacrifice. But she no longer inspired me. Except, you know, when fucking.'

Attractive yet repulsive. Perhaps Peg should have that engraved on her tombstone. He'd wanted a relationship to inspire him to greatness, and she'd wanted an inspiring, great relationship. She could see why they were doomed. Peg remembered, in the weeks after that breakup, smashing her magnolia tree painting. That had felt good. Why hadn't Peg picked up on Ed's conceit? Maybe the warning bells were drowned out by the grunts and moans, screaming his own name when he came. Prick bastard. Good riddance.

She turned the page.

Harry Slolem
Married: August 2002
Wife: Suzie Levitt, stay-home mom
Children: Moe, two; twins Larry and Curly, one

He'd named his kids Moe, Larry and Curly. This Suzie must be either the most acquiescent woman on the planet, or she was severely impaired, thought Peg.

Address/phone: 543 Court Street, Brooklyn;
              718-555-8512
Profession: Owner of Little Peanuts Clothing
              Store, 543 Court Street, Brooklyn

He worked and lived in the same building, the wife at home with three babies. Peg smiled to herself. When

Harry had ended it, he said he wanted to see the world, not be tied down.

Reason for breaking up with Peg: 'I loved Peg, even when I ended it. But I had to do it. She turned me into a freak. I developed a one-track mind. I used to be a contractor, and I'd pound nails and think of Peg. I'd use the power drill, and think of Peg. I'd polish wood and think of Peg. I guess it's fair to say that our relationship was sexually based.'

Peg scoffed at that. It might have been for Harry. Peg considered him the worst lover of the bunch. He fucked with the imagination of a hammer – a ball-peen hammer. He continued:

'Peg was my first long-term girlfriend, and she taught me some stuff. It was so exciting, I started thinking about sex 24/7. She turned me into a walking hard-on. I had an erection twenty hours a day.'

So this was her error? Granted, she could see how a perpetual erection might be painful. Embarrassing. Especially on a job site, with the other guys, pounding nails, power drilling, etc.

When did you know the relationship was over?: 'After about six months, I started fantasizing about every woman I saw. Making comments to women who walked by on the street. 'Nice ass.' 'Shake your tits.' 'Suck my cock.' I'd grab myself. I got really turned on when a woman would look at me with contempt. I started stalking girls on the subway. I'd follow them around the platform, stand too close to them on the train. I knew it was bad. I disgusted myself. And I blamed Peg. She brought out the worst in me. I had to get away from her. I started thinking about moving to Prague. But then I realized I could just break up with her instead. Three months of celibacy got my head on straight. And then I was fixed-up with my wife, who only fucks me once a week, on Saturday night. It's much better this way.'

Peg closed the dossier. She'd had no idea that Harry was a stalker pervert. Twisted bastard. Riddance, better than good.

Okay, she analyzed. Some common themes: (1) they all fell quickly, (2) six months had been the turning point, (3) the act of kindness, generosity and interest brought out the worst in them – or they blamed her for it, regardless if she was really to blame, and (4) each was better off without her. Peg thought of Stacy's explanation, that after they'd broken up with her, the guilt set in (blaming her for their own problems, she assumed), and the rebuilding of each man's romantic aspirations upon the foundation of Peg's own model of kindness, generosity and interest.

How did that work? She had to know. Having read their words, Peg did not want to speak to Ed again, and definitely not Harry. She might unleash his public masturbator tendencies. How had she missed that he was a freak? And then Peg came to common theme (5): She hadn't realized that Ed was a prick, that Harry was a fornicating sicko, that Daniel was a loser. She hadn't been paying much attention at all, had she? And yet, she'd given these men years of her life.

It was all so very depressing. Peg remembered one of Nina's little pick-me-ups: When feeling blue, call someone bluer. The idea was that his or her depression will make one feel superior. Exactly what Daniel had accused her of doing. She never thought she'd felt that way before. But she might as well see if it worked. Peg flipped through the dossier, found his number.

She dialed. One ring, two. And then, 'Hello?'

Peg said, 'Daniel? It's Peg Silver.'

Upon hearing her name, Daniel said, 'My God, Peg. Peg! I'm so glad you called. I hoped you would. I'm so touched to hear from you. I can't tell you . . . the emotions . . .'

And then the big pussy started blubbering. Peg held the phone away from her ear. She couldn't stand to listen. He might have gotten himself a wife and a job, but he still didn't have a grip.

Peg said, 'I can make a man cry in four words.'

Daniel said, 'I'm sorry, Peg. I've had these feelings about you for so long, and I've never gotten to express them. The release is . . . too much . . .'

Christ, not again. New blast of sobbing. Peg hoped she hadn't seemed as pathetic when she cried to Stacy Temple. Stacy had taken pity on her. She should do the same for Daniel. She really should.

She said, 'Daniel. Pull yourself together. We broke up a million years ago. Before sliced bread, and flush toilets. When dinosaurs ruled the Earth.'

'I can't remember the last time I cried like this,' he said.

'It was probably the last time we saw each other.'

'Hey, you're right!' he said. 'I guess hearing your voice was like pulling a trigger.'

On the gun she wished were pointed at her head. Peg decided suddenly that maybe she didn't need to have this conversation after all. She would go back to blissful ignorance. Peg said, 'Listen, I'm glad we finally reconnected. I've got a kettle on. The buzzer just rang. My bathtub is running over.'

'Don't hang up!' he said. 'Give me ten minutes!'

She sighed and said, 'I gave you a year.'

'And what did I give you?' he asked.

She paused to think. What had he given her?

Daniel said, 'I'll tell you what I gave you: nothing. I used you up and threw you aside. And the whole time, I was conscious of what a bastard I was being.'

'I was about to say that we had fun together,' said Peg. Many of their bar nights had been howlers.

'Yeah, we did have fun,' said Daniel. 'We were young and stupid. In love. We were fun. But we never fit. You must have known. You acted like you did. The morning blow jobs. Doing my dishes. Cleaning up my puke.'

'I did those things out of love,' said Peg. Had she really cleaned up his puke?

Daniel said, 'You did them out of desperation. To keep our relationship going, even when we were obviously wrong for each other. It was all wrenching for me.'

'If the blow jobs were painful, your orgasms must have been excruciating,' she said.

He paused. Didn't laugh. 'I'm trying to explain myself, Peg,' he said. 'Breaking up with you was one of the hardest things I've ever done. I want you to know, I need you to know, that I did it for you.'

Echoes of Paul Tester. Peg said, 'I don't get it.' She took care of him for a year, was his personal maid, cheerleader, hand-holder. He ended it without warning, no net, and Peg was supposed to be grateful?

Daniel said, 'You never would have ended it, so I had to. You probably would have catered to me for the rest of your life. I could have let you, but the guilt got to me. I wouldn't have cleaned up your puke, Peg. I was a jerk. Now, with the baby, I change shitty diapers. I get puked on. And I love it. I can see the appeal of taking care of someone else, the way you took care of me. I didn't deserve you, Peg. We both knew it. But you wanted to get married so badly that you would have married me. You didn't really want me. How could you have? After we broke up, I vowed to make myself worthy. And then I met Millie. Her influence turned me into the woman I didn't want to marry.'

'You mean me?' asked Peg.

'Yes,' said Daniel. 'I became selfless.'

'Selfless.'

'Giving,' he added. 'Instead of taking.'

'And now your life is perfect.'

'Pretty much.'

'So your advice to me,' said Peg, 'is to become a lesbian, because my giving, selfless style plays well with the ladies.'

'You understand!' he said.

'Thanks for the insight,' she said.

'Don't thank me.'

'I take it back.'

'A burden has been lifted,' he said. 'I am at peace.'

Peg said, 'Me, too.'

'Truly?' he asked. 'Have I really helped you?'

Peg thought about it and said, 'More than you know.'

She hung up, genuinely at peace. Resolved. The conversation with Daniel had shown her the light. Peg wouldn't date or be dumped by another Daniel or Ed or Harry or Paul. She wouldn't be selfless and giving and more than these men deserved. Daniel said it explicitly: 'We didn't fit.'

New York City men would never fit. And Peg was finished with them.

May 31, 2005
To: Peg Silver
From: Jack Silver, vice president, Citibank Private Bank
Enclosed: Contract on sale for 102 Grand Street, #4F

Peg, here's your signed contract. Keep for your records.
You owe me for this. I'm not supposed to pick up the
phone for clients with less than a million dollars. And I'm
waiving my fee, only because Mom said that if I made a
penny on you, she'd make me do my own laundry for a
month. A couple of details:

1. Mr Yamaguchi sent a personal check for his ten per
cent deposit of $100,000. I've got it in escrow.

2. Closing date is, tentatively, July 1. Mr Yamaguchi
will pay the $900,000 balance at the closing.

3. At the closing, I will handle the payoff of existing
mortgage ($80,000), taxes, fees and commission. Mom is
waiving her fee for representing you. But the Corcoran
Group broker gets six per cent ($60,000). City transfer
taxes will be approximately $20,000. Capital gains tax
(fifteen per cent of profit beyond $250,000) is $98,000.
Your net profit for the sale is $740,000, give or take a
few grand.

4. I will also arrange a wire transfer to your new

account at Solomon Smith Barney. Thanks for hiring Rich Spawn. He's an excellent money manager, and now he owes me a kick-back for the referral. He'll give you good advice. My two cents: I recommend triple-tax-free bonds, providing a guaranteed annual income of about $28,000. Enough to live like a princess in Vermont.

5. Once the wire transfer clears (twenty-four hours), you can go get drunk, throw a party for yourself, and everyone you know, at the Four Seasons, whatever your little heart desires. You are now a woman of means. Kind of makes me sick that I never bought an apartment in the days when Mom and Dad were doling out the down payments. How could anyone have predicted that a crappy one-bedroom in Soho would increase by 900 per cent in ten years? For the first time in my life, I am jealous of you. I expect that makes you feel pretty fucking good.

6. On a personal note, Stephanie and I are over. I have you to blame (thank?). She thought your leaving New York would inspire me to leave Mom and Dad's. I said, 'My Mom cooks dinner, does my laundry and pays my phone bill.' She said, 'I suck your dick and mix your drinks.' I said, 'Unless you do laundry, too, I'll be trading down.' That was the last thing I said before the slap heard round the world. She'll come crawling back. When she sees what's out there, I'll look great in comparison.

June 15
To: Peg Silver
From: Pru Silver
Attachment: Five photos

Peg, some photos from Bertha Billows, the broker at McLaughlin Realty. I think this place looks fabulous, and

Bertha has staked her reputation (very good – I made inquiries) on this farm. It's in the Upper Connecticut River Valley area, right near the border of New Hampshire. FYI: Bertha says locals call it the Upper Valley for short. It's on the outskirts of Manshire (the town you mentioned specifically), on a dirt road. Ten acres, a pond; the farmhouse was built in 1791. It still has its original beams. The foundation and plumbing were renovated about seven years ago. Not ideal, but Bertha swears everything is solid and functional. Price: $180,000. If you still want to buy outright in cash (Bertha loved the sound of that), she's sure she can talk the seller down to $150,000. A *very* good deal. It's not Manhattan, but apparently, all these Upper Valley towns are seeing huge rises in property values in the past few years. Since the place is empty, you can move in at any time. Not that we want you to go. We want you to stay. Just so I have that on record.

P.S. Your brother is acting strangely. Quiet, stays out late. Is taking phone calls in his room. Stephanie mailed a box to the house. I opened it accidentally – the packing tape was peeling, I swear – and it was full of shredded clothing, doused in honey. Do you think they broke up? I never liked her anyway. What kind of girl hangs out in the lobby with the doorman rather than spend time with her boyfriend's family?

Lot number 456985545
Pottery Barn bedroom set
Starting bid: $2,000
Place bid >
Time left: 7 hours and 39 minutes. 10-day listing. Offer expires 6/20/05 20:30 EST
History: 5 bids

Item location: Grand Street, Soho, NYC

Description: Five-piece bedroom set from Pottery Barn, circa 2000. All oak, in excellent condition. King-sized bed (mattress and box spring – like new! hardly used! slept on by a ninety-year-old grandmother! – included). Owner moving in two weeks and motivated to sell. See photos. Also, check out living room set (lot number 7899545), kitchen set – dinette-style table plus vintage chairs – and full day-to-day Louisville Stoneware service, along with other kitchenware (lot number 26589952), and entertainment package includes TV, VCR, DVD, stereo, speakers, 2001 iMac, HP printer (lot number 5263574). I'll pay shipping to anywhere in the Northeast, and some parts of the Midwest. And the South. Hell, I'll arrange/pay shipping anywhere, except Alaska and Hawaii. And maybe even there, if the price is right. EVERYTHING MUST GO! Sponsored by ebay.com

To: nina_pelham@goldenface.com
From: pegleg@yahoo.com
Date: July 3, 2005 7:38 EST
Subject: my dream mountain man

Nina, this is the last email I will ever send from this computer. And I'm sending it to you. I hope you are sufficiently honored. I've spent the day with the UPS man (who was NOT dreamy), tagging and shipping my bedroom to Georgia, my kitchen to Delaware and my living room to New Jersey. Rica is coming in an hour to collect all my electronics – including the iMac. Funny, I thought that stuff would sell first on ebay, but I didn't get a single bid. I'm happy to give it to Rica. She's been an excellent boss, and it was her idea that I become a perennials farmer in Vermont. I owe her. I made more $$$ than I thought I would from selling the furniture ($5,400, minus shipping). Enough, I think, to replace it all with cheaper stuff once I get to my new home. Should be enough to get a flock (?) of chickens. Maybe a goat. Or a cow. What might a cow cost, I wonder. A live one, I mean.

Anyway, the train leaves first thing. You'll get this email after I've gone. I'm not going to get weepy on you (you've been weepy enough for both of us). And, remember, Manshire is only forty-five minutes from Manchester, outlet mecca of the Northeast. Think of whole country weekends, getting ninety per cent off retail at Barney's.

I'll leave you now with an image, a picture of what I'm going to find up north. I did a quick search of men in my new zip code on match.com. The pickings were slim. But that's good. I like slim guys. Most of them had facial hair, drat. Not all of them were rugged country types. Some claimed to have real jobs at IBM in South Burlington (who knew there were corporations in Vermont?). Anyway, see attached photo of the pick of the bunch. He's a logger, with a BA. He included a poem in his posting – 'Ode to an Elm.' At least it's not a sonnet to a sheep. Note the chest (logging). The legs (mountain climbing; skiing). The face (under the beard). The shoulders (chopping firewood). The wardrobe of hiking shorts, Timberland boots, and a matt of chest hair. This is a man who can change the oil in his truck, the one he built himself with spare parts, a screwdriver and a stick of butter. And he'd love a woman with all the country goodness of fresh-baked apple pie.

Ahhhhhhhhh. I can smell it from here.

7

The train trip was tolerable so far, thanks to Peg's Gatorade bottle of vodka. Peg took a sip, grimaced and looked out the window. She was on the Montrealer, a slow crawl up the Northeast, with a few thousand stops in minor industrial New York and Connecticut towns, and a few thousand more in rural Massachusetts and Vermont outposts. The trip from Penn Station to White River Junction, Vermont, would take seven hours. She'd been on track, as it were, since 8 A.M. Not even halfway there.

Peg purposefully avoided eye contact with the other passengers. Stilted conversation with strangers would make the hours seem like centuries. Instead, she read Chuck Palahniuk's *Choke*, stared out of the window, drummed her thumbs on the armrest, drank her vodka-infused Gatorade.

She was celebrating. It was a holiday, after all – Independence Day, July 4, for the nation, and one adventurous American in a train car, venturing, blazing, striking, all those pioneer verbs, into undiscovered territory. Peg had been a dyed-in-the-wool Manhattan-ite. And now she was moving to the state where the wool was grown, to grab a virgin clump and start a new life. With new dye. Maybe green.

The train pulled into the station in Hartford, Connecticut. Another stop. Another shuffling of people and luggage. Peg watched the bustling. Several new passengers boarded her car. Two ancient ladies in support shoes were helped by a conductor. A few college girls giggled in their midriff-baring T-shirts, distracting the conductor, making him bump into one of the old ladies, knocking her into the seat next to Peg. On reflex, Peg raised her hands to catch the woman as she stumbled. For her good intention, Peg got a cane in the eye.

The conductor apologized, helped the ancient woman to her seat next to her companion and came back to ask Peg if she was okay. Rubbing her eye, Peg assured him that she would survive, and he turned around and walked out of the car.

Peg followed him out with her good eye. Just as he stepped off the train, a man stepped on. The train whistled. Peg would have, too, but her lips were suddenly dry as sand. This was not any man. Nina would say, 'A god in a mortal sheath.'

He lugged a large duffel bag as he walked down the train aisle. Peg noted his not-too-tight jeans, sunny yellow T-shirt, thick dirty-blond hair, juicy raspberry lips. A bit younger than her, Peg guessed, licking her lips. 'Sit by me,' she shouted at him telepathically. The train car, meanwhile, was about half full. Plenty of seating options. But he must have gotten her message. As he approached Peg's row, he slowed. Stopped. Heaved his duffel onto the luggage rack over her head.

He barely looked at her as he eased his lanky body into the seat opposite Peg, facing her, his feet inches from hers.

Peg reached into her snack bag on the floor, and

pulled out a big bag of spicy Doritos. She opened it, waving it subtly. Let the smell waft into his nostrils.

She said, 'Chip?' offering the bag.

He turned toward her and grinned politely. He took a triangle and said, 'My favorite.'

Peg said, 'Drink?' offering him her full backup bottle of Gatorade cocktail.

He nodded, and washed down the Dorito with a gulp. He handed the bottle back, and said, 'That's the best Gatorade I've ever had.'

She smiled uncertainly. He must have tasted the vodka. She said, 'I'll bet you're hot in those boots.'

'Should I take them off?' he asked.

Peg said, 'If it would make you more comfortable.'

This man, this babe, leaned down, unlaced his Timberlands, slowly, deliberately, and pulled them off. Miraculously, the blue socks were unholed and clean. He wiggled his toes, making a few cracks as the bones released their tension. No detectable feet smell.

'Much better,' he said. 'What about you? Those flip-flops can't be comfortable.'

She laughed. 'I'll take them off, then.' She did. 'Since we're undressing, I should introduce myself. I'm Peg Silver. From New York. I'm moving to Vermont to start over,' she said, holding out her hand, knowing and not caring if she was sharing too much. Just let the Gatorade do the talking, she thought. Maybe he'd take off his shirt next.

He said, 'Ray Quick. From Hartford. I'm moving to Vermont for a month to, uh, do some work.' He smiled at her, then looked out the window as the train picked up speed. Peg examined his profile. He turned back toward her, grinned. And then opened his newspaper.

That was it? He sat on top of her, drank her booze, removed his clothing – and then nothing? This was odd. Peg was accustomed to receiving more attention than this.

'Where are you staying?' she asked, keeping the conversation going. No wedding ring.

'In Manshire.'

'I can't believe it!' said Peg, the Gatorade making her speak too loudly. 'That's where I'm going. We'll be in the same town. And it's a pretty small town. Smaller than a single grain of rice. We're bound to bump into each other. Rub elbows at the general store.'

He turned to look at her head-on, finally, proving that using the words 'bump' and 'rub' would intrigue any man with a functional penis.

'Any more of that Gatorade?' he asked.

She passed him the bottle.

Ray said, 'I may not get into town much. The place I'm staying at, I'll be closely monitored.'

'You're staying at a prison?'

'More like a spa.'

'A prison spa?' she asked.

He said, 'A retreat.'

'And you're working there?'

'I'm doing some work on myself.'

Sizing up his perfect profile, Peg said, 'You know, in New York, if someone says he's getting work done, it's code for plastic surgery.'

'I'm not getting a new nose,' he said.

'A new what, then?' she asked.

'If I tell you, you won't want to bump into me. Or rub my elbow.'

Okay, maybe he didn't have a functional penis.

He said, 'You're cringing.'

'I'm being intrusive,' she backpedaled. 'I wonder if the dining car is open?'

'You've got a bag full of food,' he said, pointing at her groceries. 'Whatever you're thinking, you're wrong.' He hesitated, deciding whether he should say more. 'I'm doing a program,' he admitted vaguely.

'Like AA.' Oops on the Gatorade.

'No, it's not like that,' he said, still reluctant to give her the details. 'I'm not getting surgery, and I'm not an alcoholic.'

'Don't be shy,' said Peg, curious. 'You know you want to tell me everything.'

Ray laughed and shook his head. 'I'm not supposed to be talking to beautiful woman at all.'

He thinks I'm beautiful, thought Peg. She smiled, and took a swig of Gatorade and crossed her legs. She absentmindedly rubbed her knee. 'I'm sorry, Ray. I don't mean to press you,' said Peg. He pricked up with the word 'press.'

Ray watched her hand, moving up and down, skirting across the skin of her knee. He said, 'You've heard of Outward Bound?'

She said, 'They give you a fish hook, a candy bar and a piece of string and expect you to live in a forest for three days.'

He nodded. 'You're supposed to learn survival skills. Teamwork. How to scale a cliff with a rubber band.'

'So you're doing Outward Bound?' she asked, not sure why he was so reluctant to talk about it.

He shook his head. 'The place I'm going to teaches survival skills of a different kind.'

'What kind?' she asked.

He blushed, his cheeks apple red. Peg said, 'You're going to sex school.'

'Why does everyone think this is about sex?' he asked defensively. 'I've had some disappointments with girlfriends. I just had another bad breakup. A friend told me about this place. So I thought I'd check it out. And now I'm completely embarrassed. If you'll excuse me, I'll get my stuff and jump off the train.' He stood and reached for his bag.

'Don't go.' Peg sprang to her feet. Standing beside him, Peg was impressed by how tall he was. She touched his wrist, lowered his arm from the luggage rack. 'I've had disappointments, too,' she said. 'But not with sex. Never with sex. The sex is always great. I have a very healthy sexual appetite. Dorito?' she asked. 'Gatorade?'

He allowed her to smooth away his embarrassment, let her settle him into his seat. He smiled as she sank into the seat next to him (instead of opposite him). His eyes were golden brown like toffee.

'Why aren't you supposed to talk to women?' she asked.

'I can talk to women,' he said. 'But I was warned not to talk to anyone I'm attracted to. I'm supposed to be free from distraction.'

'So why did you sit so close to me?' she asked, moving even closer to him.

'Old habits,' he said. 'You were alone and gorgeous. I couldn't resist.'

'Alone sounds right,' she said. 'I've left everyone I know, my home, my job, my family and friends, to start over.'

'Running from an ex-boyfriend?' he asked.

She snorted. 'I'm running from seven of them. Each

one dumped me. And within six months of letting the ax swing, they all met and married another woman. I'm the Last Girlfriend. I'm moving to break the pattern. But it's probably unrealistic to think I can leave my problems behind. I've probably brought them with me.'

Ray blinked, toffee eyes stirring, and then he started laughing.

Peg squinted at him. 'Go on. Laugh. My misery is fucking hilarious.'

'Sorry, Peg,' he said, regaining control. 'I'm only laughing because I can. If you're the Last Girlfriend, then I'm the Last Boyfriend.'

She asked, 'How many?'

'Four,' he said.

Peg felt a rush of blood to her head. This had to be fate, she thought. Was Ray Quick her reward for taking a risk? She had no idea the payoff would be so, well, quick. But she wasn't going to question it. She would answer the call of destiny instead.

He said, 'My friends think I should start charging women to date me.'

'My friend said the same thing to me.'

'We could go into business together,' he suggested.

'I don't mix business with pleasure,' she said, pushing her right tit against his arm.

Ray shifted in his seat. He said, 'Okay, I'm officially distracted.'

'What's the name of this place?' she asked. 'The Last Resort for Romantic Misfits?'

'Inward Bound,' he said.

'No wonder everyone thinks it's about sex,' said Peg.

The trip ended three hours later in White River Junction, Vermont. Peg's next stop, after a fifteen-minute taxi ride, was the Subaru dealership in Manshire, where a brand-new Outback was waiting for her. Peg got her driver's license only a week ago. A city kid, she'd always taken the subway, cabs, or walked. She was looking forward to operating heavy machinery. She just wished that, on her maiden voyage, she weren't so tipsy.

The car salesman had her fill out the paperwork, fork over her credit card, and then walked her onto the lot. She tried to focus on his recitation about the past week's weather patterns, but Peg's mind drifted like a log on phloem back to Ray Quick. His kisses were spicy (from Doritos) and hot (from heat). They'd made out for the last two hours of the train trip. No need to talk once they'd discovered their mutual defect. Why talk anyway, when their mouths were put to better use in other ways?

They held hands exiting the train, had to pry their lips apart at the station. He asked, 'Are you going straight to your farm? Can I call you there? I'll sneak off. Whatever I have to do.'

'I'm not hooked up yet at the farm,' said Peg, 'but I can give you my cell.'

They programmed each other's number into their mobile phones. 'Reception is spotty in the mountains,' Ray cautioned her.

'Take my address, too,' she said. 'Come over, if you can make a break for it.' She scribbled her address on the back of his train ticket.

He looked at the writing. 'You live on Old Dirty Goat Road?' he asked, slaying her with his smile.

'Better than Young Dirty Goat Road,' she said. 'Those young dirty goats, they throw wild parties. Drink. Do drugs. Listen to rock-and-roll music.'

'From what I hear, the old dirty goats are just as bad,' he said. 'In these heah parts.'

'Is that a Vermont accent?' asked Peg. 'Do it again.'

He cleared his throat, and said, 'If you don't like the weathah, wait an houah.'

They giggled. She said, 'You've had quite enough Gatorade for one day.'

He did the accent again – 'I reckon' – and then planted another smooch on her. Peg dropped her suitcase on the ground to put her arms around his neck.

He pulled back. 'Where were you three months ago? I wouldn't have signed up for Inward Bound.'

'The program is just four weeks,' she said.

He looked down at her, toffee eyes sweet and gooey. 'I can't wait that long to have you,' he said, sending Peg's heart racing.

'You've got five gears, and reverse,' the Subaru dealer said loudly, breaking into her thoughts. He was giving Peg the spiel. 'This is the remote. You can lock and unlock the doors, turn on the ignition, start the heater, even switch on the CD player. It's a nifty little gadget. I tell you, they get more advanced each year.'

'You don't have to sell me,' said Peg. 'I already paid. Unless you need the practice.'

He stopped abruptly. 'Here it is,' he said. 'Two-thousand five Subaru Outback, fully loaded, standard transmission. Metallic black.'

He dropped the keys into her palm. 'My first car,' she said wistfully. 'So I put the key into the slot, and twist to turn it on, right?'

The dealer nodded, and said with all earnestness, 'Gas pedal on the right. Brake in the middle. Clutch on the left.'

'I know, I know,' she said. 'I was trying to be funny.'

'What's funny about not knowing how to drive?'

'Nothing,' she said. 'Just a little sarcasm.'

'Sarcasm?' said dealer, as if it were an alien concept. 'Oh, yes. I've heard they do that in New York.'

Clearly, they do it in Vermont, too, thought Peg. She got in her car, checked her mapquest directions and drove. She got all the way out of the lot before she stalled. Then she cruised down Manshire's Main Street – four blocks, with a white steeple church, a general store, a post office, a restaurant, an inn and a bookstore. Another few miles down a paved road, then a left (stall) and a right. At the turn for Old Dirty Goat Road (stall), the road changed from blacktop to graded dirt. Peg thought of an old *New Yorker* cartoon: an illustration of a car on a highway, passing a sign that read, 'Welcome to Vermont. Pavement ends.' She drove along the road narrowing into a single-lane squeeze under a canopy of elms, maples and oaks. Queen Anne's lace, black-eyed Susans and wild daisies dotted the ditches on the sides of the road. Peg drove slowly, getting a feel for her new car, watching butterflies and dragonflies flitting by the flowers. Peg came to a full stop (slam on breaks, stall) to avoid hitting a deer and two fawns in the road.

She watched the furry family disappear into the woods, her heart thundering from nearly killing them. She'd have to get used to living so closely with animals. But that was how the world should be, she thought, getting the car back in gear. Humans and animals, co-existing, sharing the Earth's bounty. Peg smiled to herself. Moving was the best decision she'd ever made. She could feel herself shedding the artifice of New York, the overcivilized pretentiousness that defined city life. Bring on the deer. They'd become her prancing pals. Feral pets. She could leave out food for them in a dish on her porch. This is heaven, or Eden, she thought as she turned into her gravel driveway, which was exactly where it was supposed to be, 2.39 miles from the turn.

Peg turned off the ignition and stepped out of her new car to look at her new home. The photos did not do the place justice. The small two-story house, white with navy trim, had a triangular aluminum roof, four-panel glass windows, dormers, extended eaves. It was a classic country home, modest, muscular, neat, no frills. Just like me, she thought proudly. They were a perfect match. And then, another notion: Won't Ray be impressed?

Peg approached the front door with some trepidation. Sure, the outside looked great, exactly like the photos. But she hadn't seen any pictures of the inside. All she had to go on was the word of Bertha the broker. Peg was a realist. She expected to find something wrong. Water damage. A rotting floor.

She used her key (the broker had mailed it to her in New York). No problem with the lock, or the solid oak door. She entered a square mudroom: terra-cotta brick floor, white walls with a few wrought-iron hooks. She hung up her purse and dropped her suitcase (full of clothes, some sheets and her brokerage account info – all she'd brought to start her new life). She ventured straight ahead, into the kitchen. She peeked at the deep, stainless-steel sink. She turned on the faucet. She'd expected a clattering blast of liquid rust. But the water flowed soundlessly, colorless and odorless. The downstairs bathroom looked good, too. She flushed the toilet. No muddy backflow.

Peg started to relax. Faster now, she prowled from room to room on the first floor. The ceiling beams and wide-plank floors were solid, seamless. The mantel and fireplace were swept. Peg lit a match in the flue, and watched with joy as the flame fluttered and then steadied. Chimney clear, good. Good. She walked through the French doors of the living room and out onto the deck to look at her land.

Seeing her property, that first look, almost hurt from the beauty. Ten acres, all hers. The view directly in front – the four acres of flat pasture – would be turned into her flower farm. Peg admired the swell of a hill to the left, about an acre or two, covered in a carpet of yellow, purple and white wild-flowers. A wind lifted suddenly, and she caught the scent of mint and grass. Peg cast her eyes on a pond to the right of her future garden, water surface rippling, a willow tree bending on the bank, a frog leaping into the water. More ripples. It was a small pond. Barely big enough for swimming laps. But plenty sizeable for cooling off.

Peg scanned the horizon. She couldn't believe she was the owner of all she surveyed. She had to see it up close. Deciding to take a wander through her pasture,

Peg ran back to the mudroom to grab her suitcase. She carted it up the steep, banisterless staircase (built over two hundred years ago, when people were shorter – and narrower), up to the second floor.

The upstairs had two bedrooms and another bathroom. She entered the larger bedroom, and threw her suitcase on the floor. As per her instructions, the real estate broker had arranged for a mattress to be delivered pending her arrival. And there it was, wrapped in plastic, leaning upright against the wall.

Peg stripped out of her traveling clothes. In the privacy of her own home, she stood naked, arms stretched to the ceiling. The months of planning, the excruciating decisions, the stress of selling, buying, all seemed worth it now. This was the life she wanted, in the setting of her dreams. The fact that she'd met Ray on the way up was a sign that she'd done the right thing. No mistakes, no surprises. It was all going off without a hitch. Maybe the pieces of her life were finally coming together.

Peg rummaged in her suitcase for a towel, toothbrush and toothpaste. She had a million things to do, buy and see, but first, before anything, she'd shower.

The upstairs bathroom had a toilet, a sink and a big, claw-footed tub. The window by the tub let in beams of light as the sun slowly sank into the mountains. She could gaze out of this window at her pasture while taking long soaks, smelling the minty air. Her entire body softened, her muscles unclenching for the first time in ten years. Smiling at herself in the framed mirror above the sink (she'd have to buy a medicine cabinet), Peg was bursting with pride. She loved her car, her house, her previously untapped adventurousness. She even loved her bangs.

Peg brushed her teeth quickly. She decided that, in the absence of a medicine cabinet, she would store her toiletries in the cabinet under the sink. She opened the cabinet door. Light from the window shined into the space.

What came out of the space: a gray swarm. A few at first, and then scores of mice raced out of the cabinet, darted around the bathroom, across her naked toes and into the hallway, where they dispersed like scattered marbles.

Part of her brain realized how terrified the critters had to be. She was a 125-pound woman, and they were tiny creatures. The rest of her brain was going on pure instinct, instructing her muscles to jump up and down, setting off her vocal cords to emit an ear-piercing scream with the power and wind of two healthy lungs behind it.

Peg wasn't afraid of water bugs and cockroaches. She'd killed many large, hard-shelled insects, even taking pleasure as they crunched under her shoe. Rats were horrible. But Peg saw them only at a safe distance – in sewers, running along subway tracks. A rat sighting, while waiting for a train, could be entertaining.

Nothing entertaining about these mice, scurrying over her unshod feet, spilling from the cabinet as if poured from hell's bucket. Into her bathroom. The place where she would do personal, naked things. She watched a mouse crawl across the toilet seat. This unleashed a surge of horror in Peg. The surge careened inside her blood and bones, like the mice on the floor, maniacally and without direction or purpose, until she thought she would pass out or throw up. Or both.

Stumbling on pure adrenaline, Peg ran out of the bathroom and slammed the door. In a blind panic, she rushed back into the master bedroom and bumped into the mattress leaning against the wall. It fell to the floor with a violent splat, letting fly another burst of gray. More mice darted in wild fright from the underside of the mattress.

A new blast of screaming and the hot-foot dance from Peg as disgust crept upward from her toes to the ends of her hair. The plastic wrapping of the mattress had been gnawed away, along with a plate-sized hole in the padding. A family of rodents had fashioned a comfortable nest of stuffing and droppings there. One brave mouse hadn't fled. He remained in his nest, chewing unfettered at the padding upon which Peg was to have slept. He stopped for a moment and looked up at her with his black bead eyes, as if daring her to make him stop, even for a second.

Peg grabbed her suitcase, her purse, her pile of clothes on the floor, and rushed down the stairs, out the door and into her Subaru, where she sat in the front seat, leather sticking to her bare bottom, screaming.

She used the nifty remote gadget to roll up the windows and lock the car doors.

'You've got a little mouse problem,' said Chuck Plenet, Manshire's 'One and Only Exterminator,' or so it said on his truck.

He met her on the porch of the Manshire Inn. Peg had been living there for two days. That was how long it took to get Chuck Plenet to get out to her house and investigate the vermin scourge.

'Well, which is it?' asked Peg. 'Do I have a little mouse problem, or a little problem with mice?'

Chuck chuckled, and adjusted his baseball cap with the logo of an ant with X-es for eyes. His other style choices included bib overalls, filthy Nike sneakers, a blond mullet and a fine layer of dust. His face had more wrinkles than a Thomas Pynchon novel, but he didn't seem that old. He could have been any age from thirty to fifty, impossible to tell.

'The mice are small,' he said. 'The problem is big. That's what happens when a house is empty for too long in the warm weather. You get uninvited guests.'

'So you'll get rid of them,' Peg prompted. 'Use the strongest poison you've got. Go in there with napalm. Nuke them to vapor.'

Chuck shook his head, kicked a post with his sneaker and said, 'I don't like to kill a mouse for no reason.'

'Aren't you an exterminator?'

'Only one in town.'

'Do you exterminate pests,' she asked, 'or just the competition?'

Chuck said, 'I prefer to relocate mice. To a better place.'

'To Jamaica?' she said.

Chuck said, 'These mice were just doing what comes naturally. It's wrong to kill them for being animals. I'm sure you don't want the murder of hundreds of mice on your record when you go to meet your maker.'

'Hundreds?' Peg asked. And then, *My maker?*

Chuck whispered, 'God.'

She would have laughed, had she not been dumbfounded. 'Wouldn't the mice be in a better place, as you say, with *their* maker? Who, I assure you, is not the same one who made me.'

'Can't do that,' he said. 'Mice have souls, Ms Silver. Insects don't. I'm fine with killing bugs. But I have a strict policy about mammals.'

'You've got a gun rack on your truck!' Peg protested, pointing at his truck.

'Hunting is different,' said Chuck. 'I eat what I kill. I don't eat mice. Do you, Ms Silver?'

'Not yet,' she said, getting frustrated, missing the exterminators of New York with their crush, kill, destroy, scorched earth policy with vermin.

Chuck said, 'I recommend cats.'

'You eat cats?' she asked.

'Cats eat mice,' he explained. 'What they don't eat, they'll scare away, into the field. That way, you won't have mice dying in the walls. They're small, but the rotting bodies stink. The smell never quite goes away.

You'll need about thirty cats. Should take a month.'

'Where am I going to get thirty cats?' she asked. And then, 'A *month?*'

'I can rent you the cats,' he said. 'For two hundred a week.'

'Eight hundred dollars,' she said, incredulous. Chuck obviously thought her a rich urbanite – or, in the native Vermont tongue, a 'flatlander' – who would pay anything.

She said, 'I can go to an animal shelter and get thirty cats for free.'

'Four hundred?'

'Two hundred,' she said.

'I can work with that,' he said. 'I'll bring the cats over sometime next week.'

'Next week?' she asked. 'Do it today!'

Chuck said, 'It takes some time to rustle up thirty cats, Ms Silver.'

It takes Vermont time, where everyone moved at the speed of tort reform. The concierge at the Inn made Peg wait two hours for her room. The bartender took half an hour to mix a martini. Bertha the broker, who'd sold her the mousetrap, hadn't returned her multiple urgent phone messages for two days. Chuck Plenet, forty-five minutes late for their appointment, apologized by saying, 'Inside an hour is on time' to her, before shaking his head in bald disgust at her impatience. Manhattan to Manshire was like going from sixty to zero in one second flat. She felt the emotional skid marks on her soul. Despite the martinis and Jasper Ale (the Inn's home brew), both of which she'd been guzzling since she checked in, nothing erased the sight of mice rampaging around her bathroom, the sensation of their claws on her toes.

'Do it,' she directed to Chuck. 'Send in the cats.' Peg reached into her purse, removed her wallet and slapped some twenties into his open palm. He wrote her a receipt.

Peg glanced back at the Inn. Charming, quaint, floor-to-ceiling floral. It was enough to drive a city mouse insane. Plus, her room wasn't cheap at $100 per night, and at the rate she was going, she could look forward to another fifty dollars a day in bar and restaurant charges. She was flush, but Peg Silver hadn't been raised to throw her money out the chintz-curtained window. 'Where am I going to live?' she asked herself out loud.

Chuck arranged his cap again and smiled, showing off his countrified dentistry. He said, 'You can stay with me if you like. I've got an attic room that's comfortable. Shower behind the barn. Clean outhouse. No charge.'

Peg could see it now. Chuck, the mammal lover, trapping her in the attic. Spying on her barn showers. Doing what came naturally. 'Tempting offer, Chuck,' she said. 'But I'm partial to indoor plumbing.'

'Suit yourself,' he said. He got in his truck and drove away.

Hating the idea of going back into the Inn, Peg wandered off the porch, and across the parking lot to Dombit's general store. The store's slogan, painted in big letters on the side of the building, read, 'If we don't have it, you don't need it.' She'd see about that.

Peg perused the organic produce aisle, the Cabot cheese department, the racks of flannel wear (from panties to slacks). She picked up a hummus-and-sprouts sandwich and a Diet Coke and took them to the register. The cashier, skinny in a tank top (no bra), flipped her three-foot-long braid and asked, 'Need anything else?'

'You don't have it,' Peg said.

'Then you don't really need it,' chirped the cashier.

Peg said, 'In which aisle can I find a habitable place to live? A friend? A man who will love me unconditionally?'

The cashier blinked. 'I can check our inventory,' she said.

'Don't bother,' said Peg.

After paying, Peg left with lunch. The cashier was glad to see her go. Raw emotional vulnerability unsettled the locals (it was stock-in-trade in New York). Once outside, Peg noticed the giant bulletin board on the wall of the store. By rote, her eyes scanned the colored flyers tacked on the board, selling used tractors, teams of draft horses, cords of wood, steer slaughter service. She took out her cell phone. No service.

Suddenly exhausted, Peg leaned back against the bulletin board. All her plans had gone to shit. Her farm was a disaster. She couldn't start furnishing a house with a horde of cats inside it. The huge stretches of waiting had left her free to fantasize about Ray Quick, which only served to deepen her impatience and loneliness. She wanted to contact him. Get some sympathy. Some TLC. But she had no way to contact him. Her cell was useless. Inward Bound wasn't in the Upper Valley phone book.

Peg would have to rethink her course of action. Nina would give her ideas. She'd call New York on the landline in her room. Maybe she'd let Nina convince her to move back to the city. Except, how humiliating would that be? Admitting defeat after only two days? No, Peg would have to be tougher than that. She would call Nina anyway. Get some pity. She'd feel better.

Leaning forward, her shoulders lifting off the bulletin board, Peg caught her hair on a thumbtack. Pulling the strand free, she watched a red flyer flutter to the ground at her feet. She found the tack on the ground, picked up the piece of paper and read it.

TIRED OF REPEATING THE SAME MISTAKES?
HAD ENOUGH OF FAILED RELATIONSHIPS?
YOU CAN CHANGE YOUR ROMANTIC DESTINY
TAKE THE MOST IMPORTANT JOURNEY OF
YOUR LIFE
GO INWARD BOUND
SPOTS IN THE JULY SESSION STILL AVAILABLE
FOR MEN AND WOMEN
JULY 5 THRU AUGUST 3
CALL 802–555–4089
INWARD BOUND, INC. MANSHIRE, VERMONT

Holy shit, she thought. Coincidence, she wondered, or was this destiny? To be thinking of Ray, frustrated not to be able to reach him, only to have the number drop from the sky (bulletin board, whatever), and land at her feet? Coincidence, she'd once read, was merely the work of synchronicity, the cosmic spheres spinning at exactly the right speed and directions at the right time. As if everything in her life – the years in New York, the move, the mice, the stay at the Inn, buying lunch at the general store – had been leading to this moment, this message on red paper in 14-point Geneva. As advertised, Dombit's did have exactly what she needed. And Peg, a woman in touch with her needs, was not going to ignore this gift of fate.

She raced back to the Inn, and up its steep stairway to her room. As she climbed each step, an image clicked through her consciousness like a slide show: the faces of her exes, breakup scenes, at a bar, the movie theater, over dinner, in bed. A flash to freshman English at NYU. 'The best laid schemes of mice and men often go wrong. And they leave us nothing but grief and pain for promised joy,' she recited the Robert Burns poem to herself as she rushed down the corridor to her room. Each word of it was suddenly packed with new meaning (especially 'mice' and 'men').

Peg would invent a new scheme – impulsively laid, for promised joy. It wouldn't work to just call and ask to speak to Ray. He wasn't supposed to have romantic contacts. The Inward Bound directors might not even give him the message. No, if she was going to get close to him, she'd have to enlist. Four weeks to demouse her house. The program lasted four weeks. Logistically, it couldn't be more perfect.

She called the number on the flyer. She had a twenty-minute conversation with a woman on the other end. She gave her credit card number, took driving directions, packed her suitcase and checked out of the Inn.

Ten minutes later, Peg pulled into the gravel driveway of a huge Federal brick mansion, shaped like a box, with white-trimmed windows and a red-painted door. She found it easily. Only stalled twice on the drive from the Inn. The woman on the phone, a Wilma McGrup, gave her simple and clear directions. 'Take Main Street out of Manshire until you reach a stone bridge. Make a left turn – socially, environmentally and politically – to stay in Vermont. New Hampshire is to the right. The far right,' said Wilma. 'Do not cross the bridge.' The rest of the way was a straight shot on River Road, about half a mile.

Peg stalled to a stop and stepped out of her Subaru. A woman appeared in the doorway of the Federal, and waved. Peg waved back. She grabbed her suitcase from the backseat. She walked by another Subaru in the driveway (was it the state's official car?), and up to the front door.

'Welcome, Peg,' said the woman. 'I'm Wilma.'

Up close, Wilma's smile seemed pinched. Just another client greeting for her, thought Peg. She appeared to be in her mid-twenties, but she could have been deceptively young-looking due to all that high altitude clean living. Wilma's blond hair was tied back in a tight ponytail, her skin, free of makeup, was bronzed and glowing. The thighs sticking out of her cutoff shorts were unshaven, and hard as granite. She was either a hiker or biker. She pumped Peg's hand with the grip of a man. Wilma's tanned forearm was knotty with sinew, also unapologetically fuzzy.

Peg said, 'What, no complimentary cocktail?'

'Complimentary cocktail?' asked Wilma, pinched smile collapsing. Even with the dour expression, Wilma was a living, breathing advertisement for effortless beauty, in a muscular, oddly sexless way. Peg could easily see her sweating and groaning on a bike, but not on a man.

'Whenever you arrive at a resort hotel, they greet you in the lobby with rum drinks,' said Peg. 'Sometimes they give you mango on a stick.'

'We're not a hotel,' said Wilma. 'I can get you some organic apple cider.'

'I wasn't serious. I was just trying to be . . .'

'Critical?' asked Wilma. 'Demanding?'

'Apple cider sounds great,' said Peg.

Wilma nodded and invited her inside. 'The others are waiting outside. Let's dump your suitcase in the women's suite first and go join them.'

'How many others are here?' asked Peg, not realizing she'd be sharing a suite.

'Two other women, and three men,' answered Wilma. 'We had a cancellation last week. A woman. You took her spot.'

'I got lucky,' said Peg.

'You sure did!' said Wilma buoyantly.

Peg had to shut her lips with her fingers. All this earnestness would take some getting used to. Accepting people's comments at face value? Not searching for hidden meanings or making the assumption of irony? Yikes. Peg was unprepared for this kind of braintease.

Wilma led her through the Federal's interior, the perfectly skimmed white walls, exposed ceiling beams, low ceilings, tiny rooms for optimal fireplace heating. Doorways led to doorways, and Peg wondered if she'd get hopelessly lost in the maze. Wilma took her up the staircase to the second, then the third floor. Finally, they came to a suite of rooms. And then, into a private bedroom.

'This was once a walk-in closet,' said Wilma. 'Two hundred years ago.'

A walk-in closet? Peg had seen smaller Manhattan one-bedroom apartments. The wallpaper – a rose, lime and cream floral – was a replay of the onslaught at the Inn. But the room was bright and airy, three windows, a bouncy bed with a white eyelet coverlet and an oak dresser with crystal pulls. Except for the wallpaper, Peg liked it. She could easily stay here.

'Do you have mice?' she asked, just to be sure.

'Black flies, but no mice,' said Wilma.

'Where do the other women sleep?'

'There are two more rooms on this floor, and a common bathroom across the hallway.'

'Where do you and Dr Bester sleep?' Linus Bester was the founder, organizer and head instructor of Inward Bound. Masters in sociology, doctorate in psychology, a through-hiker of the Appalachian Trail and native son of Manshire. Wilma, herself, was a doctoral candidate in psychology. She'd rattled off her and Bester's credentials on the phone earlier. She'd also mentioned to Peg that she and Linus Bester were 'partners.' Under questioning, Wilma admitted that they were 'a couple,' which forced Peg to say, 'A couple of what?' in a Groucho Marx voice. Wilma replied, 'Psychologists.' Peg knew then that she and Wilma would not become close friends.

Peg bounced her suitcase on the coverlet and started to unpack. The blonde watched, didn't offer to help, and said, 'He prefers to be called Linus.'

'Linus,' repeated Peg.

'We sleep on the first floor, off the kitchen,' said Wilma. 'Let me go over the daily schedule with you. Breakfast at 6 A.M., lunch at noon. Dinner at six. We eat every six hours for optimum functioning.'

Peg looked at her watch. She'd get dinner in five hours. That seemed a long way off. 'Are naps scheduled?'

'Naps?' asked Wilma.

'Put head down, close eyes?' said Peg.

Wilma nodded. 'Bedtime is early. Ten o'clock,' she said. 'You'll get plenty of sleep.'

'Meals and sleep times are planned. Do you schedule bathroom breaks, too?'

'You can use the bathroom whenever you like,' said Wilma.

'Do we eat with the men?' asked Peg, thinking of Ray, his lips parted to taste.

Wilma nodded.

'Where do the men sleep?' asked Peg, thinking of Ray, his eyes closed in slumber. Or lying on his back in bed, jerking off and thinking of her.

Her host wasn't too quick to answer that. 'The men sleep one flight below. But you aren't allowed on their floor,' she said. 'For obvious reasons.'

Peg asked, 'Are the men allowed on the women's floor?'

Wilma had had enough. 'Our clients have come here to learn, not to date. If you think this is some kind of Catskills singles weekend, you've got it all wrong.'

Catskills? Was that a Jewish slur? Peg said, 'So orgies are out of the question.'

'We don't currently have them on the schedule.'

Peg was led back downstairs. If she'd suspected some subterfuge would be necessary to get what she was after from Ray, she'd underestimated how much. But she was not one to back down from a challenge. Peg smoothed her bangs as Wilma took her through a living room with three large couches and a grand piano, out the rear of the house and onto the back porch, where two other women sat on rocking chairs, gazing at the river – or the scull of shirtless crewmen skimming by upon it. No sign of Ray anywhere.

'Look at the guy on the end,' said the chestnut brunette. 'He must be the cock swain.'

'He has a nice stroke,' said the butter blonde.

'Ahem,' said Wilma.

The two women spun around. The blonde smiled hesitantly; the brunette frowned, as if annoyed by the distraction from a more satisfying diversion. Peg guessed both women were roughly her age, within a five- or six-year radius. Attractive. On the surface, neither seemed like a misfit of love. And yet here they were, paying $2,000 for a month of live-in, eat-in, breath-in romantic intervention.

Peg introduced herself. The blonde said, 'Gloria Martin.'

The brunette said, 'Tracy Ball.'

Wilma said, 'Everyone ready?'

Gloria and Tracy rose from their chairs. Peg got a

better look at both. Gloria was at least six feet tall. The only thing stopping her legs from going on forever was the porch floor. Along with her hiking boots, Gloria wore a cute little sundress, cotton, spaghetti straps, cone-shaped tits that didn't need a bra and jutting collarbones you could put a hanger on. She was a goddess, really, a stunning figure of Nordic perfection, the arched eyebrows and glacial blue irises, pale poreless skin and fine-fettled bone structure. The flame of female competitiveness flared within Peg. Couldn't be helped. She swallowed hard, the lump of envy burning all the way down.

Tracy was easier on the ego to look at. A busty brunette, she had curly hair and a curvy body, with dark eyes and pink lips. She could benefit immeasurably from better posture, and a few thousand sit-ups. Peg guessed she was the oldest of the group, around thirty-four or thirty-five. She wore a Lacoste short-sleeve shirt, yellow (did nothing for her), with khaki shorts and hiking boots.

Wilma glanced at Peg's feet. She said, 'Are you comfortable hiking in sneakers?'

Peg wore New Balance running shoes. She didn't have appropriate footwear for hiking, so she said yes. Wilma slipped a backpack on her shoulders and pointed the women to the left. They started walking in a tight cluster toward a trail along the riverbank.

'What about the men?' asked Peg.

Gloria the goddess said, 'We don't do activities with them for the first week.' Hearing her speak, Peg guessed Gloria was in her early twenties.

That would simply not do. Peg would have to figure something out. She remembered that she would see Ray at dinner. Five hours from now.

Wilma said, 'We'll walk along the river for about a mile, and then we'll turn up that mountain, and hike to the top.' She pointed at a low peak in the near distance. 'Round-trip, it's about six miles.'

Peg was glad to hear it. She hadn't been running since she left New York, and she needed the exercise. It was one of those things: With all the time in the world to go for a long jog, Peg had killed the hours in the bar of the Manshire Inn instead. Five minutes of hiking and Peg surrendered to the sensation, legs churning, heart beating. Some of the tension of the past couple of days eased as she marched. The sun shone through the trees. Peg listened to her own breathing, and the birds. The women fell into a line. Wilma, Peg, Gloria and, last, Tracy.

Wilma said, 'Tracy and Gloria have already been here for a day, Peg. They filled out a questionnaire. I'll leave one for you in your room. If you start right after dinner, you can finish it before bed.'

'I'll need three hours to fill it out?' Peg asked.

'It's a very thorough questionnaire.'

Peg turned and noticed Gloria and Tracy rolling their eyes.

Wilma said, 'I'd like each of you to tell the group why you've come to Inward Bound. Peg?'

Peg didn't feel like talking. She was hiking. And she didn't think Wilma would appreciate the truth, that the combination of nowhere to live and raw lust were what had propelled her to enlist. So instead, Peg drew a thumbnail sketch of her romantic history, her serial dumpings, her Last Girlfriend-itis, her escape from New York. She concluded by saying, 'I'm into change. Change of scenery. Change of mind-set. I want all the change I can get, especially in my relationships. Never thought

I'd say this: I am red hot for some hard-core learning and growing.'

Wilma said, 'Tracy?'

Peg turned toward the brunette. She was already sweating. The shine on her forehead attracted a fly. She swatted at her forehead and said, 'Did you bring water? How far have we gone? Only half a mile? Jesus, I'm already getting a blister.'

After assurances from Wilma that she had water, moleskin and trail mix, Tracy said, 'I'm from Boston. Big town, tons of guys. I feel like I've systematically dated every single one of them. I've met men in bars, at clubs, blind dates, fix-ups, on the Internet, at parties, at work. I've used every dating resource available. I am out there. Out There. Capital 'O,' capital 'T.' I will go to my grave knowing that I exhausted every last possible means to find a man. Can we slow down, please? We're not going to jog up this mountain. Holy shit, look at Peg. She's hardly sweating. What is *wrong* with you?'

The group shifted into first gear. Wilma wasn't sweating much either, Peg noticed. Gloria was breathing shallowly. She was slim, but out of shape. Wilma fished in her backpack for water. She handed a bottle to each of them, and Tracy insisted on stopping to take a drink. They'd reached the foot of the mountain, with miles to go before they got to the top.

Tracy said, 'If I talk and drink and hike at the same time, I'll get a cramp.'

This could be bad. Tracy might complain and bitch the entire way up and down the mountain. Wilma tried to calm her. Gloria stared into the distance, seemingly in her own universe. Finally, Tracy was able to continue walking and talking.

She said, 'So I've dated, dated and dated some more. I've been on hundreds. But I haven't had one – not one – bona fide relationship. I've managed to hold on to a man for a few months here and there. But never with the understanding that we were a couple, that it was ever more than a casual sexual connection, a wait-and-see kind of thing. And even those arrangements ended prematurely. He'd say he met someone else, or was getting back together with an old girlfriend, or he wasn't that in to me. Or I'd end it because he wasn't worth the five minutes of my time anyway. No man has ever told me he loved me. I've never been in love. Never been with a man I know will be around in a month or a year, who cares about what I do all day long. Which is merchandising. I work for the Boston Red Sox organization – another losing proposition. So that's why I'm here. In the spirit of leaving no stone unturned, I've come to Inward Bound.'

She paused, gasping. 'It didn't say in the literature that we would have to hike,' Tracy managed to say. 'Christ, my foot. I'm getting a hot spot on my big toe.'

Wilma agreed to stop and tape up Tracy's foot. While they rested, Peg sipped her water, careful not to gulp. Her thighs were warmed up, jumpy, wanting to run. The woods were quiet, except for the sounds of buzzing insects and chatty birds. Gloria leaned against a tree. The sun shining through the leaves turned her blond hair a light shade of green. Peg and Gloria made eye contact, smiled awkwardly and looked back at the ground. Peg was struck by the inherent contradiction of the situation – the natural setting, the unnaturalness of confiding one's fears and failings to strangers.

Tracy was finally patched up and the women

continued the hike. Gloria was asked to speak. Peg was impressed by her matter-of-fact tone. 'I live in Darien, Connecticut, but I go to parties and events in New York every week. That's how I meet dates,' she said. 'My parents and their friends make introductions. I'll find myself sitting next to a man at a dinner party on Saturday, and on Monday, he'll send me flowers and jewelry. He'll pursue me relentlessly for a month or two. I'm always reluctant at first. These guys never try to get to know me. They want me for other reasons. I'm aware of it, but all those Tiffany boxes and phone calls and invitations to box seats at the ballet – they can wear a girl down. And the talk, too. How much they want me, how they can't stop thinking about me.'

A stark contrast to Tracy's story. Peg glanced at the curvy brunette. Tracy seemed to be distracted by a tree root on the trail. Gloria went on. 'I'll tell you about Brandon. He was the most recent. Brandon worked for my father, and Daddy insisted I date him. We did the circuit together. A charity ball in the Temple of Dendur, dinners at Daniel, bungalows at the Ocean Club. He bought me a diamond necklace, and sent a dozen white roses every day for a month.'

'What a bastard,' said Tracy.

'He never talked to me,' said Gloria. 'He'd sit next to me, or across from me, look into my eyes and stroke my forearm. And then he'd take a cell phone call for an hour. He was after me because I'm the boss's daughter. My parents didn't believe me, even after I told Mom that Brandon never tried to kiss me. He didn't seem attracted to me at all. Mom refused to listen. She said he was a gentleman. But I knew the truth. One night, I insisted Brandon come to my bedroom with me. I put on a nightie and pranced around. He sat on my bed, frozen. I had to grab his dick before he'd admit he was gay. He ran out. I felt bad for him, but relieved. My parents didn't believe me when I told them what happened. They must have had their hearts set on him for me. I had to get out. I made the arrangements to come here in secret. I left a note at home saying I was going to Canyon Ranch for a month.'

Tracy said, 'What was your last name again?'

'Martin,' said Gloria.

'I *knew* it. You're the heiress to the Martin Pharmacy chain. I've seen your picture in gossip columns. You're worth millions! Your mother is Anastacia Martin, former supermodel. And your father is Trevor Martin, megamogul. He's bigger than Trump.'

'He's much shorter, actually,' Gloria said, 'I'd appreciate your discretion.'

'Of course, you have it,' said Wilma, giving Tracy and Peg a warning.

The women climbed on. Peg stole glances at Gloria. One could be born to every advantage, and still struggle with the most elemental human need. Peg felt sorry for the heiress. But she didn't know what to do with her pity, or what to say to her, and found herself slowing down so she wouldn't walk next to her.

Wilma kept up with Gloria, though, and the two women spoke quietly to each other. Peg and Tracy were a few paces behind. Tracy was breathing too heavily to speak, and Peg was glad not to have to talk anyway. With each step, her thoughts traveled away from her romantic plight, and into her body. Peg hadn't done much hiking before. But she decided she liked it, especially the sense that she was moving closer to the sky.

Tracy groaned suddenly. 'For God's sake. We've been hiking for over an hour. Are we there yet?'

Wilma said, 'Just another few minutes.'

True to her word, Wilma led the small group over one last tricky patch, and they were at the top.

The surface at the summit was rocky, a flat granite slab with sparse grass poking between cracks. The sun was hotter, brighter, the trees gone. Peg was blinded for an instant, and when her eyes adjusted, she could see for miles. Hills, meadows, the river below. Everywhere lush and green. Wilma pointed out a red house with a silver roof in the river valley below.

'That's the Federal,' she said. 'Look how far we've come.'

The Inward Bound mansion was the size of a Monopoly hotel. Seeing it, how tiny and abstract it was (she could line it up to sit on her fingertip), filled Peg with a warm glow. Even Tracy smiled at the idea, the measurable accomplishment of hauling one's ass from point A to point B.

Wilma invited them to sit down, to pull up a rock, any rock. She unzipped her backpack and took out three small round mirrors.

She said, 'When you look in the mirror, it's usually to fix your hair or put on makeup. To examine your body, searching for problem areas. We look at ourselves to see the flaws, not beauty. And we look at predictable times. In the morning, after using the bathroom, before bed. We hardly ever see ourselves when we aren't prepared for inspection. But only when you're unprepared can you see your true self, your true beauty.' Wilma handed a mirror to each woman. Peg held it in her palm, the sun reflecting on the surface, making a plate of light.

'Hold it up. Look at your faces,' Wilma said.

Peg did as she was told. Her skin was red. Beads of sweat rolled down her forehead and the sides of her face. In the direct sunlight, she could see every wrinkle, every pore. The landmarks – eyes, nose, mouth – were in their usual places. But something about the whole face, her expression, maybe, looked completely different. Peg was surprised by the image. She gazed at the floating foreign face in the mirror. It was her, but not her.

Tracy and Gloria seemed as transfixed by the strangers in their mirrors. Wilma said, 'The light does funny things on top of a mountain.'

'Are these trick mirrors?' asked Tracy.

'Do you like what you see?' asked Wilma.

Peg blinked, testing the image. Objectively, she should be horrified by the bumps and lines. But she wasn't. Her face was stripped down, no protective smirk or practiced seductive stare. She smiled at herself, liking the way her lips and eyes moved, the shadows on her cheeks. The image was clear and honest, her expression empty. She wasn't quite sure this was the standard definition of beauty. But Peg liked the woman looking back at her.

Placing the mirror in her lap, Peg said, 'Is this Lesson One?'

'What do you mean?' asked Wilma.

'Being honest and natural is sexy.'

Wilma shrugged and said, 'We'll take a short breather and then head back. Don't worry. It's all downhill from here.'

11

'**D**inner in an hour,' Wilma announced before leaving the women in their suite to shower and change after their hike.

'Black tie?' asked Peg.

'Hardly,' said Wilma, already halfway down the steps.

Peg suspected that there hadn't been a black tie event in Manshire in this century – or any. The official Vermont dress code could be Casual Everyday, or A Fleece for All Seasons.

Freshly showered and powdered, Peg milked her lighter-than-a-marshmallow mood. She chose her red sundress, acutely aware that in minutes she'd see Ray Quick. And he would see her. Red was the only color for the situation. Plus, she wanted to show off her legs. Unlike every other female in the state, Peg's thighs were as smooth and hairless as plastic. Tonight, she would forgo her usual three concealers and gloss. After what she'd seen in the mirror on the mountaintop, she decided she didn't need it.

Tracy and Gloria, also in sundresses, were in the bathroom, fighting for mirror space. Peg watched them apply copious foundation, blush, lipstick and eye shadow. She said, 'You two completely missed the point on the mountaintop.'

'I got the point,' said Tracy. 'I'm just not brave enough to take it.'

Gloria added, 'If I don't wear makeup, I'm transparent. You can see right through me.'

The blonde was a paler shade of white. Peg asked, 'Have you met the male Inward Bounders yet?'

'We have,' said Tracy. 'Wine and cheese meet-and-greet yesterday, orientation day. About an hour, but most of it was taken up listening to Wilma go over the course schedule. After that, Linus gave the men a tour of the basement. We hardly got to talk to the guys. Nonetheless,' she said, lips smacking, 'I have one scoped out.'

Had to be Ray. 'What's his name?' asked Peg, nonchalantly.

Gloria said, 'Has to be Luke.'

Tracy laughed. 'Was I that obvious?'

'He has a certain mysterious, smoldering appeal,' said Gloria.

'What about the others?' asked Peg.

Tracy shrugged. 'Ben is short, balding, fortyish. An insurance wonk from Hartford. Not the kind of guy who grabs you by the libido. There's a guy named Ray, also from Hartford. He's great-looking – sublime body – but he seems shiftless. I don't trust him.'

'We're not here to hit on men,' said Gloria. 'I'm not anyway. You two can do what you want.'

Peg felt herself relax. Her fellow female In-mates weren't after Ray. Was he shiftless? She hadn't thought so. He seemed sweet, passionate, searching to answer life's grander questions. Peg leaned on one foot, and then the other. Both bore blisters (she would have to buy a pair of proper hiking boots). But she didn't mind the pain. Not when the prospect of rubbing, bumping and pressing against Ray loomed. If he was receptive (and why wouldn't he be?), they could arrange a late-night rendezvous. The thought of sneaking around with him in the dark made her nipples hard as cherry pits. Good, she thought. She hoped they'd stay that way.

Gloria said, 'Are you okay, Peg? You're smirking.'

'I'm fine.'

Tracy said, 'Actually, you know who was surprisingly hot?' She snapped her compact closed.

'Who?' Peg asked, hoping she wasn't changing her tune about Ray.

'The director. Linus Bester,' said Tracy. 'If you like the scruffy intellectual type. But I hate scruffy.'

'I hate intellectual,' said Gloria.

'Shall we go?' asked Peg, who didn't want to hear about Linus Bester when she had her heart (and nipples) trained on Ray Quick.

Tracy and Gloria appraised their mirror faces one last time, and the three women headed for the stairs. As they walked, Peg felt a degree of camaraderie with them. She probably wouldn't have sought out either woman for friendship in the real world. But, then again, her new reality was under construction. She'd be wise to take all comers. Tracy was affable, if whiney. Gloria was fragile and remote, but refreshingly caustic. The two of them had already formed a friendship. Despite their differences in demeanor and background, Tracy and Gloria shared elemental problems and desires, and that was enough – more than enough – for a friendship. Peg liked the idea of being the odd woman out, the third wheel. She felt more comfortable on the near outside.

The men were standing in a tight circle by the

bookcases in the living room. They smiled at the women as they descended the last flight of stairs. Peg spotted Ray immediately. He looked steamy in jeans and a navy blue shirt, bare feet. She watched his eyes travel from one woman to the next, pausing too long on leggy Gloria (forgivable – no man could help that), before landing on Peg. He smiled blandly at her, the way a stranger would. And then the out-of-context recognition clicked in. He let out a gasp, and rushed to her side, taking her hands in his and leaning down for a kiss. On the cheek. They were in a roomful of people.

'Peg!' he whispered excitedly. 'What are you doing here?'

'I thought I might get some work done,' she said.

'You know, in some circles, that's a euphemism for plastic surgery,' he said, grinning.

'I'm getting an emotional lift,' she said. 'A bad-pattern tuck.' He laughed. She relished the sound. She asked quietly, 'Have you been thinking about the train?'

'Nothing else,' said Ray. 'I can't believe you're here! This is so fucking fantastic! I have to get you alone. When? Tonight.'

'Fraternization between campers is strictly forbidden,' Peg said.

'Meet me on the back porch at midnight,' he whispered.

'My thoughts exactly,' Peg whispered back.

'Excuse me, Peg Silver?'

She turned to the man who'd stepped up. He was around forty, tall, his long brown hair had a touch of gray. His eyes were intensely blue, thickly blue, like anti-freeze. His shorts and T-shirt were a size too big. Clean-shaven, tan cheeks. He wore Birkenstock sandals. A string of leather with a red bead was tied around his ankle. He looked like a preppy hippie.

'I'm Linus Bester,' he said. 'Your host.'

He smiled at her, creasing those tanned cheeks. Tracy nailed it when she said he was a scruffy intellectual type. Peg smiled and shook his hand. Ray excused himself with a secret wink, and went to chat with the others, leaving her alone with Linus.

'Wilma tells me you had a positive experience on top of Sacatosh Mountain,' said Linus.

'I had a blazing epiphany,' she said. 'And I've got the sunburn to prove it.'

Linus, grin never fading, said, 'Wilma also mentioned that you have a bad habit of sarcasm. We're going to have to beat that out of you. With a stick. It may hurt.'

'No pain, no gain,' she said.

'You are a runner?' he asked.

'Does it show?' she asked. He was one, too. She could tell. The runner's equivalent of gaydar. Rundar?

Linus pointed at her legs. 'Your overly developed calf muscles,' he said. 'I noticed them from across the room.'

They weren't that big. She said, 'Now I'll be overly self-conscious about them.'

'Be proud of them,' he said. 'I'm sure you are. I run down the logging road to a mountain lake and back every morning. Four miles round-trip. Care to join me?'

'I'm slow,' she said.

'I thought New Yorkers did everything fast.' Was it her imagination, or did he glance at Ray?

Peg said, 'What time?'

'Five-thirty.'

'In the morning?'

'Sunrise on the lake,' he said.

'We run in the dark?' she asked.

Linus said, 'Only at first. On the way back, everything is beautifully illuminated.'

Did Wilma and Linus talk in metaphors on purpose? Did they realize? Or was this just Peg's New York hangover of searching constantly for hidden meanings? She would take him at face value, as pledged.

'Okay, Linus,' she said. 'I'll plod slowly through the darkness of confusion, until we come to the baptismal purity of the lake, at which point, the light of truth will shine into a new dawn.'

Linus said, 'That's a lot to ask of a morning jog.'

From across the room, Wilma announced, 'Dinner is served.'

The group filed into the country kitchen (sink basin, butcher-block countertop, baker's racks with plates and cookware), and sat around a big farm table. Conversation seemed intentionally steered toward soft subjects, like the weather, the food (vegetarian chili on cracked brown rice), the house (built in 1789), Linus's background (earned his Ph.D. in psychology at Dartmouth three years ago), Wilma's credentials (she was in Dartmouth's psychology program currently, had finished her course work, but hadn't completed her dissertation; Linus had been her mentor/advisor until they hooked up last year).

Gloria said, 'I heard about your program from one of your first clients, from two summers ago. She was my private ski instructor at Killington this March. She couldn't have recommended you more highly, Linus.'

'Claudia McKinney?' he asked.

'Yes,' said Gloria. 'She's married now. To a man she met almost immediately after she left here.'

Peg let the others carry the conversation, choosing instead to observe her fellow programmees. She knew first impressions were superficial and probably inaccurate, but one had to start somewhere.

Ben, insurance executive from Hartford, Connecticut, was, as reported, balding, about 5'8", wearing black socks with Nikes, in his early forties. He seemed nervous, self-conscious. He stole glances at Gloria as if she were a luscious morsel of some outlandish foreign delicacy – mouthwatering and scary at the same time. Peg sat across from Ben, and once tried to engage him. He said, 'Yes, insurance is a growth industry. But if you'll excuse me, Gloria was just saying something fascinating about river silt.'

Luke, pro golfer from Providence, did smolder mysteriously. But Peg couldn't imagine feeling attracted to him. True, he was fit, neat (too neat: pressed khakis and white shirt, mink-brown hair cut short). Around thirty, Peg estimated. But his expression was impenetrable, like a rock. He chewed without cracking that stone face. When he smiled (hardly ever), only his lips moved. Peg theorized that he'd be as exciting in the throws of passion as he was currently, in the throes of eating.

Ray, meanwhile, was even more sparkling and gorgeous than Peg remembered. He sat between Luke and Wilma. Peg between Tracy and Linus. She enjoyed watching Ray from across the table, taking in the way he held his fork, the length of his eyelashes, his careful table manners. Ray's shirt was unbuttoned enough to show a peek of sun-kissed chest. His sleeves were rolled up to show nearly hairless and well-muscled arms with the long, graceful fingers of a pianist. His neck! Ropy, but not too thick, eminently suckable. She'd have to get a grip on herself if she was to make it through the meal without sliding off her chair.

After dessert (fresh fruit and nuts), Linus stood and said, 'It'll be an early morning. I suggest we go to our rooms for private meditation and reflection.'

Tracy said, 'It's eight-thirty.'

Wilma said, 'Most of us are used to getting by on just six hours of sleep. I can show you a dozen studies that reveal the long-term hazards of REM deficiency. Linus and I recommend nine or ten hours a night.'

Peg and Ray locked eyes. Ray said, 'You are absolutely right, Wilma. I can't remember the last time I got a decent night's sleep.'

Grumbled acknowledgment – yes, they were all in profound need of unconsciousness – led to tablewide chair scraping and a chorus of 'good nights.'

Wilma called after Peg and gave her a booklet. On the cover, Peg read, 'The Big Five Personality Test.' There was a separate answer sheet with bubbles to be filled in, like the SATs. Peg flipped through the booklet. 'This questionnaire is fifty pages long,' she said.

'It's thorough,' said Wilma, handing her a number 2 pencil. Tracy, Gloria and Peg wandered back upstairs. The men followed in a group behind them. Wilma and Linus remained in the kitchen to clean up.

As soon as they'd reached their suite, Tracy said, 'I don't know about you, but there is no way I could possibly go to sleep now.'

Peg said, 'You can always reflect and meditate.'

Tracy said, 'Like that's going to happen.'

Gloria said, 'I've got pills.'

'The drugstore heiress has pills,' said Tracy. 'Why am I not surprised?'

'Doing this survey will knock me flat,' said Peg. 'I'll pass.'

Gloria said, 'Tracy? Are you woman enough?'

Tracy said, 'Oh, all right. I'll succumb to peer pressure.'

Gloria went into her room and brought out a bottle of Xanax. She said, 'I'd better give you a half. Otherwise, there'll be no hiking mountains tomorrow.'

'I'll take a whole,' said Tracy. 'I'm never hiking again.' She popped her pill and swallowed it with water. Gloria, a seasoned prescription-drug abuser, took hers dry.

The three women went to their separate rooms. Peg lay on her bed and listened as the sounds of the house quieted. Then she opened the questionnaire. There were over a thousand questions. She was instructed to weigh each statement on a scale from 1 (strongly disagree) to 5 (strongly agree). Each question started with the phrase, 'Do I see myself as someone who . . .'

1. Sees a project through to the end?
2. Sacrifices her own happiness for others?
3. Is relaxed, handles stress calmly?
4. Is emotionally unstable, easily upset?
5. Is sometimes rude to others?

Six hundred questions and three hours later, Peg rubbed her throbbing forehead. She should have finished an hour ago. She was taking this too seriously, spending five solid minutes trying to determine if she was 'easily distracted.' After giving herself a 5 (strongly agree) for being 'spontaneous,' she filled in answers for the last four hundred questions with 3, 'neither agree nor disagree.'

With relief, she threw the booklet and answer sheet on the dresser.

She checked the clock. Five minutes before midnight. Should she just go to sleep – she was so very tired – or keep her rendezvous with Ray?

Do I see myself as someone who pursues sexual gratification, even if it means breaking the rules to get it? she wondered.

'Strongly agree,' said Peg to her floral wallpaper, and crept downstairs.

12

Peg's head still hurt, so she decided to go in search of Tylenol or Advil before meeting up with Ray. Nothing in the bathroom upstairs. Nothing in the common bathroom on the first floor. She'd go foraging in Gloria's room, but they weren't that friendly just yet. Peg would try the kitchen. She crept silently, knowing that Linus and Wilma's bedroom was somewhere nearby. Her ears on high alert, she stole into the kitchen and began opening cabinet doors. She found nothing. But she heard the soft murmur of voices coming from a closed door by the refrigerator.

She wondered, Do I see myself as someone who eavesdrops on other people's private conversations?

Strongly disagree, she thought. And then she moved closer to the door, as if pulled by a mysterious force. Not so mysterious, really. It was curiousity. What did Linus and Wilma have to say to each other in the dark of night when they should have fallen asleep hours ago, or risk their tender health to REM deprivation?

Ear pressed against their bedroom door, Peg listened as hard as she could.

Wilma's voice: 'She's going to be a problem. I was wrong to accept her on such short notice.'

Linus's voice: 'She's fine. A bit defensive, but that's not surprising.'

Wilma: 'You don't have to deal with her.'

Linus: 'We can't kick her out. She already paid. And we need the money.'

Peg inhaled sharply. So Wilma thought she was an insurgent. How flattering, thought Peg. Smiling wickedly, she leaned closer into the door to spy.

Linus: 'She and Ray are already acting out.'

Wilma: 'It's amazing how easily they get into it. Every session, same thing.'

Peg had surmised as much. Inward Bound was a romantic biosphere: The programmees would inevitably fall into their bad patterns with each other. And, in the process, their issues would be splayed naked on the table, prepped for dissection. It was just like standard group therapy. Nina was a huge fan of circle shrinking, and she'd tell Peg stories about accusing the young men in the group of callousness – regardless of their own behavior – thereby making these unsuspecting guys the stand-ins for her shitty boyfriends.

Naturally, Peg didn't want to think of Ray as the clay she'd use to sculpt the model of her neurosis. She also didn't like being singled out by Wilma.

Do I see myself as someone who is intentionally disruptive? she wondered. Disagree somewhat.

'Ready for bed?' That was Linus.

'I'm going to get a glass of water,' said Wilma.

Peg's heart went thud. Was Wilma coming into the kitchen?

Linus saved her. 'I have water right here,' he said. 'Take off your clothes and get in bed.'

Wilma said, 'I have to shower.'

'You showered before dinner.'

'I'm too tired to fuck you for hours tonight.'

'We can fuck for just one hour,' said Linus.

'Why do you need so much sex?! It's been over a year already. I can't do it every night. The hour-long makeout session, the protracted back rub, your insistence on performing oral sex on me, all the hugging, and whispering and excruciating eye contact during intercourse. And your penis is too big. It's not normal.'

'I do put a lot of pressure on you,' said Linus.

'You do.'

'After tonight, I won't do it again.'

'Will you . . . stop it. Stop touching me!'

A creak sound, someone getting out of bed. Peg flung herself into the cranny between the fridge and the wall. The bedroom door slammed open, hiding Peg even better. Wilma, in a dowdy cotton nightshirt, burst out of the room, kicking the door closed behind her before dashing across the kitchen and into another room, closing that door and locking it. She hadn't noticed Peg. Seeing an opportunity to escape, Peg peeled herself out of her cranny, and crept toward the living room.

Peg made three steps before Linus opened his bedroom door. The light from his room shining a spotlight of yellow on the kitchen floor. Peg stood, on tiptoes, right in its center. She smiled nervously and said, 'I didn't hear a thing.'

Linus was naked except for blue flannel boxer shorts. The light was behind him, so Peg couldn't see his face. She'd hazard to guess that his expression wasn't the same sagacious calm he'd shown at dinner.

Linus said, 'Those who can't do teach.'

'I didn't hear a thing,' repeated Peg. 'But if I had, I'd

say that you're doing just fine.' An hour of making out, a back rub, oral sex, a slow screw with a big cock, eye-locking and dirty talk? Wilma was turning that down? Just the thought of it gave Peg a crotch-twitching reminder of what was waiting for her on the porch.

Peg said, 'I'll be going now.'

'Early run tomorrow,' said Linus.

'I'm not a big conversationalist when I jog,' warned Peg.

'Me neither,' said Linus. 'Good night.'

'Good night,' she said, and walked back into the living room. The porch door was the first on the left. She opened it, and stepped outside.

At the threshold, she caught a big waft of smoke. Sweet, distinct and earthy. She turned toward the source. Dear Ray, handsome Ray of the crunched abs, sat in a rocking chair, smoking a joint. Peg beamed and sat in the rocker next to him. Wordlessly, he passed her the pot, and she inhaled deeply, deep enough to forget Linus and Wilma, the program, everything except the moon on the water, crickets chirping, the smell of pot smoke and the dewy New England summer night air.

Ray said, 'You're late.'

'I hope you were planning to save some of this for me.'

'Plenty more where that came from.'

A tiny bell rang in Peg's head, a ding of warning. But only for a second. She said, 'We climbed a mountain today.'

'We played touch football.'

'How did Ben do?'

Ray said, 'Surprisingly fast on his feet. He made some grabs.'

'What's the relationship lesson of touch football?' asked Peg. 'We got six miles' worth of metaphor. Love is an uphill climb, but once you know yourself and like yourself just as you are, it's all downhill from there.'

'Wilma said that?' asked Ray.

'I extrapolate,' said Peg.

'Linus wasn't explicit. I think – and I admit that my thinking may be temporarily impaired – the touch football game was to show us our competitive natures. That pursuing women is like a game to play and win.'

'That's not your problem, though,' said Peg. 'Luke maybe.'

'Who knows with that guy,' said Ray. 'He's too aggressive. He actually knocked me down. Tackled me like a fucking Marine.' He smoked some. 'Tell me about Gloria and Tracy,' he asked.

'I like them both,' said Peg. 'Tracy more than Gloria, but it's early yet. I reserve judgment.'

'Sit on my lap,' said Ray.

Paul, her most recent ex, had said the same thing to her the night they met at a Village dive. She'd been sitting at the bar, Nina on her left, sipping a Bailey's. He'd been on her right, and they started talking. Three or four Bailey's later, Peg was in a back booth, sitting on his lap, exploring his dental work with her tongue. In the months that followed, they spent scores of nights making out in public places. That had been his particular predilection, and it had been exciting for Peg, too. She smiled at Ray as he patted his thigh.

'Your lap doesn't look very comfortable,' she said. 'There's a big bump in the middle.'

'Pay no mind,' he said. 'Come here.'

He took her by the wrist, and pulled her over. She sat

down on his legs, hers dangling over the side of the rocker, and leaned against his chest.

'All my relationships start this way,' she said.

'Isn't that how it should be?' he asked, stroking the side of her breast.

'They move quickly,' she added.

'First-date fast?'

'Second.'

'Me, too,' he said. 'Is that how it's going to be with us?'

Peg nodded. 'So we both have a tendency to rush into things.'

Ray kissed her ear. 'Yet another thing we have in common.'

'And then we try to mold what we've got into something we want,' she said.

He stopped kissing her to think for a second. 'I see what you mean. By kissing you, and touching you like this, or like *this*, we're just repeating what we've done wrong in the past.'

'Right,' she said, her breath shortening. 'We're letting history repeat itself. Letting attraction take over.'

'Attraction is hard to resist,' he said, placing her hand on the bump of his jeans. 'Harder by the second.'

Peg was panting now. 'It might be useful to draw upon new experiences, for learning purposes. Since I haven't had any experience in months. Many months.'

Ray licked her neck and said, 'My old mistakes seem like a million years ago. In fact, I can't remember any of them. I'm having trouble remembering my own name.'

Peg turned toward him for a smashing kiss, arms around his neck, squirming on his lap, getting the excitement, the rush, remembering why she was always chasing after men.

He pulled back suddenly, and asked, 'Why did you come here? To Inward Bound.'

'My house has mice. I had nowhere else to go,' she said.

'You came for me,' he said. 'Admit it.'

She nodded, too drugged by pot and kissing to deny the truth. 'I came for you,' she said.

13

Dreamily, Peg's eyes opened in the morning. She felt refreshed and rested. Turning toward the night table and her travel clock, she saw that it was 10:04 A.M.

'Shit and double shit,' she said. She'd slept through her planned run with Linus, breakfast and half the morning activity, whatever that was. Peg knew Wilma would demand an explanation for Peg's sleeping four hours late, that this would only reinforce her reputation as a delinquent. Throwing her clothes on, Peg tried to get a story going. 'I was up until three in the morning,' she'd say. True. 'Doing the questionnaire.' False.

Did she see herself as someone who'd lie to get out of trouble? Peg wondered.

What kind of idiot wouldn't?

She did feel bad about missing the morning run. Linus's feelings might be hurt that she'd blown him off. She wondered if Ray had made it downstairs for breakfast at six. But that would be impossible on three hours of stoned sleep.

But, apparently, he had. When Peg finally located the women, meditating in lotus positions on the river's edge, Wilma looked at her and said, 'There's one in every group.'

'Just one?' Peg asked for confirmation.

'The kitchen is closed until lunch,' said Wilma.

Peg slapped her own wrist. 'I'm sorry. I didn't mean to sleep late. I don't see myself as someone who is irresponsible,' she defended. She remembered Linus had described her as defensive. 'Not that I'm defending myself. I'm admitting guilt freely.'

'Sit down and shut up,' said Tracy, opening one eye. 'Can't you see we're in a state of deep relaxation? And, just for the record, you didn't miss much at breakfast. Bran muffins the consistency of sand, and weak coffee.'

'I made the coffee,' said Wilma.

'Try grinding the beans first next time,' said Tracy.

All of the women were in yoga shorts, tank tops, barefoot and hair back in ponies. Peg had on tight jean cutoffs and sneakers. 'I didn't get the wardrobe memo,' she said.

'We sent out a clothing list with the literature prior to arrival. I'll get one for you,' said Wilma. 'Did you do the questionnaire?'

'Up all night working on it. It's on my dresser.'

'I'll pick it up before lunch,' said Wilma. 'I'll have the results for all of you by the end of the week.'

'I can hardly wait,' said Tracy.

'It'll be worth it!' bubbled Wilma in earnest excitement.

Tracy and Peg blinked at each other. Gloria, meanwhile, remained in her yoga posture, eyes closed, breathing rhythmically, either ignoring the conversation or swimming in the recesses of her mind. Wilma gestured for Peg to find a spot, and bend her legs into a lotus.

Once Peg had twisted herself adequately, Wilma said, 'We're doing a relaxation technique. Imagine you're breathing in a glittering blue light of health and fulfillment. Exhale the dark red of rage and confusion.'

Peg swallowed a groan. Having watched Soho transform into yoga central in the last few years with women trading in their art portfolios for rolled-up mats, Peg reflexively distrusted Eastern 'exercises.' And did she have to visualize, too? On an empty stomach? Guilty for her lateness, she didn't protest. She closed her eyes, and tried. She really did. But her thoughts drifted away from the glittering blue light and toward the wispy mental snapshot of Ray's hand, pushing the fabric of her dress higher and higher up her legs, until his fingers disappeared between them.

'Your mind may wander,' said Wilma. 'Gently bring it back to focus.'

After what seemed like ten hours (only thirty minutes), Wilma asked the women to stretch in a Salutation to the Sun, and then they got to lay flat on their backs and Contemplate Their Navels. Peg contemplated with her eyes open, watching the streams of clouds float in the sky with impressive speed.

Tracy was cloud gazing, too. She said, pointing upward, 'That cloud actually looks like a navel.'

Gloria said, 'ZZzzzzz.'

Wilma said, 'While Gloria takes her nap, you two can quietly reflect on this question: What do you want out of a relationship? We can discuss your thoughts in the canoes. We launch after lunch.'

'Tell me they have an outboard motor,' said Tracy.

Peg wondered if Wilma ever prescribed self-reflection and contemplation about her own relationship, which, from what Peg had heard last night, was bathed in the dark red light of rage and confusion. 'It might help,

Wilma, as our fearless spiritual guide, if you could tell us what you want out of a relationship,' said Peg.

Tracy said, 'Excellent idea.'

Wilma paused. 'This isn't about me,' she said.

'But you must think about it,' said Peg, rolling onto her stomach (rumbling now), to look directly at Wilma. She wasn't sure why she was pressing the matter. Wilma's love life was none of her business. Nor did Peg believe that a guide or mentor had to serve as a role model. In fact, famous experts in history were their own worst example. Dr Spock was a neglectful father; Dr Atkins died obese; Dr Freud had the sex drive of a smurf. Those who can't do may be resigned to teach (as Linus said last night), or they were attuned to others' shortcomings because they clearly saw their own.

Wilma said, 'I want my relationship to be a caring partnership.'

Gloria said, 'ZZzzzzzzz.'

Tracy said, 'I want to be taken care of.'

'I want to take care of someone,' said Peg.

Wilma said, 'In several French studies, researchers concluded that women who want to be taken care of are looking for a father substitute; women who want to take care of men are playing mother.'

'That may be true,' said Tracy. 'In France.'

'So what do you want in a relationship, Gloria?' asked Wilma, nudging the young blonde awake. 'We were talking about how relationships sometimes mirror the parent-child—'

'I heard you,' said Gloria, eyes still closed. 'I don't want a father. The father I've got is enough for ten lifetimes. And I don't want to be the mother. I guess I'd want a sibling. I'm an only child. My parents try to control me. I always wished I had someone to share the burden, or just divert their attention.'

'Can I ask, and I don't mean to be intrusive,' said Tracy, 'what is the deal with your father's hair? Is that a wig, or creative combing?'

Gloria said, 'Wig. He has five of them on a two-week rotation. The fresh haircut wig, the two weeks' grow out and so on, until the 'in desperate need of a trim' hairpiece. My mom hates that one. She thinks he should downgrade to four.'

Wilma said, 'On that note – giving us all a lot to think about, in quiet reflection – I'm going to set up lunch. I'll call you in an hour.'

Time for Wilma's break. Once she'd gone, Tracy said, 'Is anyone else wondering what hiking and meditating have to do with relationships? I thought we'd get analysis, on a couch. With a box of tissues.'

'I never expected to get much out of Week One,' said Gloria. 'Next week should be more revealing, when we do the simulated dating. But I think Peg may be getting a jump-start on that front. Tell us, Peg, where were you until three in the morning?'

'Simulated dating?' asked Peg. 'You guys got a week-by-week breakdown?'

'With the clothing list,' said Gloria. 'In the packet.'

'I want a packet,' said Peg.

'You were up at three?' asked Tracy. 'I was out cold like a frying pan to the skull on that Xanax. I nearly collapsed with a toothbrush in my mouth.' To Gloria: 'You took one. And you were up at three?'

'I've built up a tolerance,' said Gloria.

' "Tolerance" being a euphemism for addiction?' asked Tracy.

'Not addiction. *Dependence*,' corrected Gloria.

'Addiction versus dependence. That's like defining the difference between an accident and a mistake,' said Tracy.

Peg said, 'Addiction is a mistake; dependence is an accident.'

The three women thought about that.

'I'm addicted to men,' said Peg.

'I'm dependent on them,' said Tracy.

'I'm building up a tolerance,' said Gloria.

The three women thought about that, too.

Peg said, 'Back to the packet.'

'Week One: Acclimation and Self-Analysis,' recited Gloria. 'Week Two: Interpersonal Exercises. Week Three: Group Dynamic. Week Four: Incorporation and Evaluation.' And then, 'Back to what you were doing at three in the morning.'

Peg said, 'I couldn't sleep after filling out that monstrous questionnaire. So I got some fresh air. On the porch. I acclimatized. And self-analyzed. Very hard work.'

'Liar,' said Gloria.

'Okay, okay. The truth is, I was with someone.'

'Who?' asked Tracy.

Peg said, 'I was with . . .'

'Yes?' they prompted in unison.

'The ghosts of relationships past.'

'More like the specter of relationships future,' snorted Tracy.

Tracy and Gloria dropped the subject. The three women talked and cloud-gazed until Wilma called them in for lunch. The men were already seated and eating ravenously, having spent the morning digging a septic sewer in a neighbor's field.

Peg sat next to Ray at the table. He gave her thigh a squeeze, high up. She said, 'You smell like dirt.'

He said, 'According to Linus, digging is like getting to know someone. Shoveling on the surface is easy. Unearthing gets harder the deeper you go.'

'Ah,' said Peg.

'Say that again, in my ear, but more like a moan,' he whispered.

'Next week, we get to go on a simulated date,' she said.

'I don't want to simulate anything with you,' he said.

Peg felt like she was being watched. Sure enough, both Wilma and Linus had their eyes on her and Ray. Peg plowed into her bean-sprout and eggplant wrap.

'I missed you this morning, Peg,' said Linus.

'I not used to getting up so early,' she said. Meanwhile, Ray continued to stroke her thigh under the table.

'Maybe tomorrow?' asked Linus.

'I'll try,' she said.

Linus smiled amicably. Peg watched him glance over at Wilma, who assiduously avoided making eye contact with him. Meanwhile, Tracy stared at Luke, who kept a watchful eye on Gloria, who was staring blankly into her plate. Ben, unable to get Gloria's attention, took to gnawing on a carrot like it owed him money.

Ray leaned toward Peg and whispered, 'I'm still hard from last night. We need a second date. Tonight. At ten?'

She nodded slyly, her heart already pounding in anticipation. Peg put a hand on Ray's leg, and thought smugly, I'm the happiest woman at this table.

14

That afternoon, the women took a five-mile canoe trip, first downriver, with the current, Wilma making comments like, 'You see how easy it is in the beginning? Everything flows in the right direction, you glide along, not a care, paddling easily.' On the way back, upriver, against the current, their arms aching, Wilma said, 'When things get harder and the current runs against you, it's tempting to stop, to give up, to park on a nearby island, to forget the whole journey—'

Tracy shouted, 'There's a nearby island!' She pointed her paddle toward a tiny dot of land in the middle of the Connecticut River. 'Let's stop. Let's give up. Let's forget the whole journey.'

Peg said, 'Yes, let's. We get the message, Wilma. Relationships are easy at first, but challenges inevitably arise and one has to be willing to paddle through them, no matter how hard things get, even if you're pulling muscles in your forearms, or your neck is in spasm, or your back is sunburned.'

'And you're dying of hunger,' said Tracy. 'What I wouldn't give for some of that tasteless trail mix from yesterday.'

Gloria, still digging deep with her paddle after Peg and Tracy had taken theirs out of the water, said, 'Are my arms supposed to be numb? Look, I can pinch myself.'

Wilma agreed to take a break, so Gloria steered the canoe toward the little island. They pulled up on a mud beach and lashed the canoe to a tree branch overhanging the river. They got out, and invaded the island – twenty feet in diameter, nicely shaded, with a carpet of dry pine needles and a dozen sappy trees. Tracy and Peg lay down on the ground, enjoying the sunlight through the branches. Gloria stood next to the canoe, paddle in hand, like a conquering hero. Wilma sat on a rock by the beach, surveying the river.

Gloria said, 'The reason relationships are easy at first is because everyone is on his and her best behavior. You get comfortable, and then the ugly truth emerges.'

Wilma nodded. 'According to research, people let down their guard, on average, after six months.'

Six months was usually when Peg's relationships went bad. 'It would make more sense if people showed the ugly truth from the start,' said Peg. 'That way, you can only improve.'

'Only, who's going to get involved in the first place with the ugly truth? Men want the beautiful lie,' said Tracy. 'So do women. We want illusion. Reality is a disappointment.'

Wilma said, 'Or maybe you can be your true self, develop a friendship that can deepen over time, building trust and familiarity, and then shift into a romantic relationship that's based on something real.'

'Once you're friends, you can't see a man the other way,' said Gloria.

'Besides which, where's the passion?' asked Peg. 'If you can keep your hands off him long enough to become friends, that's a sign that there's no attraction.'

'You can have passion with a friend,' said Wilma.

'Are you speaking from personal experience, or research?' asked Peg, again trying to draw her out, satisfy her curiosity.

Hesitantly, Wilma said, 'Linus was my mentor when I was a grad student. We established a friendship before getting involved.'

'And that's when the passion emerged?' asked Peg. Tracy turned her head toward Peg, giving her a questioning look.

Wilma said, 'Study after study proves relationships that begin as friendships are three times as likely to result in marriage.'

'Will yours?' asked Peg. Wilma didn't respond.

Gloria said, 'I've never had a close male friend.'

Tracy said, 'I've got busloads of them. Every man I date wants to be my friend.'

Peg and her brother, Jack, were friends, sort of. But he didn't count. Otherwise, she'd had some friendships with men in college, but she either slept with them and, thus, killed the friendship, or decided she would never sleep with them and moved on. She'd always worked with women, and refused to let ex-boyfriends stay in her life. She believed wholeheartedly that men and women could be friends. Nina and Jack, for example, still met for drinks, and had managed to form a friendship despite their failed romance. But Peg knew that if she were to make friends with a man, she'd have to be completely indifferent to him as a potential lover.

They got back in the canoe and paddled to the mansion's dock. They showered, had dinner (turnip and parsnip soup, with radish and celery salad) and were sent to their rooms.

*

Peg was a bit bolder about leaving the women's suite that night, at ten. Since Tracy and Gloria knew she'd sneaked off last night, she wasn't compelled to be as stealthy about it tonight. They were busy anyway, pouring over Gloria's personal pharmacy (besides Xanax, she traveled with Valium, Paxil and Xenadrine, among others), and Tracy's collection of vibrators (the Princess Rabbit, Pocket Rocket and Dancing Dolphin, among others). Gloria was into pills, Tracy was into plugs. Gloria could give Tracy relaxation; Tracy could give Gloria satisfaction. Peg would rather find what she needed on Ray's lap. And he was saving the seat for her right now.

She bounded down the stairs. Tonight, she'd do him. Putting off what they both craved seemed like a waste of time. Peg was quite certain she wouldn't go to her grave wishing she'd had *less* sex. Why deny herself? One should fill her life to the brim with sensual goodness.

With such thought in mind, Peg strode through the living room and punched the porch doors open. She smelled smoke immediately, and looked to her right, expecting to find Ray with a joint – ideally, shirtless. And pantless. Instead, she found Linus Bester – fully clothed – in the rocker, a cigar between his fingers.

Busted. Peg kicked herself. Actually, got her feet tangled, and stumbled onto the porch. The railing stopped her from tumbling over the side.

Linus said, 'Expecting someone else?' Eyebrows up, smiling, pleased with himself.

She said, 'This might be a good time to discuss my reservations with the Inward Bound program.'

'Hold those thoughts, and let me ask you something first.' Not giving her a chance to object, he said, 'A woman possesses a rare and unusual sexual confidence she's grown accustomed to using. When she's attracted to a man, she immediately seizes on how 'right' it feels, how she should follow her instincts. That denying a mutual attraction goes against nature. They jointly decide that there's no point wasting time, since they're clearly meant to be together. They become intimate. From that moment on, they spend every night together. She lets her friendships slide, cancels family plans because she'd rather be with him. After several months, they are essentially living together. And then, once they've settled into a domestic union, the man starts doubting his feelings. The magic of the first months has faded. He chafes at her expectations. He starts to pull back. In response, she goes into full-pursuit mode by catering to him, trying to make him happy. He finds the extra attention suffocating. In her desperation, she brings up the subject of marriage. He feels a combination of pressure and guilt. Eventually, he ends the relationship, telling her, "You're the greatest woman I've ever known." '

Linus took a long puff of his cigar. Peg said, 'I didn't hear a question in there.'

'What do you think you're doing with Ray Quick?' he asked.

'Where is he?' she asked, hoping he wasn't within earshot.

'He's not coming,' said Linus. 'We had a talk.'

'You gave him a thirty-second relationship profile, too? Which was spot-on, by the way.'

Linus said, 'Ray's took fifteen seconds.'

'This is your special gift?' she asked. 'Sizing up people's relationship patterns at a glance?'

'I *am* a doctor,' he said, waving the cigar a bit, smiling as usual.

'My profile could apply to millions of women,' she said.

He said, 'Not many women have your sexual confidence, but I'm sure millions rush into relationships,' he said. 'The difference between you, Peg, and the teeming, hormonally driven millions is that you're here and they're not. You have the opportunity to break your cycle of excitement, illusion and rejection.'

'You make it sound bleak,' she said.

He ventured, 'Ray Quick came here with goals. He deserves a chance to get something out of the program.'

'We are consenting adults,' she said.

'You can't possibly be that selfish, Peg,' said Linus. 'But if you are, I'll refund your money. You can leave tomorrow.'

It was one thing to leave a party. It was another to be shown the door. And Peg wasn't selfish. On the contrary. Hadn't Daniel described her as self*less*?

She asked, 'Do you have to throw ice water on a couple every session?' she asked.

He paused. 'Not every session. But many people start off thinking Inward Bound is some kind of sex retreat.'

'You might consider changing the name,' she said.

Linus smoked quietly. She fumed at him.

'Not many runners smoke,' she said.

He laughed. Linus would laugh at anything. 'I have one or two cigars a week. But you don't inhale cigar smoke. My lungs are fine.'

Peg leaned off the porch railing and took a seat in the rocker next to him. She said, 'Let me try that.'

He handed her the cigar, coaching her about drawing

and exhalation. She tried it, keeping the smoke in her mouth as instructed, and then blew out. It was strange not to inhale.

She handed the stogie back. Linus held it in his fingers, and said, 'With cigars, you have to unlearn everything you know about smoking. It's odd at first, doing things differently, but you get used to the change. You might even decide you like the new way better.'

Peg sighed. 'With the exception of Wilma, you are the biggest metaphor whore I've ever met,' she said. 'You, Linus, are a metawhore.'

Linus chortled, which was a refreshing change from his usual titter. He said, 'Here,' and handed her the cigar.

They passed it back and forth until it was gone, without saying another word.

15

Dear Nina,

Sorry I haven't called. Exhausted, unshaven, forced to eat raw vegetables daily. While my farm is being worked on (euphemism for mouse-lift), I'm living in a big house on the river. I signed up to do an elucidation program – adult shrinkage retreat – to figure out why I'm the Chronic Girlfriend. I had to give them $2,000, but what's more important than my emotional well-being? The host shrink is named Linus Bester. He reads me like a fortune in a cookie. Very annoying. I met a guy named Ray Quick. He's the Chronic Boyfriend. I'd love to take him up on his offer to fuck me raw, but Linus says he'll kick me out (thereby leaving me homeless) if I interfere with Ray's emotional development. I have no doubt that he'd do it. He's already threatened to beat the sarcasm out of me with a stick.

Must go. If I miss breakfast, they starve me for six hours. I'll try to call, but we can't use cell phones up here.

Learning and growing,
Peg

Through the blur of sweat, tears, sore muscles, bulgar wheat pancakes and tabouli-stuffed cabbage that defined the first days at Inward Bound, Peg managed to get with the program. It was all development, all the time. She knew she'd return to her regular (yet completely changed) life at the end of it. But the surrealism of the current situation – living in a mansion with seven strangers (stranger by the day), eating truckloads of vegetables, ignoring her grooming habits, denying her libido – made Peg question her very identity. Maybe this was just a vivid, masochistic dream.

Did she see herself as someone who avoided sexual contact with a gorgeous man who wanted her desperately?

Strongly (she couldn't emphasize the strength of that 'strongly') disagree.

This particular morning, Wednesday, after dashing off her note to Nina, Peg made it downstairs in time for breakfast (first she'd seen in three days). Ray was there, of course. Studying her, watching her closely over his granola and organic yogurt. She didn't dare look at him, or smile or massage his balls under the table as she longed to. She was at Inward Bound to learn. And if that meant twisting the coil of sexual frustration tight, she'd try to do it. She'd try hard. Hard as a block of ice. Or as hard as a giant throbbing erection you could cut diamonds with. *No*, she chastened herself. Stop thinking about sex. She grabbed a bulgar wheat muffin and ran outside to get away from Ray. Wilma was herding the women in that direction anyway. Time for the customary post-breakfast meditation and body part contemplation.

Wilma said, 'Pick a tract, any tract,' as the women arranged themselves lotusly on the grass.

A half an hour of this, and Tracy announced, 'While traversing through my intestines, I've come to realize that men have habitually treated me like shit. But, then again, I have a toddlerlike fascination with my own feces. I always look at them. In the bowl. Appraise their size and consistency.'

Wilma nodded and said, 'Very normal.'

Gloria said, 'While on an imaginary journey through my fallopian tubes, I've come to realize that I've never had good sex, ever, but I'm certain I'm attracted to men, because I often have sexual fantasies about large dogs with huge, hanging balls.'

Wilma nodded and said, 'Very healthy.'

Peg had taken a walk up her spine, thinking of each vertebra as a step along a ladder she felt compelled to climb, believing each bony rung took her closer to a universal truth that couldn't be revealed to her consciousness at this juncture. She said, 'I admire my own shit, too. And I have sexual fantasies about being gangbanged on a park bench in the middle of the afternoon by jugglers and clowns, with an audience cheering me on.'

The three other women looked at her strangely. Wilma said, 'I'm glad you've sought help, Peg.'

After lunch of fresh-picked berries and Cabot cheddar, Wilma took the woman to a lumberyard and had them swing axes, chopping cord, for three hours, practically applying the lesson that they were capable, no matter what they might think, of spotting and cutting out the dead wood in their lives. After dinner of fresh-killed rabbit stew, the women retired to their suite to pack their arms in ice.

The next morning (Thursday), Wilma announced at

breakfast that the morning meditation was canceled. 'We're going biking,' she said.

Riding on the hills of Vermont was pleasant but painful. Peg welcomed the ache in her thighs. Anything to keep her from thinking about sex. Although pumping for hours on a phallic-shaped bike seat might not do much to distract her.

They rode fifteen or so miles to Lake Fairlee. Tracy bitched and complained the entire way out, even though the ride was mainly downhill (going back would be absolute hell). Wilma directed the Inward Bounders into the main entrance of Aloha Hive, a girls' sleepaway camp.

'Maybe we can mooch a lunch,' she said. 'The director is a friend of Linus's.' They sat at a table with eight seventh-graders and pigged out on fried chicken and mashed potatoes.

The girls were thirteen or fourteen. At first, they were pretty shy. Not saying much, but watching in awe as three grown women tore into fried chicken like tissue paper.

A girl with braces and yellow hair tapped Gloria on the arm and said, 'Are you good with makeup?'

'I'm not good,' said Gloria when she finished chewing. 'I'm GREAT!'

That was all the girls needed to hear. They grabbed Gloria, Peg and Tracy by the hands and tugged them toward their bunk, leaving a plate of brownies and a pitcher of bug juice on the table. Along the way, the braces girl said, 'We have a social tonight with the boys' camp across the lake.'

'And you want a makeover,' said Gloria.

'Can you make us hot?' asked a scrawny girl with pimples and dishwater hair.

'Absolutely,' said Gloria.

The pharmacy heiress, who'd gotten every cosmetic in her dad's store for free from age six, knew her way around a blotter and blush brush. Peg watched from a cot as Gloria gave each kid an overhaul, expertly transforming the ducklings into ducklings with painted faces. Tracy fixed their hair into French braids that were doused with spray to hold them until later that night.

Peg smiled and watched, listening as these pubescent kids bubbled with excitement at the idea of spending chaperoned hours with a bunch of awkward and, probably, far less mature-for-their-age boys. Out of the bunk's screen door, Peg noticed Wilma sitting by herself, face to the sun, on the mess hall porch. Eating a brownie.

Peg realized then that they'd been setup. Wilma had made it seem spontaneous. The 'Oh, let's go this way' on the ride out. Her 'Maybe we can mooch a lunch.' The 'Extra seats at this table' when they entered the mess hall. Peg assumed the lesson of the day was to show the In-mates just how early in life this whole business started. Socials, boys, decorating ourselves for their approval. To count up from thirteen how many years of excitement, rejection and disappointment every woman had to log in by the time she hit an age when marriagelessness became genuinely frightening.

On the ride back, Peg was taken over by it – the ignorance and innocence of thirteen. Gloria and Tracy must have been subdued by it, too. No one spoke much as they pedaled home, nor at dinner.

Once they returned to their suite before bed, Gloria said, 'I envy those kids. Being with boys, men, should be excitement and butterflies. All the rest of it, the things it becomes – anxiety, confusion – that's the opposite of fun.'

Tracy said, 'Right now, one of those girls is standing alone while all her friends are dancing.'

16

'Not dates exactly,' said Linus. 'We call them "interpersonal exercises."'

The Inward Bounders – having suffered through one more day of metawhorisms while weeding the flower beds surrounding the mansion ('Weeds grow quickly and choke off nutrients for the plants that grow slowly and bear fruit,' said Wilma while Peg stabbed the wet earth with her trowel) – sat in the living room for their intro to Week Two. It was already afternoon.

'You will be paired off each night,' said Linus. 'Wilma or I will chaperone and observe your behavior. The next day, you'll be evaluated on your performance, and given goals to enact the following night.'

Tracy said, 'Three couples, only two of you.'

'I'll have auxiliary chaperones,' said Linus. 'Friends of mine.'

They ate an early supper, and Linus instructed each Inward Bounder to find a quiet spot and make a list of goals for Week Two. The list was supposed to reflect any new thinking about relationships gained during Week One.

Peg decided to swim across the Connecticut River to New Hampshire (less than a quarter-mile distance), and hang out on the Dartmouth College boat dock. She'd take in some sun, gawk at the undergraduate crew guys. Think. Ideas might flow if she was away from the Federal, away from Ray.

The time spent with the Aloha camp girls had dislodged long-buried hurts in Peg's mind, blackening her mood for two solid days. As she changed into her bikini and went outside, Peg realized that her adolescent miseries had only been extended in her adult dating life. All along, she'd been chasing the approval of men. Searching for the thrill of puppy love, the uncomplicated joys of attention, being asked to dance, not being the girl alone in the corner. Except, for all the male approval she'd won, her relationships hadn't moved beyond puppy love. She'd never had a mature love, one that was founded on solid ground. This was exactly what Wilma and Linus had been beating into her head for a week.

The message had reached its target. And now, if her intellectual reckoning could squelch her unrelenting sex drive, maybe she could – by luck or will – lift the Curse of the Ultimate Girlfriend. Maybe, one day, not too many years from now, she'd find lasting happiness.

She dove off the Federal's puny dock. The water was cold at first. Peg swam in long strokes, reaching the other side quickly. She hoisted herself onto the Dartmouth boat dock, the floating cubes of plastic held together by thick wire, and found a spot on the end to dangle her feet, far enough away from the score of college kids on summer session to avoid eavesdropping on their conversations. She lay back, enjoying the bobbing sensation as the dock rose and fell with the waves of a passing motorboat.

Minutes later, a shadow darkened her eyes. She

opened them, having to blink, and saw a male figure standing over her, arms at his sides, wet hair dripping, surfer-style swim trunks.

He said, 'I like your bikini.'

'Ray, we're supposed to be alone, in quiet contemplation of the various ways we've fucked up all our lives,' she said.

He sat down next to her, his feet splashing into the water. 'I watched you swim over here.'

She said, 'Linus told me he'd kick me out if I didn't back away from you.'

Ray said, 'You let that stop you? I thought you came here for me.'

Was he hurt? 'I did,' she said. 'But since I'm in this program, I thought I'd try to get something good out of it. You should, too.'

'I haven't been impressed so far with Linus's methods. I've sawed tree branches, hauled well water, milked cows,' he said. 'The only good thing I'm going to get out of this is you.'

Before she could respond, Ray leaned back on his elbow and kissed her.

When he pulled away, Peg said, 'You milked a cow?'

'It was pretty cool,' he said. 'I tugged an udder.'

Peg asked, 'What was the relationship moral?'

'Something about naked vulnerability.'

'Don't say "naked."' Peg barely had any clothes on as it was.

'Can we find a more private spot?' he asked, glancing back at the students.

'Are you sure you want to walk past all those college girls in your condition?' She looked at his swim trunks.

'I'll give them the thrill of their lives,' he said,

laughing. 'The suit has a pretty good lining. And it's baggy.'

Peg would have loved to go off with Ray, find a spot among the trees on the hill behind the boathouse. But what of her inchoate insight? She said, 'Maybe we should wait until the program is over. It's only three weeks.'

Ray said, 'I can't wait.'

From the look in his eyes and the tightness of his voice, Peg knew he meant it. Of course he *could* wait. Sexual frustration wasn't, as yet, a high-ranking killer among American males. He just didn't want to. For the first time, instead of being swept up by a man's urgency, Peg was able to think first. A clear sign of progress! She would have to tell Linus.

She said, 'I think we should stay right here and have a nice conversation. We could get to know each other better. Become friends. Did you know that relationships that start as friendships are more likely to end in marriage?'

He said, 'And relationships that begin with passion are bound to fail?'

'Of course not,' said Peg.

'Okay, then,' said Ray.

He leaned down and kissed her again, a sweet brushing of lips and the touch of cheeks warmed by the sun.

He said, 'Let's take a walk.'

'I'm not going anywhere,' she said. A couple of the students were looking at them now. 'The kids are watching us.'

He said, 'If you won't leave, we'll have to frighten the children.'

He lay down next to her and started sucking her ear. Sucking, nibbling, licking just the fleshy lobe. The sensation, the snapping to of her nerve endings. He might as well have been sucking (nibbling, licking) her in another place, the way she responded. A moan of lust and defeat escaped her lips, and Peg gave in. She'd let him. But they'd stay on the dock. How far would he try to go in full view of a dozen people? A simple kiss wasn't diving feetfirst into disaster. It was nothing. A trifle.

When they came up for air, the sun had disappeared behind the mountains, and the dock was dark and deserted. Hours had gone by.

He said, 'Finally, we're alone.'

He went for her bikini strap.

What now? Peg wondered.

He unhooked her top, and pulled it off. He moved on top of her, whispering, 'This is right, you know it is.' It was a beautiful night. Warm, quiet, the water lapping gently on the dock, silvery clouds against the black sky.

Did she see herself as someone who would fuck on a college boat dock a man she'd met a week ago?

In her previous life, that would've been 'strongly agree.' When she'd swum out here, it would've been 'strongly disagree.' And now? Ray put his hand inside her bikini bottom and her resolve melted. She couldn't be strong all the time. Peg closed her eyes.

Suddenly, a beam of light hit her lids, as if the sun had been turned back on.

Ray said, 'What the fuck?' and rolled off.

She pulled herself up on her elbows, and squinted. She and Ray were trapped in a white circle, the beam coming from a point at the top of the dock. The light was so bright, when she looked at Ray, and at her own half-nude body, she could see every detail, as if it were high noon.

'You two!' said a voice behind the beam. 'You're trespassing on private property.'

Peg fumbled for her bikini top.

Ray stood. He said, 'Turn off the fucking flashlight.'

Flashlight? It was a klieg light. The policeman, security guard, whatever, said, 'Leave the premises immediately, or I'll arrest you for indecent exposure and lewd behavior.'

'You can't arrest us,' said Ray defiantly. 'We're citizens, with rights!'

This was not the time for civil disobedience. Peg said, 'Ray, let's just go.' But where? Back into the water? It was black as ink. Walk over the bridge and the additional half-mile to the Federal in a bikini and bare feet? Peg tried to look across the river to locate the mansion, but from within the beam of light, she couldn't see anything.

The next sound Peg heard was the squawk of a walkietalkie. The policeman talked again. 'I've got two trespassers on the crew dock. They're giving me a hard time. Better come on down with the squad car. And the stun gun.'

Peg didn't like the sound of that. She slid into the river. Ray shouted to the cop, 'Come and get me if you've got the balls!' and dove off the dock. The white beam stayed on them as they swam, making it nearly impossible to see where they were going. As they made some distance, Peg thought the light would fade. But no. It was just as bright from halfway across the river.

And then, as if one klieg light wasn't enough, another tracker beam hit them, this one from the Vermont side. Instinct told her the second beam was coming from the

Inward Bound Federal. She swam toward it. Ray swam next to her, continuing to shout insults at the cop.

A bullhorn sounded from behind them. 'Don't come back to New Hampshire if you know what's good for you!'

That blast made all the houses along the river light up. Suddenly, more beams were on them. Three, four, five. Aimed right at them as if they were fugitives on the run. Peg thought she could hear laughter and whistles bouncing across the water.

Finally, Peg and Ray made it to the other side. They couldn't find the boat dock, so they had to wade through slimy weeds to get up on the bank. Once there, the whoops and whistles got louder. Standing next to her in the circle of light, Ray took a bow. She could hear applause and laughter from all directions. Ray waved at the spectators he couldn't see, pumping his arms over his head like a prizefighter. Peg left him in the spotlight, and trudged up the hill. She got her bearings and found the footpath along the river.

When she reached the Federal's dock, she was hit anew by a massive flood of light.

Pinned in it, she said, 'I can explain everything.'

An eruption of laughter. The light clicked off. When her eyes adjusted, she saw all the Inward Bounders lined up on the porch. Wilma, Linus, Luke, Tracy, Gloria and Ben, each holding a bottle of Magic Hat. Except Linus. He was holding an enormous flashlight.

Ray appeared at her side, took a few more bows, to great applause. 'Thank you,' he said. 'Thank you very much.'

Dripping wet, the swimmers took the stairs up to the porch. Peg accepted a beer from Linus. Ray wandered toward Luke and Ben to receive high fives and a cigar.

To Linus, Peg said, 'Are you going to kick me out?'

He said, 'Nah. I like having you around.'

'You called the cops on us?' she asked.

He said, 'I was concerned for the safety of my charges.'

'What is this thing?' she asked, pointing at the flashlight.

He handed it to her. It was at least five pounds with a bulb the size of a saucer. He said, 'It's a SuperLight. Two million candle power, five-thousand-watt bulb, with a visibility range of one mile. They're great for hiking at night, spotting deer and bears. Everybody's got one. But you've probably gathered that by now.'

'You called the neighbors, too?'

He shook his head. 'The bullhorn caught their attention.'

Wilma said, 'How's that list coming, Peg?'

'List?'

'Of your goals for Week Two. What you want to get out of your interpersonal exercises.'

She looked at Ray, still charged from his turn in the spotlight(s).

Peg said, 'I'm working on it.'

Wilma said, 'Sometimes it helps to figure out what you don't want first.'

'Way ahead of you, Wilma,' she said.

17

'Pretend I'm a typical man,' said Linus Bester. 'For the moment, I want you to forget that I'm a psychologist and relationships expert.'

From her seat on the couch, Peg would not have a problem with those instructions. Linus looked nothing like a Ph.D., or an expert in anything but hugging trees. He wore a tie-dye T-shirt, cargo shorts with Birkenstocks and the red-bead leather anklet. Peg studied Linus's feet. She liked them, the long toes, and callused heels from running. He had sweet legs, too. Long. Ripped. He was smiling at the women, as usual, Mr Friendly with the anti-freeze blue eyes and shiny brown hair. He was the picture of earnest good intentions.

He'd last ten minutes in New York, thought Peg. Then again, who was she to talk? She'd run screaming from the city and come north, just for the chance to meet a man like Linus. But not him. Definitely not him. Peg had her heart set on a woodsy guy, not a crunchy one.

'Now,' said Linus. 'As a typical man, what do you think I want out of a relationship? Write a list. Feel free to draw from personal experience.'

Tracy and Gloria sat on either side of Peg on the living-room couch. Those two immediately scribbled on their legal pads. Peg doodled. She just couldn't go there yet. It was simply too early on a Monday morning to crawl down memory lane.

She'd had a proper Sunday. Peg walked to the Manshire Inn for a saturated-fatty and nitrate-laden breakfast of bacon, eggs, buttery toast, dark coffee, OJ, hash browns, sausage and honey buns. She sat alone. Ate and ate. Then rolled herself out of there, and checked her cell phone messages in the parking lot of Dambit's. She got service, miraculously. A dozen messages from her parents, Nina, Jack, the exterminator, the real estate broker. Peg called mice-sympathizer Chuck Plenet and got his voice mail. She called Bertha the Broker, who was in Woodstock at an open house. She tried to call her parents, to assure them that she hadn't been carted off by deer hunters, but the signal died. Peg considered driving over to her farm. But she was afraid of the carnage.

On the walk back to the Federal – belly painfully full – Peg vowed to get control of herself. Eat right. Exercise. Avoid Ray. Peg would get up early, join Linus for his dawn jog, no matter how tired she was the next day.

That being Monday, today, which began when Tracy and Gloria dragged her out of bed to catch the final minutes of breakfast before Linus's seminar on what men want.

Tracy raised her hand first. Linus called on her. She said, 'What men have wanted from me, in descending order of importance: an ego boost, a sounding board – and I do mean *bored* – a last-minute escort, a drinking buddy. And cab fare.'

Gloria said, 'I have ego boost on my list.'

Peg said, 'I have drinking buddy.'

'What else, Gloria?' asked Linus.

Gloria said, 'Arm candy, clout, bragging rights, an empty vessel, masturbatory tool.'

'Jesus, Gloria,' said Tracy. 'It hasn't been that bad.'

'Oh, yes,' said Gloria. 'You have no idea how hard it is to be me.'

Peg might have been turned off by Gloria's self-pity. But, then again, she didn't know what it must be like to have a famous father, to be heiress to a fortune and trotted around society like an exotic animal. Gloria the giraffe.

Linus called on Peg. She recited, 'Men want me to be their sexual co-adventurer, drinking buddy, cook, maid, cheerleader.'

He said, 'Very good. Now take that piece of paper, all of you, crumple it into a ball and throw it away. That's right. Over your shoulder.'

'Now you're going to tell us why our lists are fucked up, and how to change,' said Peg. 'We're symbolically throwing away the mistakes of our past, and you're going to point the way toward future happiness.'

'How should I know what will make you happy?' he asked.

'You're not going to give us the answers?' asked Tracy.

'I can't do that,' said Linus. 'That would be cheating.'

Gloria asked, 'So what are we doing here?'

Linus held up his finger, imploring the impatient heathens to wait. 'My job is not to give you answers,' he said. 'It's to ask the right questions.'

Tracy, Peg and Gloria heaved couch pillows at him.

Holding up his arms to ward off the throws, Linus said, 'I guess I deserved that.'

'Since we're to draw on personal experience, why don't you tell us about what you want in your relationship,' said Peg.

'I'll speak as a typical man,' Linus said. 'Sweeping gender generalizations can be useful sometimes. First and foremost, men want reliability. Women get into a relationship hoping a man will change, and he never does; men get into a relationship hoping the woman won't change, but she always does. Men want their partners to be consistent. That they won't make impromptu impossible demands nor baffle him with classically female sudden-onset hysterical behavior.'

'You just made yourself very unsympathetic, mister,' said Tracy frostily.

'I'm not speaking for myself,' he defended. 'I like sudden-onset hysterical behavior. It can be educational, from an empirical anecdotal research standpoint.'

Peg said, 'So what do you recommend? That women should be completely accepting, ask for nothing, expect nothing from the men we give everything to?'

Linus sat down on the coffee table, right in front of Peg. He leaned in close, his knees touching hers. 'Your language,' he said. 'It's plaintive.'

'I've been wronged,' said Peg.

'You think relationships are about give and take.'

'Doesn't everyone?' she asked, appealing to Tracy and Gloria, who dutifully nodded.

Linus said, 'The typical man suspects that his girlfriend gives to get. He appreciates all the giving at first. Eventually, he starts to wonder when all this giving will turn into demands and ultimatums. Every time she volunteers to get him a beer, he worries she'll expect something in return. A gift. A dinner with her parents. A commitment to love and honor each other until death. His anxiety builds, and the typical man can take only so much before he cracks.'

The women on the couch listened, horrified.

Linus continued. 'I'm not suggesting that women

consciously scheme. A woman in love wants to demonstrate. She's not necessarily giving to get. But the typical man will think otherwise.'

Gloria said, 'I've never put pressure on men. I barely ask for anything.'

Linus said, 'Have you ever pursued a man?'

Gloria looked surprised. 'Men are supposed to pursue the woman.'

'Your answer is no,' he said. 'Do you flirt?'

'I flirt,' said Gloria.

'What's your style?' asked Linus.

'I'm rude and snotty,' said Gloria. 'The ruder I am, the harder they come after me.'

Linus nodded sagaciously. He said, 'Did you bring your other list? What you hope to achieve from your interpersonal exercises this week?'

Gloria had her list folded into a small square, tucked into the bib pocket of her pinafore dress. Tracy took hers out, too. Peg hadn't completed hers at this time. She'd have to improvise when her turn came.

Linus said to Gloria, 'What's the first thing on the list?'

She said, 'I want to feel excited. To have fun. Like those girls at camp.'

'Has being rude to men made you feel excited?'

'No.'

'Was it fun?' he asked.

'Kind of.'

'What would be exciting and fun?'

'Something else?' Gloria ventured hesitantly.

'Tracy,' Linus said, turning to the brunette, 'what's on your list?'

Gloria said quickly, 'You're not going to tell me what

to do? You expect me to figure it out for myself? And how am I supposed to do that?'

Linus said, 'Trial and error. Your date tonight is with Ray. Use him, experiment on him. You can start by smiling and talking to him instead of being rude and snotty.'

Gloria seemed mollified by that.

Linus said, 'Tracy?'

Tracy said, 'The first thing on the list?' He nodded. She read, 'I want to learn how to turn a first date into a second date.'

Peg said, 'Sleep with him and have breakfast the next morning.'

Tracy said, 'That may work for you, Ms Perfect Runner's Body. But I can barely get a decent good night kiss. I can wave them in with semaphore flags, and they don't get the message.'

Linus said, 'How does that feel?'

'It's humiliating! Every time.'

'So why do you do it?'

'If I didn't, I'd never get laid.'

'And you're getting laid how often?' he asked.

'Never.'

'Ah.'

Tracy said, 'So you're saying that I shouldn't humiliate myself, since it's not working anyway?'

'I didn't say a word,' corrected Linus. 'But you might be on to something there. You're with Luke tonight.' Tracy liked the sound of that. She smiled brightly and settled back into the couch.

'Gloria should do more, and Tracy should do less,' said Peg. 'What about me? How should I handle gentle Ben?'

Linus asked, 'What is the number one thing on your list?'

'I, uh, I'm not fully prepared to make a statement,' she said. He stared at her, not letting her off the hook. Peg said, 'The dog ate my list.'

'The dog named Ray?' asked Tracy, and then she and Gloria giggled at the memory of Peg's late-night swim.

'I don't know what I want to learn,' whined Peg. 'I'm sure I need to learn something, and that, once I've learned it, I'll be eternally grateful to have the information.'

Linus gave her a cryptic smile, nodding weirdly at her confusion.

Peg said, 'Are you going to help me, or what?'

He said, 'I'm going to help you.'

'I'm waiting,' she said, her annoyance growing. She didn't want to sound vexed. She knew she was impatient. She would dearly love to be Zen-like, as in, 'All things will eventually become evident.' She would like to be recalibrated to Vermont Time. She would also love a beach house in Bermuda.

Linus said, 'You wouldn't feel so lost if you took the time to familiarize yourself with the surroundings.'

'Meaning?' she asked.

'Stop running,' he said.

Jesus Christ. 'From this day forward,' Peg said, her sardonic tone gooey, 'I will chew my food thirty-two times before I swallow. I'll crawl from room to room. I'll count pennies, daisies and blessings. I'll wait until my wedding night to have sex.'

'That sarcasm,' said Linus. 'Where the hell is my stick?'

'Can we stop talking about Peg?' asked Gloria. 'And get back to me?'

Linus said, 'You want to know what you should wear tonight.'

'How did you know?' asked Gloria.

'Linus knows everything,' said Peg. 'It's his special gift.'

He said to Gloria, 'You and Ray are going to a potluck dinner at a church in Chelsea. Wilma will take you. Tracy, you and Luke are going to a cornhusking bee at Billings Farm in Woodstock. With me. Peg, you and Ben are going to dinner at Poule au Dent on Main Street in Manshire. It's walking distance.'

'Who's our chaperone?' she asked.

Linus said, 'The chef is a friend of mine. He's going to observe.'

'I still don't know what to wear,' said Gloria. 'I've never been to a potluck. I've never been to a church.'

'And I've been to a cornhusking bee?' asked Tracy. 'Which doesn't sound very romantic, whatever it is. How am I supposed to be seductive on a farm?'

Linus said, 'You're not supposed to be seductive at all, Tracy. Just be. If there aren't any more questions, you can have the afternoon off. You'll leave for your dates at five o'clock.'

Then he left the women in the living room to their collective and individual bafflement.

Gloria said, 'Potluck? I'm supposed to bring a pot to get lucky?'

'Don't worry,' Peg said, 'Ray will bring the pot.'

Tracy said, 'What the hell is sexy about corn?'

'Pretend it comes with batteries,' suggested Gloria.

'How's the soup?' asked Ben.

Peg sampled the strawberry bisque. 'Fruity yet wet,' she said.

'You don't like it,' said Ben.

Ben seemed to take her slow spooning of summer soup as a rebuke of him personally, even though he hadn't picked the restaurant, composed the menu, prepared the dish or ordered it.

'It's delicious,' she reassured him.

'Do you like the décor?' he asked.

'Very nice,' she said.

'Beautiful night, don't you think?'

'Hot yet dry.'

'We've had meals together every day for a week, but we haven't had a single conversation until now,' said Ben. 'Tell me about yourself.'

She cringed. Peg hated talking about herself. Maybe that was why, on most of her first dates, she skipped the talking part, and moved immediately to the not-talking part. Her goal tonight, however, was to practice patience.

'I grew up in Manhattan,' she started.

'New York! Great town. Lots of energy. Lots of buzz. So you've traveled from Manhattan to Manshire,' he said. 'You're really moving north in the world! Tell me more.'

He leaned forward, eyes big, forehead shiny, in the grip of anticipation for her next utterance. Or faking it as hard as he could.

Peg paused. 'Linus gave me an agenda for tonight,' she said, choosing her words. 'I'm supposed to take things slow, be relaxed. Not to disrupt the natural unfolding of events with my ego.' Or libido. Not a problem there, though. Ben didn't do it for her. He could for someone else, though. In a cerulean shirt, lavender tie, linen jacket that concealed his belly, he looked dapper. His hair was well-trimmed (where there was hair) and his face was open. For a chubby guy, his chin and cheeks were well defined. He had nicely shaped lips, puffy but not too feminine, and streamline brows over large, almond-shaped hazel eyes. When he smiled, dimples appeared in his cheeks.

Ben said, 'Wilma talked to us about date strategy, too.'

'She told you to ask me a lot of questions?' guessed Peg. 'To show an interest in me.'

Ben said, 'I have a tendency to override my nerves by talking about myself, and before I realize it, I've alienated my dates.' He took a sip of Bordeaux. 'Are you alienated?'

He asked with such seriousness that Peg had to laugh. Ben said, 'You're laughing. That's better than crying. Or falling asleep in your soup. That's happened to me. I was with this girl from work. She was a secretary. Too young for me, but she was impressed by my title. I'm executive vice president for SafePath Insurance. We're the third-largest supplier of home-owner's policies in the Northeast. My specialty had been earthquake and tidal wave. But lately, I'm selling insurance against terrorist attacks. Believe it or not, one out of seven New Englanders believe there are terrorist sleeper cells living somewhere in their community, despite the fact that this part of the country has a negligible Islamic population. In Vermont, it's about one-quarter of one per cent. This state is ninety-nine per cent Caucasian, with a sizable Cambodian population. But they're not Islamic.'

Ben's speech was hypnotic. Trance-inducing. Peg's eyelids were growing heavy. She felt drowsy.

He said, 'Are you Islamic? Have you ever met a Cambodian? Do you have homeowner's insurance? Why did you come to Inward Bound? Are you recently out of a relationship? Was he a bald man? Have you ever dated a bald man?'

She stammered, not knowing which question to address first, or why she should answer any of them. She said, 'Can you repeat the questions, one at a time?'

He said, 'Oh, God. I'm doing it again. I'm alienating you. We're not connecting. We're at the same table, but we exist on parallel planes that will never intersect.'

The new geometry of dating? Peg had always been bad at math. She said, 'I would love to talk about home-owner's insurance,' she said, smiling her super-watt, hoping for a discount.

Ben said, 'You don't care about insurance. You're pretending to be interested.'

'I do care!' said Peg.

'Don't insult me,' he said, offended now.

'Okay, you want the truth?' she asked. 'The truth is, I hate the soup.'

'What the hell is wrong with me?' he blurted suddenly, his list of questions ceaselessly growing. He stared meaningfully at his plate for a few seconds, and then, as if it just occurred to him that food lay upon it, he scarfed his crab cake in three aggressive bites.

Peg, abandoning her bisque entirely, reached for the wine. Ben got there first, and gave her a refill. She gulped the wine, then drained the bottle into her glass. She said, 'We need another bottle.'

'I'm incapable of shutting up,' said Ben. 'It's like my mouth has a mouth of its own. And I know I'm not saying anything charming or endearing or even intelligent. But the words just keep on coming, even though I realize nothing I say will get you to remove a single article of clothing. Words won't undress a woman.'

Peg must have looked startled. He said, 'Not you, necessarily. I mean *any* woman. The world is full of women. They're everywhere! Literally billions of them the world over. And each one – every single one – has a vagina.'

'I guess your penis has a mouth of its own, too,' said Peg.

'I'm not greedy. I only need one,' pleaded Ben.

'One vagina?'

'Yes!' he admitted. 'With the rest of the woman wrapped around it.'

The waiter brought out their next course, braised venison with sherry and mushroom sauce, wild rice and apricot chutney. It looked and smelled delicious. She thanked the waiter and apologized for not finishing her soup. He cleared the appetizer dishes and left them alone.

She said, 'Isn't the chef supposed to be watching us?'

Peg and Ben looked back toward the kitchen. No sign of the chef anywhere. 'I prefer it this way,' said Ben. 'I feel self-conscious enough already.'

It *was* awkward. Two people who wouldn't have picked each other for a romantic dinner in a million years. And yet, they sat at a table laden with tapered candles, fresh lilies, wine and nouveau country French food. If Ray were here instead of Ben, he'd be groping her under the table. She'd swat at his hand. Ray would persist, she'd give in, and they'd screw in the bathroom between courses.

The thought of it sent a flash flood to Peg's panties. She looked at Ben (he was about as appetizing as the soup), afraid he'd notice her sudden blush. She needn't have worried. Ben's insecurity made him blind to anything else.

Peg decided to take advantage of the MIA chaperone. Her helper instincts kicked in.

Peg asked, 'Of the three women in the group, who are you most attracted to?' Ben squinted at her, unsure or unwilling to confess. She said, 'Our secret.'

He relented. 'Gloria is stunning,' he said.

'Tracy is very cute, don't you think?'

'I'd put you second,' he said, searching her face for the right reaction. Not getting it, he said, 'Wilma is hot. We've all talked about her.' He leaned forward. 'She likes to touch us. On the shoulders, the back. She's touched my knees five or six times. She grabbed Luke's ass.'

Peg kept herself from demanding details about where and how Wilma had touched Ray. 'Maybe Wilma flirts to boost your confidence,' she said.

It could be true. Wilma wasn't affectionate with the women. She seemed to shrink from the prospect of closeness, physical or otherwise. Then again, women often acted differently in the exclusive presence of men. Nina, for one, dropped twenty IQ points as soon as a good-looking man walked in the room. Their biggest fight was about Nina's stupid-girl routine while on a double date with Peg. Peg said to her: 'You shouldn't change for a man, regardless. But for God's sake, don't make yourself worse.'

Ben said, 'I guess it's possible Wilma is touching us with an ulterior motive. Can't say I mind.'

Peg steered him back in the right direction. 'Tracy is a very genuine person. Funny. Smart.'

'I'm sure she is.'

'She has a vagina,' dangled Peg.

'No doubt.'

'And it's well attended to,' added Peg, thinking of Tracy's vibrator collection.

'I'm just not attracted to her.'

'What if I told you she was attracted to you?' asked Peg. A lie, but Peg might be able to talk Tracy into it.

He shook his head. 'No sale. Just for the record, I would gladly join any club that would have me for a member. I'm a member of a dozen different organizations: a bowling team, a cheese-tasting society, a neighborhood watch, a gardening club, to name several.'

'Gardening club?' asked Peg with interest.

'I breed hybrid roses.'

'I'm an interior landscape designer,' she said. 'Was. In the city.'

'I dated a nursery owner once,' he said. 'From the club. She was sweet. But her fingernails were filthy, and she smelled like fertilizer. She had wrinkles from working outdoors. Her hair was a disaster.'

Dirty nails and mulchy aroma. Story of Peg's life. She wondered if any of her boyfriends had said as much about her.

'She blew me off,' said Ben, 'after two dates.'

'Maybe she didn't like the way *you* smell,' snapped

Peg. Her charitable impulse toward him had evaporated.

'You're angry. Alienated, for sure,' he said. 'I should have stuck to our common interest in gardening, instead of saying something critical about another woman.'

'A good idea for future dates,' said Peg.

He paused, and then asked, 'Under what circumstances could you possibly see us getting together?'

'You and Tracy?' she asked.

'You and me,' he said. 'Be honest.'

She said diplomatically, 'We both have a lot of Inward Bounding to do before we could have that conversation.'

'So it's possible,' he said.

Eyes on plate, fork busy, she shrugged. She chewed to avoid speaking. But she was running out of food.

He said, 'Just theoretically, Peg. What would it take for a woman like you to be attracted to me?'

'A woman like you,' he'd said. She was struck by the notion that, for most men, all females were of a type. To him, she was 'beyond reach.' She could be (had been) a demanding neurotic who woke up her boyfriend at 3 A.M. crying and begging (Linus would call it 'sudden-onset hysterical behavior'). She could be (had been) a clingy succubus who drained her lovers of emotional pulp. Or she could be (hadn't been yet) a deranged hatchet killer, or brain-eating zombie. But that didn't matter to Ben. All he saw was long shiny hair and an athletic body.

She said, 'A woman like me could be attracted to you exactly as you are.' Which was the kindest thing Peg had ever said.

The waiter appeared (thankfully), and asked if they'd like to meet the chef. Ben was hesitant. He didn't want to veer away from his favorite topic – what was wrong with him – but Peg said yes, they'd love to.

A spiffy man approached their table from the kitchen, wiping his hands on a cloth apron. Under it, he wore khakis and a pink oxford shirt. He was about forty, his face wide and weather-worn, red hair turning a soft silver. Half expecting the chef to be French (another New Yorker assumption), Peg was surprised by his Vermont accent.

'Albert DeWitt,' he said. 'I hope you're enjoying the meal.'

Peg and Ben assured him they adored every bite. Albert smiled amicably, soaking it up like sauce on bread. She said, 'I thought you were going to join us.'

'Linus told me not to,' said Albert. 'I do exactly what Linus tells me. I have since we were three years old, and things have worked out pretty good for me so far.'

'Have you lived in Vermont your whole life?' asked Ben.

'Not yet,' said Albert, deadpan, waiting for a laugh.

Peg and Ben laughed.

'Or, I should say, so far. I can't imagine leaving. I'm a native. Fourth generation Vermonter.' He was obviously proud of that, too, along with his cooking, and his jokes.

As a native New Yorker, Peg understood the cachet of being born and raised in the city. Vermonters, apparently, were just as snobby.

Peg said, 'Linus is a native, too, right?'

Albert shook his head. 'Technically, Linus is a flatlander. His parents were from Boston, and they moved to Manshire a couple of years before Linus was born.'

'Before?' said Peg. 'He's not a native even though he was born here?'

'If a cat crawls into the oven and has kittens, that

don't make 'em biscuits,' replied Albert with an exaggerated Upper Valley-ese, of which he was also proud.

'How unfair,' said Peg. 'To live in the same town for decades, to be born here and still to be an outsider.'

Albert laughed loudly at that. 'No one in Manshire thinks Linus is an outsider,' he said. 'They wouldn't have elected him mayor if they did.'

'Linus is the mayor of Manshire?' asked Ben, as surprised as Peg was.

'He adjudicated at my wedding,' said Albert. 'He's married a hundred couples at least, but never been married himself. Everyone in Manshire is waiting – praying – for that day.'

Peg felt herself blush, not sure why. Albert seemed to notice, his eyebrows rising.

She quickly changed the subject. 'If Linus told you not to sit with us, how are you going to report back to him about our date?'

He said, 'I'm not reporting anything. Your date is none of my business. I'm just giving Linus the tape.'

Ben said, 'The tape?'

Albert reached under the tablecloth, and ripped something from the bottom of the table. He brought his arm back into view, and showed them the microcassette recorder, duct-tape tacky, the spinning wheels inside still recording.

Ben stammered, 'That's . . . that's an invasion of privacy!'

Albert frowned at Ben's reaction. He said, 'You knew you were being monitored.'

'Not covertly,' said Ben.

Peg sympathized. Ben had said those things about

Wilma. She tried to remember if she'd said anything inflammatory.

'That's the way we always do it,' said Albert. 'Linus likes an element of surprise.'

Ben said, 'This is an outrage!'

Albert wasn't up for Ben's outrage. He said, 'Tell you what. I'll send out some white chocolate mousse, with a raspberry sauce and a sugar cookie.'

'And coffee,' said Peg. 'If you please.'

Albert left the table, the tape recorder in his pocket. Ben dropped his head in his hands. He said, 'Great! This is just fucking great. They'll hear everything I said. About Wilma. Vaginas. Cambodians. They'll hate me! My bad dating has reached a new low. Now I can alienate people *who aren't even on the date.*'

'Wilma and Linus are professionals,' said Peg. 'They have the necessary detachment. This can't be the first time they've been gossiped about over dinner.'

'This is all your fault,' said Ben, his once kind eyes sizzling with anger. 'You made me talk.'

Hadn't he been saying that he couldn't shut himself up? Peg said, 'I didn't know we were being recorded. Honestly, Ben, I'm sure they won't care what was said. Everything is fodder for them. They won't take it personally.'

'You believe that?' he asked.

'I do,' she said, not too convincingly.

'Under these circumstances,' said Ben, throwing down his napkin, 'you can forget about us ever getting together.'

The waiter arrived with their dessert on a silver platter.

19

When Ben and Peg returned to the Federal (he walked three paces behind her), the place was quiet. Where was everyone? she wondered. Clearly, the others were having a better time on their dates. Without a word, Ben walked straight up the stairs, into the men's suite, slamming his door. Peg wandered through the living room, toward the back porch.

She thought of turning on the outside light, but then again, why attract a swarm of mosquitoes? She pushed the screen door open, and stepped outside.

A yelp, the creep of floorboards. Peg turned toward the noise. Even in the dark, she could make out two figures on the wicker love seat. On reflex, Peg averted her eyes. But then she had to turn back out of sheer amazement.

Tracy sat astride Luke, his hand up her shirt, her arms around his neck. 'A little privacy,' said Tracy in a raspy voice Peg hadn't heard from her before.

Peg immediately backed herself into the living room. Tracy's evening of stripping corn had ignited vegetative passion in Luke, a man who, until that point, appeared to have the sex drive of a potato. Peg was glad someone was having a good time. And jealous that she wasn't.

If Tracy and Luke were back from the farm, Peg

figured Gloria and Ray had to be done with their church potluck. Might they be lip smacking in a dark corner, too? The thought unleashed another blast of jealousy. Fearing the worst, she went in search of them.

Starting with the living room. All couches clear. The kitchen, empty. The light under Linus and Wilma's bedroom door was on, though. She tiptoed closer, her ears prickling like a cactus. She crept closer, slowly, stealthfully, until she was pressed against the door, her cheek resting on its wood panels, listening.

Soft voices. Wilma's clinical tone. The shuffling of paper. Linus must be in there with her, she thought (he'd been Tracy and Luke's chaperone). But that begged the question: If Wilma was home, where were Ray and Gloria?

Suddenly, the sound of footsteps, the door handle jiggling. Shit, she thought, jumping away from the door as it opened. Peg zipped back to the cranny between the wall and the fridge.

She kept her mouth shut. She was impressed by her ability to do this, especially when she saw Ray exit Wilma's bedroom. Wilma of the touch-feely hands. Wilma who'd stroked Ben's knee and grabbed Luke's ass. What had she just touched of Ray's in her bedroom?

Jealousy, flaming, hot, burned in her marrow. Wilma was her rival? She'd tear her apart, she'd cut out her eyes. Then again, Peg was having some doubts that Ray was right for her. But even if he wasn't, that didn't mean she wanted him to be right for someone else. Or maybe it wasn't jealousy she felt. Maybe it was anger, at Wilma, for cheating on Linus. He didn't deserve to be deceived in his own room, his own house.

Did Peg see herself as someone who would tell a

friend about his or her partner's infidelity?

Strongly disagree. Although, as she knelt in her cranny, Peg pictured herself telling Linus the truth. His shocked expression and instant grief. Her comforting him, holding him, rubbing his back. Guiding his head into her neck, knitting her fingers in his unruly hair, whispering softly to him, planting kisses on his shoulder, lifting his head to access his lips . . .

To *what*? Kiss Linus? Peg screeched that fantasy to a halt. Clearly, she was coming undone. Too much Inward Bounding had knocked the sense from her mind. Peg crawled out of the kitchen, and dashed to the front yard. Still wearing her date dress, Peg kicked off her sandals and started running.

She ran along River Road, back toward Main Street. She stayed on the grass or the soft dirt bunker to protect her feet. But it didn't matter. Peg barely felt the ground. She was aware only of the up and down of her legs, the warm air filling her lungs, the steady thudding of her heart. The movement of bones and muscles in coordination, faster than usual, erasing mental activity, feeling only physical strain and release.

She was back at the restaurant in minutes. Slowing after the half-mile sprint, Peg jogged by Poule au Dent, looking in the windows out of curiosity, like a murderer returning to the scene of the crime.

Inside, at a table by the open front window, she spotted Albert DeWitt in his pink shirt, sipping a glass of wine. Across from him, smiling as always, was Linus Bester.

Before Peg had a chance to duck, Albert spotted her.

'Look who's back,' he shouted out the open window.

Peg had no choice but to respond. 'I think I left my sunglasses here.' Only as the words were exiting her mouth did she realize they was true.

'I've got them,' said Albert, holding up her sunglasses, and his wineglass. 'Come on in. Join us for a drink.'

She nodded, and went for the restaurant's front door, all the while in a slight panic. Could she act normal? Could she pretend she hadn't seen Ray exiting Linus's bedroom?

Linus and Albert watched her approach them. Albert looked bemused; Linus smiled cheerfully. Poor oblivious sucker, thought Peg.

The two old friends invited Peg to sit. Linus said, 'Night run?'

She said, 'Just meandering.'

'You're sweating. And your face is red.'

'Okay, I was running. Yes,' she said.

Albert poured her a glass of the same Bordeaux she'd had at dinner. 'Do you always run barefoot?' asked Albert. 'Like those Kenyan marathoners?'

Linus said, 'Let me see your feet.'

Peg crossed her bare legs and lifted her left foot for inspection. It was dirty, but otherwise unharmed. She'd been on grass, after all.

Linus whistled. 'That's some foot.'

Peg had always been self-conscious about her extra-large hooves. 'You were expecting dainty lady's feet?'

He said, 'I wasn't expecting the leathery sole of a Hobbit.'

A party of six entered the restaurant. Albert excused himself to seat them. Peg said, 'I didn't know you were here.'

'I dropped off Luke and Tracy and came over. Albert and I have a weekly cigar date.'

'Is Wilma still at church with Ray and Gloria?' she asked smoothly.

He shook his head. 'They're back. I said hello and good-bye to them, then drove over here. I saw you and Ben on the road walking back together.'

'So Wilma knows you're here?'

'Every Monday night,' he said.

Albert rejoined them. 'Shall we?' he asked. They all rose, and Albert led them to a garden patio behind the restaurant. The patio had a full bar, benches and tables, a trellis with pink roses and a potted lilac bush, still blooming in July. Peg inhaled the summer scents, wishing she'd eaten out here instead of inside. Albert must have read her thoughts. He said, 'The tape recorder picks up conversation better indoors.'

She nodded and said, 'Can we sit at the bar?'

'You like the bar?' asked Linus.

'I always sit at the bar,' said Peg.

'Even for dinner?' he asked.

'Definitely.' Peg liked the long-legged chairs, plates on lacquered mahogany, the colored bottles to look at while she ate. They pulled up stools, Peg between the two men.

'Linus would rather eat at the bar than at a table, too,' said Albert. 'Wilma never lets him. None of his girl-friends have let him.' He added, 'That's why he's never married.'

Peg asked Linus, 'Restaurant seating is a make or break compatibility issue?'

Linus said, 'I try to compromise.'

'Speaking of compromise,' Albert said, 'how is Wilma?'

Linus said, 'Very well, thank you.'

Stage-whispering to Peg, Albert said, 'I give it six months.'

'That's what you said six months ago,' said Linus.

Albert produced two cellophone-wrapped cigars. He handed one to Linus. 'For you, nothing but the best.'

The men stoked their cigars. The bartender, a pretty woman, barely old enough to serve alcohol, asked for their orders. Albert suggested they try some new vodka from Poland. The bartender poured the clear liquid over ice. A waiter came outside, looking for Albert. Trouble in the kitchen, he said. Their host excused himself, and handed his cigar to Peg.

Alone with Linus, she watched him sip his drink. Peg admired the way he drank it without grimacing, as if he genuinely enjoyed the flavor of uncut vodka. He turned toward her, his face guileless, the candles on the bar painting him in shadow.

She said, 'In New York, the tabloids call the mayor "Hizzoner."'

Linus nodded, cigar in mouth, smoke curling. 'The *Upper Valley News* calls me "Supreme Imperial Eminence."'

'They do not,' she said.

'Ask Albert.'

'Vermont humor seems to be based on gullibility.'

Linus said, 'How'd it go with Ben?'

Peg said, 'Nice trick, the tape recorder.'

'You don't have to worry,' he said. 'People gossip.'

'You get off on subterfuge. Calling the cops on me. The tape recorder,' Peg said.

'Just doing my job,' he said.

Peg said, 'Let's talk about your job. Your other job. I

could use a friend in high places if I'm going to survive in this town.'

'You'll do fine here,' assured Linus.

'How do you know?' she asked.

'Albert likes you,' said Linus. 'He's a good barometer.'

'What did he say about me?' she asked like an approval-greedy pet.

'He said, "I like Peg." '

'What does that mean?'

'It means he wants to divorce his wife and run away with you.'

Peg asked, 'He does?'

Linus laughed at her and shook his head. 'So much for your quick study of Vermont humor.' He sipped his vodka, killing it. 'Albert doesn't make many qualitative statements. If he says he likes you, that's what he means.'

Peg thought of the millions of times she'd heard New Yorkers say of someone they just met, 'I absolutely adore him. I am madly in love with him. He could not be more fantastic.' Overstatement was the norm. A slice of pizza or well-tailored jacket could provoke a declaration of undying devotion.

'I like Albert, too,' Peg said.

'He also said I should break up with Wilma and go out with you,' Linus added.

She swatted him on the shoulder. 'I'm not falling for it again, you jackass.'

He looked her squarely in the eye, and said, 'Are you going to smoke that, or let Albert's cigar go to waste?'

She took Linus up on the challenge. Sucking slowly, she got a mouthful of blue smoke.

'What was going on back at the Federal?' he asked. 'Anything I should know about?'

She spat out the smoke, and started coughing in great wracking heaves. Grabbing at the bar for relief, she picked up her glass and drank, forgetting that it was vodka.

Albert came rushing out to the bar, hearing the commotion.

He asked, 'What have you done to her?'

Linus, who was whacking Peg on the back, said, 'It was your cheap cigar!'

'I'm fine,' she sputtered. And she was. In a minute, her face returned to a healthier shade of green. She drank the glass of water that appeared on the bar.

Albert asked, 'Well, she can't smoke a cigar or drink vodka. I don't know, Linus. I may have to take back what I said about her.'

'You don't like me anymore?' she asked.

'I like you just fine,' he said.

'Then, what?'

Linus said quickly, 'He's changed his mind about leaving his wife for you.'

Albert looked momentarily baffled, then he laughed loudly, drawing looks from diners and the bartender.

'I've listened to the tape,' said Wilma. 'I'm very disappointed in both of you.'

Peg and Ben sat side by side in rockers on the back porch. Wilma scowled at them from her perch on the porch railing. She bounced the clipboard on her hand, making little *thwack* sounds.

'It was Peg's fault!' said Ben. 'She made me say those things.'

Peg said, 'I thought we were getting individual evaluation sessions.'

'Occasionally, it's more productive to do them in tandem,' said Wilma.

Ben said, 'I'm not comfortable being in the same room with her.'

'A porch is not a room,' clarified Peg.

'I'm not comfortable on the same porch with Peg.'

Peg wasn't exactly comfortable with him either. Nor with Wilma, seducer of Ray, betrayer of Linus.

'The tape disappointed me,' repeated Wilma. 'But not for the reasons you might think.'

Peg said, 'You mean, you weren't upset that Ben called you the slut of Manshire?'

'I didn't say that!' shouted Ben, his face reddening.

'In several British studies on the benefits of physical

contact, heterosexual men reported an increase in self-esteem, confidence and relaxation if they received ten skin-to-skin touches from a member of the opposite sex per day.'

Ben said, 'You stroked my knee to boost my confidence?'

'Ten times a day,' said Wilma. She flipped back a few pages on her clipboard, and showed Ben a chart. 'I got you only seven times last Wednesday, though. Just five times yesterday.'

'So that explains his abysmal self-esteem last night,' said Peg.

'Could be,' said Wilma in all seriousness.

Ben said, 'You weren't flirting with me?'

Wilma said, 'I don't flirt, Ben.'

'You touch Luke more than ten times a day,' he said.

'But who's counting?' asked Peg.

'I touch Luke exactly ten times a day,' said Wilma, showing them the chart. 'But each instance was sustained, since Luke suffers from paralytic shyness.'

He hadn't looked too shy locking lips with Tracy last night, thought Peg. When she and Linus got back from Poule au Dent around ten, Tracy and Luke were still going at it. They sat next to each other at breakfast, too. Peg tried to catch secret glances between Ray and Wilma, but they were too sneaky to let on.

'What about Ray?' Peg asked Wilma. 'How does he figure in your touch chart?'

Wilma said, 'He gets the standard dose. Not sustained, though. His confidence is already at a high level.'

'Did he get any extra touching last night?' asked Peg. 'Any post-church services from you?'

Wilma smiled at Peg, hiding nothing, and said, 'Maybe we *should* have individual evaluations.'

Ben protested, 'Can we just get on with it?'

But the two women were in a staring contest. Not blinking, nor breathing. Not until a mosquito flew into Peg's eye.

Wilma said, 'Ben, your assignment was to engage Peg in conversation, to learn about her, ask questions.'

'I did,' he whined.

'Tell me what you learned,' said Wilma.

'She's from New York.'

'Good.'

'She gossips.'

'Yes,' agreed Wilma.

'She eats really fast,' said Ben. 'And she might be an alcoholic.'

'Anything else?'

'She's a florist,' he said suddenly, as if pulling a gem from the quarry.

Peg groaned. 'I am *not* a goddamn florist. I'm an interior landscape designer,' she said.

'Isn't that funny,' said Wilma.

'I'm not laughing,' said Peg.

'I mean your wording,' said the aspiring psychologist. 'One could say that I'm also an interior landscape designer.'

Peg shook her head. 'You can't stop yourself, can you? The metawhoring.'

'Excuse me?'

'Forget it,' said Peg.

Ben said, 'Can we please get back to the evaluation?'

'You get failing marks, Ben,' said Wilma. 'Ninety per cent of the conversation on this tape is you airing out your insecurities. When you did ask Peg a question, it was only a launching pad for you to talk about yourself. You sat at the restaurant for an hour, and all you managed to learn about her is where she's from and what she does for a living. Most people get that far in three minutes.'

Ben broke out in a sweat (it was beastly hot), and seemed to shrivel and curl into himself like a pork rind. Peg actually felt sorry for the guy. But Wilma was absolutely right. Ben had performed terribly. Criticism does hurt, but in the right circumstances, it could also help.

'Don't look so smug,' said Wilma to Peg. 'You were supposed to resist your inclination to steer conversation toward the erotic, and the first chance you got, you asked Ben to talk about sexual attraction. In case you weren't clear, that is within the realm of the erotic, Peg. You also fail.'

Peg flashed to a phone conversation she'd had with one of her exes, Oleg. She'd pulled a muscle and couldn't run – could barely walk – and was trapped alone in her apartment without alcohol, pain killers or marijuana. She bitched about it to Oleg, finally telling him she'd have to distract herself by thinking about what she'd do to him later. He said (in his Russian accent), 'This is why I love you, Peg. If you can't alter your mind, you've got only one thing on it.'

Was he right? Did Peg have a one-track mind? She defended herself to Wilma. 'I was trying to help Ben.'

'Help him by acting as his pimp?' said Wilma. 'Do you think about anything besides sex?'

'I do think of other things,' she said thoughtfully. 'But they're so boring.' A line from a lesser-known John Waters movie. By the horrified look on Wilma's face, Peg figured she hadn't gotten the reference.

'Are men merely sex objects to you?' asked Wilma.

'Of course not. I have a brother and a father,' she said. 'I have male friends.' A lie. 'I liked the evaluation much better when we were talking about Ben.'

'So did I,' he agreed.

Wilma said, 'Let's go over tonight's schedule. Ben, you and Gloria are going to Waterbury. Linus has arranged for a private tour of the Ben & Jerry's factory. You'll drive.'

'How'd Linus do that?' asked Peg.

'Ben Cohen is a friend of Linus's,' she said.

Was there anyone in Vermont who *wasn't* a friend of Linus's (henceforth, FOL)? wondered Peg.

'How long is the drive?' asked Ben.

'An hour. That's a good opportunity to work on your conversation skills.'

'Will there be a tape recorder in the car?'

'I'll be in the backseat,' said Wilma. 'Peg, you and Luke will be going to the U-Pick-Em blueberry farm in Thetford with Linus. I can't image how you could turn picking blueberries into foreplay.'

Peg could easily image it. Bending over, putting the plump fruit between her lips. Letting the juice run down her chin . . . *stop it*! Stop it now, she commanded herself.

Wilma said, 'Tracy and Ray are going to a sugar shack down the road for a primer on making syrup. They'll be chaperoned by Stan Crowley, the man who owns the shack, a friend of Linus's.'

'Am I excused?' asked Ben.

'We need to go over your OCEAN scores first,' said Wilma. 'You recall the questionnaire you both filled out last week? That Big Five Personality Test? It tests you for the five major domains of personality: openness, conscientiousness, extroversion, agreeableness and neuroticism. That's where the acronym OCEAN comes from. On Sunday, I ran your answer sheets through the Dartmouth psychology department computers, and have calculated your break-downs.' Wilma gave Peg and Ben each a sheet of paper, showing their individual OCEAN scores. 'Take some time today to read the explanation, and what your percentiles mean.'

Ben nodded and rushed off with his score sheet. Peg took a quick glance at hers, pleased to see she was in the eighty-sixth percentile in openness (whatever that meant), and then folded her sheet for later study.

Wilma, interior landscape designer of the mind, asked, 'Why are you openly hostile to me?'

'I'm not hostile,' Peg said, 'I'm friendly.'

'I'm not your enemy.'

'I saw Ray sneak out of your bedroom last night,' Peg blurted. 'Not that I was spying, or eavesdropping.'

Wilma was shocked at Peg's accusation. 'I was giving him his scores,' she said.

'I bet he scored,' said Peg.

'His OCEAN scores. He was in my room for all of three minutes, while I explained the printout. And if you'd stayed in your hiding place for two minutes longer, you'd have seen Gloria come out of my room after Ray, with her score sheet.'

Peg felt herself getting smaller. And smaller, until she was an ant-sized speck. 'I've made a terrible mistake,' she stammered. 'I, uh, I have deep emotional problems. Trust issues. I need therapy. Intensive therapy.'

Wilma sighed. 'You don't need therapy,' she said. 'You need to think before you act. To think before you speak. And stay away from my bedroom door. And stop asking me personal questions about my relationship. Stick to the program, or get out of it.'

Peg nodded emphatically in her shame. With a tiny voice, she asked, 'I'd appreciate it if you didn't mention this conversation to Linus.'

'He won't hear a word of it.'

'He wouldn't like it that I was lurking outside your bedroom door. Or that I made assumptions about what you were doing in there with another man. I can see how telling him the story might be embarrassing for you, too. Especially considering that the two of you have been having—'

'Stop,' said Wilma. 'Think. Then speak.'

Peg stopped. She thought, and then she said, 'I'll see you at lunch.'

21

Dear Nina,

Guess what? Just recently discovered that I'm obsessed with sex. And I'm a provocateur, and a Nosey Parker. And I may be an alcoholic. The revelations are coming fast and furious at Inward Bound. My dating challenge this week: undo everything I've always done, the main idea being, 'If it's broke, fix it.' For starters, I'm not supposed to think about sex, much less get any. I'm successful at keeping a clean mind for about two hours a day. Nancy Mitford wrote that women obsess about men from the cradle to the grave. Is that the nature of all women, or just me? And Nancy Mitford? (And you?)

You'd think my continual exposure to nature up here would give me a clue about my own. You'd think. One thing's for certain: My libidinous attentions (those that refuse to be suppressed) seem to have transferred from Ray Quick to Linus Bester. Linus has the mad mojo. Everyone in town is slavishly devoted to him. He's got a quality, a charm. I had a fantasy about him. The only explanation: Trying to thwart sexual thought is doing strange things to my brain.

Must run now. My turn to be sprayed with poison.

Holistically,
Peg

Peg put a stamp on her letter and dropped it in the outgoing mail pile. Then she went into the front yard, where Linus waited with a family-sized can of insect repellent. Apparently, the blueberry field at dusk was a bug utopia.

Linus sprayed Peg and Luke. When Peg was sufficiently protected, she went back up the women's suite to say goodbye to her In-mates.

'Have a great time with Luke!' said Tracy, way too cheerfully. 'Not too good a time, of course. Because he's mine. You stay away from him!' Then Tracy threw herself on her bed. 'I'm sorry. This is a first for me. Liking a guy on sight, and then bagging him so easily. I should feel a surge of confidence, but I'm shakier than before. Now there's something at stake.'

'Can you fake confidence?' asked Peg. 'Practice on Ray at the sugar shack.'

'I'll try,' said Tracy.

'Don't try,' said Peg. 'Do.'

'Yes, Yoda.'

Gloria wandered into Tracy's room from the bathroom. She was a vision in a yellow dress. Stunning. Neither Tracy nor Peg could speak. Gloria said, 'I am in the eighty-ninth percentile for neuroticism.'

That was surprising. According to the sheet, high

scores in that domain meant the subject was highly-strung, worrisome, tense. 'You always seem so calm,' said Peg.

'I'm overcompensating,' said Gloria. 'Or over-medicated.'

Peg said, 'I was in the eighty-sixth percentile for openness.' Curiosity, creativity, willingness to take risks.

Tracy said, 'I hit ninety in conscientiousness. Also above average in agreeableness and extraversion.' Therefore, Tracy was organized and reliable, forgiving and sympathetic, as well as fun-loving and social.

Peg was below average in agreeableness, conscientiousness, extraversion and neuroticism. With her high score in openness, that all added up to Peg being an unreliable risk-taking loner who was okay with that. Peg didn't put too much stock in her results anyway. She'd blown off the last third of the test (low conscientiousness), had resisted taking it in the first place (low agreeableness), didn't really care what her marks were anyway (low neuroticism), while still being curious how the test worked (high openness).

Maybe there was something to it, after all.

'Speaking of Ray, having spent an evening at church with him, I'm baffled by your attraction,' Gloria said to Peg, 'He's like a kid. He spent half the night playing Frisbee with a horde of church children. He ate hot dogs in two bites. There was a crop duster airstrip near the church, and whenever a plane took off, Ray would point and yell at me to look at it.'

'So he gets excited to see a plane take off.'

'Fifteen times?'

Peg said, 'Look, I barely know the guy.'

'You practically slept with him.'

'Back off, Gloria,' said Peg. 'I'm not judging you.'

In a snarl of anger and guilt (lashing out at Gloria was like stabbing a hamster), Peg went back down to the driveway, where she joined Luke and Linus in his pickup. They drove twenty minutes to the U-Pick-Em blueberry farm in Thetford. The owner was an FOL – a craggy long-haired farmer in a Phish concert jersey, overalls and Wellington boots. While he and Linus had a Vermont Time chat, Peg wandered into the fields. She was awed by the rolling carpet of blueberry bushes, the dark leaves with bulbous, ripe fruit. She smiled at Luke, trying to share her affection for the greenery. But he ignored her, standing ramrod straight, arms at his sides, feet shoulder-width apart. He looked like a statue, concrete running through his veins. Tracy had managed to loosen him up. Peg didn't see how.

Linus ambled over and handed the two Inward Bounders large baskets. He told his charges to fill them to the top. Peg asked, 'Aren't you coming?'

He shook his head. 'You two go ahead.'

Peg and Luke walked into the field. She'd far prefer filling her basket alongside Linus to the paralytically shy Luke. But the whole point here was to face a dating challenge, not fall back on reliably cheeky conversation with her host.

Peg started picking, selecting the biggest, purplest, roundest fruit. She held each berry before dropping it in her basket, pinching to test for suppleness. Blue splotches dotted her hands. The earthy eroticism of picking – the satisfying pluck of fruit flesh, the quiver of the leaves underneath – got to her quickly. She glanced at Luke. He plundered mechanically.

'I like the big ones,' she said to Luke.

Luke said, 'The smaller ones are better.'

'You think?'

He nodded. 'My grandfather had a blueberry patch.'

Peg was amazed. They were having a normal conversation. He'd revealed an intimate detail of his personal history. She said, 'So you really know how to pick 'em?'

'I wouldn't say that,' he answered tersely.

Peg wouldn't say she knew how to pick 'em either – blueberries or anything. New York City had been like a U-Pick-Em farm for men, where she'd prowled among the rows of ripeness, squeezing and tasting along the way. Ten years of plucking (as it were), and her basket was still empty.

Luke held up what he considered a perfect pebble-sized fruit. She complimented him on his choice. They talked about fresh produce, the merits of flash-freezing, why grapes were always mushy at the supermarket. Sticking to her assignment, Peg didn't pry into Luke's business. In fact, she didn't bother asking him about his work (he was a professional golfer, she remembered), his background, his romantic history. Ordinarily (or should she say, historically), a conversation devoid of confessions, admissions or revelations would have been tedious for Peg. She was impatient with small talk. With Luke, she knew their conversation would be superficial yet full of subtext (considering the context). Despite the fertile potential, their chat would not build to a satisfying climax. But maybe that wasn't necessary. Maybe the conversation could be a means in and of itself.

While listening to Luke's description of the hepatitis A outbreak brought on by imported Mexican scallions, Peg's eyes lit on the largest blueberry she'd ever seen. As big as a golf ball, it was, in fact, two fruits sewn together by nature's stitch of aberration. It was a beautiful mistake, like a four-leaf clover. She had to tug to release it from the plant. It fit in her palm snuggly, the shape of a heart with a deep trench down the middle.

She said, 'A mutant.' Peg handed it to Luke. He inspected it, sniffed it. She added, 'We could win a ribbon at the country fair with this.'

'It is enormous,' he agreed. 'Let's take this back and show everyone.'

'Thinking of anyone in particular?' asked Peg suggestively before she could catch herself. 'Whoops, sorry. Didn't mean to provoke.' But the damage was done. Luke stopped talking. She could see the shutters go up behind his eyes, the tense flicker of his jaw. Shit. She was flunking at date school again. And Linus had chosen this moment to bear down on them. He was only fifty feet away, and closing in fast.

How to salvage this? Peg wondered. She took the blueberry back from Luke. 'Let's eat it,' she said. Without waiting for his approval, she bit into it like an apple.

Luke watched her chew. 'Good?' he asked.

Flavorless and mushy. 'Here,' she said.

He took a bite, and then chucked what was left over his shoulder. 'More appealing to the eye than the palate,' he said. 'Try this one.'

He found a berry from his basket. Dark blue, small. She popped it in her mouth. It was springy, pliant, sweet as straight sugar. 'You *do* know how to pick them,' she said.

'You have to look under the leaves, find the berries that don't get too much light,' he explained.

'Hidden treasures,' said Peg.

Linus appeared at her side. 'Baskets almost full? Good. When we get back to the house, we'll make pies. And nip at the rhubarb,' he said enticingly.

He'd been stewing rhubarb in brandy for pie filling. Raising her eyebrows, Peg said, 'Making pies? This is your plan for a rocking Tuesday night in Vermont?'

Linus laughed. 'I admit, I'm uncool,' he said. 'From a long, proud line of squares.'

'I'm a square, too,' she said. 'A square Peg.'

Linus put his hands on her shoulders and squeezed. The contact was a very pleasant surprise. When he let go, she felt a gravitational pull toward him.

'Square? Your edges seem pretty soft to me,' he said. 'Come on, we're losing light.'

The three of them picked for another hour, and then took their bounty back to the Federal. Linus led them into the kitchen. The house empty, the three of them filled the room with the sounds of baking. Linus ladled out glasses of rhubarb brandy.

He handed one to Peg. It was piping hot. 'It's ninety degrees outside. And the oven is on,' she protested.

'Hot is counterintuitively cooling. Go ahead. The brandy won't bite,' said Linus. 'Actually, it will.'

The brandy was sweet, tart and thick. She'd never tasted anything like it, and therefore Peg felt compelled to consume glass after glass. As did Luke, who obviously didn't drink much. The three of them baked five pies and drank at least that many brandies each. Peg got sweaty, but didn't care. She liked how the trickle felt on her back and neck. She openly admired how the sheen of sweat looked on Linus and Luke's forearms and collarbones. When the pies were golden brown and bubbling, Linus took them out of the oven. The three bakers ate an entire pie with a can of organic whipped cream.

They were just licking their fingers when Wilma appeared in the kitchen threshold.

Peg said, 'Wilma, thank God. Tell me you brought back Coffee Heath Bar Crunch.'

Linus said, 'Have some pie.' When he looked down at the empty tin, he said, 'Oops,' which made Peg and Luke giggle.

Wilma was not amused. She stood there, motionless, her eyes scanning the kitchen in horror.

That's when Peg first registered the flour on the floor, the sticky spills on the counter and stove, the sink piled high with used baking tools and smashed blueberries. The room was a disaster. To Peg, the mess told the happy story of laughs and sweets. To Wilma, the mess told a different story, one with a sad ending for Linus.

Linus said, 'I'll clean it up.'

'We'll all clean up,' said Peg, sobering quickly. 'Right Luke?'

She nudged him with her elbow. Luke swayed and fell off his chair. When he landed on the floor, a plume of flour rose and dusted him, sticking to his sweat. Peg leaned down (instant head rush), and poked at him. He'd passed out. And started snoring. Loudly. Peg fought back a nervous laugh.

Wilma said, 'Is he unconscious?'

Linus said, 'This is all part of my master plan.'

'Getting drunk isn't a substitute for genuine intimacy.'

'No, but it's a shortcut to it,' said Linus.

Peg said, 'It can be a substitute. Believe me.'

'I do believe you,' said Linus.

Luke snored loudly. 'He believes me, too,' she said.

Linus and Peg giggled.

Wilma scowled, and then walked through the kitchen, stepping over Luke, and into the bedroom. She gently closed the door.

Linus smiled sadly at Peg. He said, 'Well, it was fun while it lasted.' She wasn't sure if he meant his relationship, or their evening.

Linus knelt at Luke's side and lifted him to a standing position. Peg got on his other side. They managed to haul Luke up the stairs and into his room. They peeled his shirt off, and lay him down on his bed.

'Gloria,' muttered Luke. 'Where's Gloria? Must watch Gloria.'

Peg and Linus looked at each other. He said, 'Don't tell Tracy.'

She nodded and said, 'He's going to wake up, look in the mirror and scream.' Luke's face was a white mask of flour.

They giggled again. She said, 'Okay, let's go clean up.'

'I'll do it,' said Linus. 'You go to bed.'

'You've got to let me help. That's what a friend does. And I do feel like we're becoming friends. I need male friends. I don't have any. Which somehow means I objectify men, and am obsessed with sex. Not sure about the logic at the moment.'

'There's nothing wrong with being a sexually inclined person, Peg,' said Linus. 'I am, too.'

She knew that already from eavesdropping on Linus and Wilma that first night. In her drunken state, it took all Peg's willpower not to find out just how sexually inclined he was. 'We are friends,' she reminded herself. 'And as your friend, I want you to blame me entirely for the mess downstairs. And tell Wilma I got Luke drunk. She'll believe you. She'll be glad to.'

Linus asked, 'How'd you score on conscientious-ness?'

'Low. Very low.'

'Do you see yourself as someone who would take the blame for another person's mistakes?' he asked.

'Strongly disagree – usually,' she said. 'But for you, Linus, my friend – and handsome, too, especially all sticky and shiny like you are right now – I'll go against my nature.'

'Why don't you go to bed instead,' he said firmly, scooting her out of Luke's bedroom.

P eg returned to the women's suite. Hangover starting already, she would have loved to slip right into her bed, but Gloria and Tracy were sitting on it.

'What happened with Luke?' Tracy asked as soon as Peg entered her room.

'He's in bed, covered in flour, passed out drunk,' said Peg.

'Right,' said Tracy. 'Seriously, did anything happen?'

'I'm telling you what happened,' said Peg. 'Oh, I get it. You want to know if anything *happened*. Relax. He barely looked at me.'

'So you had a horrible time tonight,' said Tracy, digging for one more ounce of reassurance.

'I had a great time,' Peg said. 'With Linus. If he hadn't been there, Luke would have spontaneously combusted from ignoring me so hard.'

That made Tracy smile. 'Did he say anything about me?'

No, but he was muttering 'Gloria' when they'd taken off his shirt. Peg said, 'He said approximately six words all night long.'

'Were they, "I'm madly in love with Tracy"?' asked the brunette.

'Sorry,' said Peg.

Tracy said, 'Ray wouldn't shut up about you. We were shown the vats for boiling sap and Ray says, "If only Peg were here to see this." We got a sample of fancy-grade syrup, he says, "Peg tastes better than this." Stan told us that a cluster of maple trees is called a "sugar bush," and Ray said, "Peg has a sugar bush." I finally had to tell him to shut the fuck up, and he says, "If Peg were here, she would slap your face."'

'I would have slapped his face,' said Peg.

'I took care of that for you,' said Tracy.

Gloria said, 'Ben, meanwhile, could talk a crack addict into a coma. I nearly fell asleep in my Cherry Garcia.'

'That actually happened to him once,' said Peg.

'The secretary in his office who was too young for him, but was impressed by his title,' said Gloria.

'You got the whole story, too,' said Peg. 'How was Ben & Jerry's?'

'Carnival-like atmosphere outside the factory, bubble blowing, cows on display, tie-dying, face-painting. Inside the factory, a PR spiel about the quality goodness of Vermont dairy products and the company's charitable foundation, moving along to the gift shop and free samples.'

'Worth the hour trip?' asked Peg.

'With Ben in the driver's seat?' Gloria shook her head gravely.

Peg said, 'Poor Ben. He could go Inward Bound until he hit marrow, and still not have a clue. Guess he'll just have to keep paying for it.'

'Paying for what?' asked Gloria.

'How sheltered are you?' asked Tracy, annoyed. 'Paying for sex. Hookers. Escorts.'

'Men actually use prostitutes?' asked Gloria, wide-eyed. 'I mean, normal men?'

Peg said, 'Most just beat off a lot.'

'Welcome to my world,' said Tracy. 'Maybe Ben and I are meant to be together.'

'Can I go to bed now? I like the pajama party idea – in theory,' said Peg. 'But I'm drunk and want to lie down. I might beat off myself tonight, and I prefer to do that alone.'

'We'll get right to the point,' said Gloria. 'We have a proposal for you.'

'A proposal?' asked Peg, excited. 'Finally! I've been waiting for this moment for ten years.'

Gloria said, 'You know we're going to the Sunbridge Fair on a group date tomorrow night.'

Peg said, 'I didn't. We're not pairing off?'

'Wilma told me at Ben & Jerry's that Linus wanted to change the plans,' said Gloria.

'I wonder why,' said Peg.

Tracy shrugged. 'I'm sure he had his reasons. Maybe he wants to have some group bonding. According to Stan, sugar shack guy – he had two functional teeth, by the way, the rest having rotted from a near-constant consumption of syrup – the Sunbridge Fair is the hottest ticket in the Upper Valley. Rides. Games. Funnel cakes. Clog dancing. The showcase event is a competition to see which team of draft horses can pull the biggest pile of concrete blocks.'

'I haven't lived,' said Peg.

Tracy said, 'It gets better. They have a smash-up derby – for tractors. Petting zoo. You can milk a goat. Stan was salivating between his two teeth for the freak-show booths. He can't wait to see the World's Smallest

Woman and the World's Largest Rat. He said he'll demand his money back unless the woman is smaller than the rat.'

'The world's largest rat,' said Gloria. 'I didn't know my gay ex-boyfriend was in Vermont.'

'It's probably just a capybara, a South American rodent that weighs a hundred pounds,' said Tracy.

'How do you know that?' asked Peg.

'The Boston zoo has one,' said Tracy. 'It does look just like a giant rat. No tail, though.'

'The proposal we want to make,' interjected Gloria, 'since we hate the group date idea—'

Peg asked, 'Too much togetherness?'

'Too little freedom,' said Gloria. 'Not to project onto Wilma and Linus, but they hover just like my parents. I want to go out, unchaperoned, untethered. This fair is my chance.'

Her chance to get kidnapped, thought Peg. Tracy said, 'If we go as a group, I won't be able to sneak off with Luke. We assume you'd like to have some privacy with Ray, since you haven't had time alone since your swim across the Connecticut.'

Peg wasn't so sure about that. She kind of liked the idea of going to the fair as a group. Linus would probably sweep in like a visiting dignitary. She pictured him leading her around the fairgrounds, smiling, as usual, pointing out the two-headed calf, the pygmy horse. The county's fattest twins. They would laugh, eat cotton candy and caramel apples. Go down the potato sack slide together. Skip hand in hand to the roller coaster. In the haunted house, he'd squeeze her tits in the dark.

Tracy said, 'Earth to Planet Peg. Come in, Peg.'

'You want to bust up the gang date,' said Peg. 'What

do you have in mind? Tell Linus you don't like his plan?'

'No,' said Tracy. 'We don't think a polite request would work.'

'So what will? Locking Linus and Wilma in a closet?'

'We're going to crush Xanax into their cider at dinner,' said Gloria. 'My idea.'

'Is that safe?' asked Peg.

'I've searched their medicine cabinets and night-table drawers for any drugs that are incompatible with Xanax, and checked through their file cabinets for medical records that would indicate an allergic reaction.' That was Gloria. In response to Peg's stunned expression, she said, 'It only took a minute. Wilma is a highly organized person.'

'So you drug them, they fall asleep. We go to the fair anyway?' said Peg. 'Why go at all?'

'The men will expect it,' said Tracy. 'And it *is* the hot ticket of the Upper Valley.'

'I am curious about the smash-up tractor derby,' said Gloria.

Peg nodded. 'I do love a funnel cake.'

'So you'll help?' asked Tracy.

Do I see myself as someone who colludes to drug two innocent people against their will? Peg wondered.

'Who's slipping the mickey?' she asked.

'Me,' said Gloria of the high neuroticism.

'If it all goes wrong, you'll tell the authorities I had nothing to do with it?'

They nodded.

'In that case, I neither agree nor disagree,' said Peg.

'Meaning?' asked Tracy of the high conscientious-ness.

'I'll go along with your plan.'

The two women left Peg's room, and she immediately fell into a deep, silent sleep. When she woke up the next morning, she didn't think she'd moved in her bed, the sheets still tight against her body. She checked her travel clock. Nine. She'd missed breakfast again. She quickly showered, dressed and rushed downstairs.

She found Linus sitting alone at the table in the kitchen with a pile of bills and his checkbook. When she saw the room, immaculate now, she felt a fresh pang of guilt for not helping clean up.

Peg stood at the table and waited for Linus to smile up at her. But he didn't. He just kept writing checks. She puttered over to the fridge and got herself a piece of five-grain wheat bread with a spoonful of home-pulverized raspberry preserve. She put it on a plate and sat down across from Linus. Who continued to ignore her.

Peg said, 'I'm sorry I slept late.'

He didn't respond. She said, 'Are things okay with Wilma? Is she still pissed off? Did Luke surface yet? He must have a killer hangover. I'm okay. Physically. I feel like shit about leaving you to clean up the mess by yourself.'

Linus glanced up. Not smiling. His mouth forming an unfamiliar straight line. It was the first time in their short acquaintance that Linus seemed unhappy to see her.

He said, 'Shall I give you your evaluation?'

'My evaluation?'

'Your performance last night.'

'My performance? I was pretty drunk, but I thought I remembered everything we did. Maybe not.'

He said, 'I'm talking about your performance interacting with a member of the opposite sex.'

'I know,' said Peg. 'I was teasing you. Trying to

lighten the mood.' He didn't seem lightened. She added, 'Yes. Please. Evaluate. I'm ready. Don't hold back. I'm paying good money for brutal honesty.'

Linus cleared the space in front of him on the table. He said, 'You were magnificent last night. You were natural, easy to talk to. You controlled your tendency to pry, and restrained yourself from being intentionally provocative. You successfully kept your sexual confidence to yourself instead of waving it around like a flag in space, a habit which has won you the attention of a long line of men who were only too happy to let you take the lead in every aspect of your relationship, surrendering to you the responsibility of maintaining it and pushing it forward, without giving you a moment to consider whether you wanted it in the first place. In fact, by not flirting overtly – one might say *theatrically* – you transmitted a sexual allure that came from who you are, not what you can do with your hair and eyes and lips. You glowed last night in the kitchen. You were irresistible.'

A fantastic review. But Linus delivered it with such severity, Peg wasn't convinced. She said, 'I guess my glow has worn off.'

He said, 'You also got high marks on companionability. Simply put, you were fun to hang out with. If Luke wasn't utterly smitten with you, it's because he has serious social phobias.' Abruptly, Linus returned to his pile of bills.

Peg said, 'So I did good.'

'You didn't do anything,' he responded. 'And therefore, you did well.'

'So Luke's not smitten with me,' she said.

'I wouldn't know,' said Linus.

'Are *you* smitten with me?' she asked.

Linus said, 'The kind of man who is worthy of you, Peg, won't respond to rote flirtation.'

'Are you worthy of me?' she asked, not able to stop herself.

He sighed.

'There I go again,' she said.

'Wilma is out on the porch,' Linus said, pointing in that general direction with his pen. 'She's leading a morning meditation.'

He was being cold, terse. She had to ask. 'We're still friends, right? I'll just assume you're in a bad mood because of last night. You can tell me what happened with you and Wilma. It might make you feel better.'

Linus grinned. Just a little, and then it was gone. 'Peg, I have to maintain a professional distance,' he said. 'I can't get personally involved with clients. I must stay detached.'

'In other words, back off,' she said. 'What if I can't? I got a low score in agreeableness.'

He said, 'Astoundingly low. The lowest I've ever seen.'

Somehow, this made her proud. She took her plate with her to the front yard, avoiding the navel contemplation on the back porch. The day was bright and hot, the usual ninetyish, clouds zipping across the blue sky, ducking behind the mountains and then emerging in streaks as if the trees had brushed them straight. Peg watched a frenetic chipmunk popping out of his hole in the garden, darting aimlessly, then returning to his underground sanctuary.

Linus said she was magnificent. Irresistible. He also said a man worthy of her wouldn't be swayed by flag-waving flirtation. Ray responded to it like a bull in a ring. By Linus's logic, that meant Ray was unworthy.

Standing there in the sun, Peg revisited her fantasy of Linus in the haunted house, gripping her tight while ghosts and ghouls moaned on the ride's sound track.

23

The Inward Bounders were lined up by the riverbank. Wilma was issuing orders.

'Down Dog,' she barked.

Tracy said, 'I hate that one.'

'Come on, hands on the ground, make a V with your body, feet shoulder-width apart.'

Ben said, 'I think my Achilles tendon just tore.'

Luke sat on the porch, refusing to participate. Peg had wandered around back. She sat next to Luke and asked, 'How's your head?'

He completely ignored her. She shrugged and watched.

Wilma said, 'Now, eyes closed, rocking slightly, I want you to contemplate the joys of solitude. The blessing of privacy. The uncompromised splendor of living alone.'

Tracy said, 'The joys of solitude? I came to Inward Bound because I'm sick and tired of rationalizing the upside of being single.'

Wilma said, 'Part of the process is to embrace who you are. To be happy in the now.'

'In the now? My muscles are popping, and all the blood is rushing to my head.'

Wilma snapped, 'If you think you can guide the

meditation better yourself, be my guest.' And then she stormed past the Down Doggers, up the porch steps, and slammed into the living room, leaving the programmees alone. Tracy, Gloria, Ben and Ray collapsed on the grass. Luke stared across the river. Peg finished her breakfast and brushed the crumbs on the porch.

Linus came out suddenly, and said, 'Wilma and I have some errands to run. We'll be back in a few hours. Serve yourself lunch. We'll have dinner at the fair.'

And then he, too, was gone.

Thirty minutes later, Peg floated, belly-up, on the Connecticut River, the sun darkening her face and limbs, burning her midsection. Tracy and Gloria joined her for the swim. Like dolphins, they glided along the bank, splashing, mindlessly relishing their relief of not having to explore their psyche, at least for a few hours.

Ray, who'd gone to change into his suit, returned to the river-bank with several fat joints. He said, 'Anyone fancy a smoke?'

He needn't have asked. Peg climbed out of the water, Tracy and Gloria close behind. Taking a joint, she sat at the river's edge, lit up, inhaled and passed it along to Tracy.

Gloria said, 'My drug-testing doesn't usually include non-prescription varieties.' And then she partoked.

Ben and Ray shared one on the porch. They offered it to Luke, but he refused.

Tracy whispered, 'Luke hasn't said a word all morning. He hasn't moved from that spot.' Fully dressed, Luke sat on the porch, ignoring everyone.

Peg said, 'He's hungover. Possibly embarrassed.' She imagined his horror, waking up shirtless and dusted with flour.

'He won't talk to me,' said Tracy, pouting. 'He hates me.'

'He doesn't hate you,' said Peg. 'I'm telling you, he's hurting. I'm an expert on hangovers.'

Gloria, who had commandeered the joint, said, 'These rocks are so smooth.' She'd started collecting some of the river stones, making neat piles.

Tracy said, 'Perfect for skimming.'

An hour later, Peg's arm was stiff from skimming rocks. Her record was six.

Ben got eight skips – the day's record. 'And that's not all I can do,' he said suddenly, before plowing into the river. 'Not too long ago, I was a member of a synchronized swimming society. The only man in the society's twenty-year history.'

He started to do some water ballet moves. When his head was above water, Peg yelled, 'Did you date any of the other members?'

He said, 'Yeah, but at sixty-four, she was just a little too old for me,' which made them all howl, including Ben, who had a charming, ringing laugh.

For the group's entertainment, Ben performed a water ballet routine while Tracy hummed 'Dance of the Sugar Plum Fairy.' By the magic of luck (or pot), Ben's routine matched Tracy's accompaniment perfectly, even though he hadn't heard a note of it.

Ray sat down next to Peg. She said to him, 'You told Tracy I had a sugar bush?'

'Well, you do,' he defended.

She laughed. He put his arm around her shoulder, and she didn't shrug him off. The sun was hot, the water cooling. The morning slouched into the afternoon, and still no sign of Wilma or Linus.

The Inward Bounders decided to walk into Manshire for lunch at Poule au Dent. Albert ran toward them as they entered. 'Peg! My favorite flatlander! You've come back to me.'

Albert might be a bigger flirt than Peg. She smiled. 'I've brought friends.'

Ben pushed through the group. He said, 'Mr DeWitt, I was an imbecile the other night. I hope you'll accept my humble apology.'

The two men shook hands, and Albert showed them a table on the patio. On the way out back, Tracy whispered to Peg, 'What was that about?'

Peg shrugged, and said, 'Ben on drugs is a changed man.'

'It's a vast improvement,' said Tracy.

'He should be on a continuous cannibus drip.'

Gloria said, 'I could eat a horse. Do they eat horse in Vermont?'

Albert said, 'We just sold out of horse tartar. But I can get you a lovely fennel salad.'

And it was lovely. Especially with all the Chardonnay. Lunch finished, the Inward Bounders were ready for a nap. They walked back to the mansion, and, once home, up to their respective suites.

Ray pinned Peg against the stairway wall and kissed her neck, breathing against her skin. He said, 'Take a nap in my room.'

The pot, sun, food and wine had lulled her misgivings about him to sleep. She said, 'We won't nap.'

'We can talk,' he said. 'We haven't talked in days.'

Had they ever? She said, 'I've been focusing on my development.'

'I've been focusing on your development, too,' he

said, eyeing her chest. He rubbed himself against her. Like a frozen cucumber, he rubbed.

She asked, 'You wouldn't relinquish the responsibility of our relationship to me, making me do all the work of maintaining it and pushing it forward?'

'I have no idea what you're talking about,' said Ray. At least, that was what she thought he said. She couldn't hear him very well with his face buried in her cleavage. Then he lifted his head, took her by the wrist and said, 'We're going to bed. Now.'

'What about Linus?' she asked.

'Linus?' said Ray. 'This is the wrong time to be thinking about Linus.'

'This is precisely the right time to be thinking about Linus,' said Linus, materializing at the bottom of the stairs.

Peg said, 'We're napping. Before the big night out.'

'Napping. Is that what you call it?'

'I'm going to my room now,' she said.

Linus said, 'You do that. Ray, would you give me a hand? I've got supplies in the truck.'

Ray said, 'Be right there.' It was a dismissal line. But Linus didn't leave. Ray stared down at him. Linus squared his feet and folded his arms over his chest.

If she didn't know better, Peg might have thought these two men were staging a body language battle over her. But that wasn't possible. Linus was a professional. With detachment. And distance. He wasn't going to let Peg get personal with him. He was simply acting as a stopgap, preventing Peg and Ray from plunging into actions that would flatten their learning curve. Speaking for herself, Peg knew that if Ray got inside her body, she wouldn't be able to get inside her head.

Ray whispered in Peg's ear: 'Tonight I am getting you alone, if I have to clobber him with a pitchfork.'

And then he left, loping down the steps, slapping Linus (too hard) on the back. The men walked off toward the driveway, and Peg went upstairs to the women's suite, surprising herself by slipping easily into a dreamless sleep that lasted for over two hours.

Linus called everyone downstairs to the kitchen around five. Gloria came into the room with sneaky eyes. If Peg didn't know something was up, she would have known something was up. Subtlety hadn't been on the curriculum at any of Gloria's private schools. Peg glanced around, seeing if anyone else noticed Gloria's tightly balled fists, her flopsweat, that her voice had gone up two octaves. Luke kept his eyes on her, even with Tracy sitting next to him. But if he noticed a change, he didn't let on.

Linus said, 'We should go over the plans for tonight.'

Tracy said, 'I'm thirsty! Mind if I put out some drinks?'

Wilma said amicably, 'Let me help.'

Gloria said, 'NO! I will.'

Peg sat next to Wilma. 'And how was your day?' she asked casually.

Wilma said, 'Very productive. I went to the psych library at Dartmouth and did some research on personality development. New studies out of Berkeley have confirmed that the bedrock traits are, contrary to widely held theories, mutable after age thirty.'

'People can change,' said Peg.

'If they can't, we have no business being in business,' said Wilma. 'The new research has flaws, though. It could be wrong.'

'That's pessimistic.'

'A dominant trait of mine,' said Wilma, her eyes shifting toward Linus. 'Not an attractive one, apparently.'

'The research will hold up. Of course people can change. Throughout their lives,' said Peg.

Wilma looked squarely at Peg. 'People *strive* to change throughout their lives. Self-improvement is the American religion. Research may or may not conclude that change is possible. Regardless, the question should be, are alterations always improvements? If I train my behavior and become optimistic, for example, does that make me a better person?'

'It doesn't make you better,' said Peg. 'Just different.'

'Different to my essential nature,' said Wilma. 'That's another thorny issue. If we can change who we are and become different – not qualitatively better – then does personality and identity even matter? And why strive to change? For yourself? Or for someone else? To please someone else?'

'You're talking as if change is a finger snap. That you could decide to be optimistic, and then' – *snap*. 'Change may be possible, but it ain't easy,' said Peg of the low neuroticism.

'What are you two talking about so intensely?' asked Ray, sitting down next to Peg.

Wilma took the intrusion as a way out, turning to her right, to talk to Ben. Ray saw his opening and said, 'You look beautiful tonight.'

Peg was wearing a tank dress – orange-and-pink-striped – flip-flops, her hair in a high ponytail. Standard summer wear. She said, 'You never say anything except how beautiful I am and how much you want me.'

He frowned. 'We talked for hours on the train.'

'We talked for forty-five minutes, tops,' she said. And even then, their conversation was ninety per cent rote flirtation, as Linus would call it.

'What else is there to say?' asked Ray, annoyed. 'What else do you need to know?'

He had a point. Did she want to discourse with Ray – or intercourse with him? His intentions were honest. She smiled at him apologetically and said, 'You can say anything you want, or say nothing at all.'

Ray leaned toward her and whispered what he wanted, explicitly.

Meanwhile, Tracy and Gloria were placing glasses of apple cider around the table. Gloria nearly spilled Linus's glass, which made her gasp way too loudly. Linus's blue eyes sharpened. His instincts had perked up.

Peg said quickly, 'So what's the agenda for tonight?'

Linus continued to watch Gloria while he spoke. 'Figured we'd go to the fair. Eat there. Hang out for a few hours. Come home.'

Tracy pushed a glass in front of Wilma.

'Pile into the pickup?' asked Ben.

'Room for eight,' said Linus, nodding. He took a long drink of his cider – Gloria, Tracy and Peg registering every swallow.

'I'm not going,' said Wilma, pushing her glass aside. 'I've got some notes to compile.'

'Your notes can wait, can't they?' asked Linus.

'I'm taking the night off,' she said.

'This morning, you said you needed the afternoon off.'

'And now I need the night off.'

'Frankly, Wilma, I can't remember the last time you

had an "on" night.' The hosts seemed oblivious to the other people in the room.

Peg said, 'Where's professional detachment when you need it?'

Linus said, 'We're demonstrating a healthy argument style. Conflicts are inevitable in every relationship. Learning to deal with—'

'Drink up, Linus,' said Tracy. 'The fair won't wait all night.'

Tracy looked at Peg, then at the full glass in front of Wilma, then back at Peg. 'I sure am parched,' said Peg. 'Wilma, aren't you parched? Your throat must be dry as a martini.'

'I'm fine.'

'You look thirsty.'

'For blood,' said Ray in Peg's ear.

'If you'll excuse me,' said Wilma, getting up and disappearing into the living room. They could hear the porch door opening and slamming closed.

Linus said, 'Pardon me,' and followed Wilma outside.

Tracy caught Peg and Gloria's eyes. She cocked her head toward the living room. The ladies made their excuses and adjourned to the other room.

When they were out of earshot of the men, Tracy whispered, 'Linus should be out cold in about half an hour. We'll have to wait. We can't let him behind the wheel now.'

'Does anyone know how to get to the fair?' asked Peg. 'We can't very well ask for directions if Linus thinks he's driving.'

'I know the general direction,' said Gloria. 'It's close to where we went to the church potluck. We also need the keys to the truck.'

'We can take our own cars,' said Peg, seeing an opportunity to log a few more miles on her Subaru.

'Good idea,' said Tracy. 'We *should* take separate cars.'

'Why?' said Gloria.

'You could not be more clueless,' said Tracy. 'Here comes Linus.'

Their blue-eyed guide approached. Peg asked, 'Are you okay?' He looked dejected but resolute.

Linus said, 'Change of plans. I'm going to stay home tonight, too. I've written out directions to the fair. You can take the truck, or your own cars. It's pretty easy. Drive down River Road into Chelsea. Make a left by the ol' knotty oak, then a quick right at the alpaca farm, bear left by where the mill used to be—'

Tracy snatched the directions from his hand. 'We'll find it.'

She marched back into the kitchen, announced to the men that they were leaving now, and herded everyone out the front door.

In the driveway, Peg pulled Tracy to the side. 'Maybe I should stay, too. Linus doesn't look good.'

'What's wrong with you?' asked Tracy. 'Don't you want to be with Ray?'

'Of course I do,' said Peg. She glanced back at the Federal. 'Who else would I want to be with?'

Peg got into her Subaru, Ray in the passenger seat. The group caravaned in three cars to the fair, not getting lost once. Upon arrival, Ray pulled Peg away immediately.

They bought tickets, and entered the fairgrounds. Peg had never been to a country fair before, but it was exactly as she'd expected. The rides, food trailers, dart games, tents selling T-shirts and macramé plant hangers, big barns with berib-boned pigs and cows. She was taken aback by the crush of Vermonters. Peg started counting mullet haircuts, but had to stop at fifty. The crowd was a walking parade of 'befores' – cropped jerseys, acid-washed jeans – as if the population of the state (Peg suspect that all 600,000 might be at the fair) had never seen a copy of *Vogue* or watched a three-minute clip of *Queer Eye for the Straight Guy*. None of the women wore makeup, nail polish or jewelry. Peg wasn't much of an accessories or makeup maven herself, but in New York, eschewing the finishing touches was a style choice in and of itself. And even if a New Yorker didn't wear makeup, her skin had the healthy glow of five kinds of moisturizer and anti-wrinkle cream. Peg's version of jewelry-free was to wear diamond studs, and a diamond solitaire on a gold strand around her neck. Next to these Vermonters, her minimalism was maximism.

Botox and laser facials hadn't come this far north either. Deep wrinkles and infected blemishes were the rage in Sunbridge. Many of the women were either scary skinny, or dumpy fat, carrying the excess weight in the middle, not bothering to slenderize with fitted clothing, just throwing a housecoat over the bulge and calling it a day. The men seemed, as a whole, slimmer, with cavemanlike bushy beards and mustaches. The men were bulking up with facial hair for a long cold winter. In July. They could house the state's squirrel population in their faces.

Granted, not every woman was a visual calamity. Not every man. Large pockets of fairgoers looked clean and fit, like hippie farmers or poetry-writing peaceniks – trademark Manshire style. But rednecks held the majority. Apparently, the fair brought the backwater hicks to the forefront.

It occurred to Peg that, in this mass of humanity, she could very well be the only Jew. She clutched Ray's hand at that frightening thought. There were more Jews in New York than in Israel. And in Vermont? Maybe five? Now six, counting her?

While Peg examined the crowd, she felt the sting and shame of her own snobbiness, not just about style but also sophistication. If she was going to live in Vermont, she'd have to get over that yesterday. Look at Linus. An Ivy-educated, intellectually inclined civil libertarian, he was best friends with Stan the sugar shack man. The Vermont ethos was acceptance and tolerance. And Peg would get started on developing hers right away. But first, she'd steer clear of the three-hundred-pound, bearded, sauce-stained slob heading her way with a rack of dripping ribs in his hand.

Ray said, 'I want a bloomin' onion. And then I want to go on that Ferris wheel and make out.'

'Can we make out before you eat the bloomin' onion?' she asked. The vegetable in question, she had just learned, was an onion julienned into the shape of a flower, dipped in batter, deep-fried in bacon grease and served on a paper plate with spicy mayonnaise. The sight of it made Peg's stomach lurch.

'I've got mints,' he said. Ray purchased his gassy treat, and they walked to the Ferris wheel. He ate as he walked, making 'yummy' sounds.

They waited for a turn on the wheel. Ray ate most of the onion on line, and took the rest onto the ride. They asked for a private car. Ray winked at the conductor, who winked back. As soon as the herky-jerky process of loading all the ride's cars was finished, they took off and up in circular flight.

Peg said, 'I can see the clog dancers from here.'

'Kiss me, baby,' said Ray.

She did as she was told. They smooched cutely, lips and tongues, no heavy-duty grappling. It seemed a bit too lazy, too slow. Not Ray's usual urgency. And then he stopped kissing her back at all. She pulled away, and saw to her shock and horror that Ray was out cold.

She slapped his cheeks. Pinched his leg. Nothing. He was still breathing, much to her relief. Peg checked her watch. It was about forty minutes since they'd left the house. Ray had been seated at the table near Wilma. He must have downed her Xanax-spiked cider when Peg, Tracy and Gloria left the room.

'Do you hate me? Am I evil? Do I deserve this kind of treatment?' Peg asked the heavens, fists shaking in fury. She sat in her creaky car at the tippy-top of the Ferris wheel, Ray slumped against her shoulder, snoring in staccato blasts like a duck, the remains of a bloomin' onion squashed into his shirt.

Peg braced herself for the downswing. The wheel kept turning, fast enough to flip-flop her stomach. She looked at the throngs of people below, cramming the fairway. 'And I didn't even get a funnel cake,' she sighed to the breeze.

Ray slipped off her shoulder, and collapsed on the floor of the car, his head nudging open the little doors. Peg screamed, and pulled him back inside before he fell to his death, or got his cranium squashed by a spoke. When she found Tracy and Gloria later, she would have to kill them.

Do I see myself as someone who would murder her

only two friends in this entire state? she wondered.

Strongly agree, if the murder was quick and painless.

The ride ended. Not a moment too soon, because Peg's arms were getting tired from holding Ray upright. When the conductor stopped their car at the exit platform, Peg whimpered that she needed help.

The conductor sized up the situation, and helped her drag Ray out of the car, down the entrance steps and off to the side, where he lay Ray down on the dirt. With an apology, he returned to his duties at the ride. The people waiting on line to board the Ferris wheel watched the incident. Unlike a New York crowd, who would have glanced at Peg's torment and then, with studied ennui, returned to their own conversations, the Vermonters gawked openly, pointing, laughing. A few hick kids got off the line, and circled Peg and Ray.

'What's wrong with him?' asked a nine-year-old boy. 'He's drunk!' he answered for himself.

'He's not drunk,' said Peg.

'He fainted,' said a little girl, maybe ten. 'The ride was too much for him. Or maybe he's got vertigo.'

'He might have narcolepsy,' said another boy. 'We've got a narcoleptic cow. You can tell when she falls asleep because she stops chewing.'

Peg said, 'He's not narcoleptic. And he doesn't have vertigo. At least, I don't think he does.'

The children nodded silently, trying to come up with another possible explanation for a grown man losing consciousness on a sissy ride.

'Maybe he's pretending,' said the first boy, nudging Ray with his sneaker.

The other kids said, 'Yeah!' and joined in with the prodding of prostrate Ray.

Peg said, 'Stop that!' The kids were laughing now. 'I'm calling a cop.'

'No need, ma'am,' said a baritone voice.

The kids ran back to their parents on the Ferris wheel line. Peg looked up at the voice. It was a cop. Middle-aged, sun-glasses at dusk, stuffed into a cardboard-brown-colored uniform, fully loaded with hat, billy club, gun, walkie-talkie. He was holding a corn dog in one hand. The other rested gently on his holster.

She said, 'Those children were harassing my friend.'

'What do we have here?' asked the cop, pointing at Ray with his corn dog.

What to say? He'd been drugged with prescription sedatives? That might lead to more questions, which she didn't want to answer. For all she knew, this country cop might haul her in to his station house, and she'd never see the light of day again. It'd be like *Midnight Express*, but not in Turkey. In Sunbridge.

Peg said, 'He's drunk.'

The cop – 'Officer A. M. Call,' read the stitching on his shirt pocket – said, 'This is a dry fair, ma'am. If he's drunk, I'll have to search you both and confiscate your alcohol. And give you a fine.' His gun hand reached behind to his back pocket. He whipped out a mini-clipboard with silver hoops. The ticket pad.

'He's not drunk. I lied,' said Peg. 'He's a vertiginous narcoleptic.'

'A *what*?' asked the cop, getting a pen from his front shirt pocket.

'He gets dizzy. And sleepy. Suddenly. Without cause.'

'He's dizzy,' said the cop. 'And sleepy.'

'Exactly. Without cause.'

'I know the cause,' said Officer Call. 'He's drunk.

Fine for being publicly intoxicated at dry fair is four hundred dollars.' Corn dog propped in his mouth, he started filling out the ticket form.

'He's not drunk!' said Peg. 'Test him! You'll see.'

'If you want to contest this fine, you can take it up with the county registrar in White River Junction. Call the number on the ticket to schedule a hearing.'

Peg said, 'I can't help feeling like you're giving me an unusually high fine because I'm from out of state. I've heard that this happens. You're trying to drive flatlanders out of the area with trumped-up charges.'

'That's an interesting theory,' said Officer Call. 'For sharing it, I'll have to charge you with disorderly conduct. Fine of two hundred dollars.'

She turned toward the people on line at the Ferris wheel. They were all watching and listening. Some seemed sympathetic. But, for the most part, the Vermonters were grinning, enjoying this part of the evening's entertainment.

This wasn't a fair. It was an unfair. This 'officer' should be fired for extortion.

'You should be fired for extortion,' said Peg, exercising her constitutional right to free speech. 'I'm going to schedule a hearing. And the judge is going to get an earful from me.'

'That's nice. When you see Judge Call, tell her that her nephew Artemis says hello,' he said. 'Name.'

'Peg Silver,' she spit.

'Address,' he said.

How to answer that one? 'I have a farm in Manshire, but I haven't moved in yet.'

'Address where you're staying,' he said.

'I'm not sure of the exact address,' she said, making

this process a difficult a possible for the bastard.

'Describe the place,' said the cop.

'It's a big Federal on River Road in Manshire. Right before the bridge into New Hampshire.'

Officer Call stopped writing. He looked at her, and then at Ray. 'Linus Bester's?' he asked.

'Yes,' she said.

'Wait a minute,' said the cop. 'You're that topless girl I turned the SuperLight on last week on the boat dock at Dartmouth. And this fellow is the one who said I had no balls.'

'That was you?' asked Peg. 'Small valley.'

'You have no idea,' he said. 'I didn't recognize you.'

'I look a lot different with my clothes on?'

The crowd laughed. Officer Call pointed his corn dog at them. They stopped laughing.

He said, 'Since you're a friend of Linus's, I'll let you off – this time.' He ripped the tickets off his pad and put them in his pocket. Officer Call ate the remainder of his corn dog in one big bite. While chewing, he bent down and lifted Ray in his arms, carrying him like a sleeping child toward the parking lot. Peg hurried to keep up.

The cop said, 'Where's your car?'

'Mention the name Linus Bester and I get out of jail free?' she asked.

'That's right,' said the officer. 'Plus a police escort back to Manshire.'

Peg couldn't find her Subaru in the parking lot full of other Subarus. She had to use her nifty remote to locate the car. Officer Call loaded Ray into the passenger side and buckled him in. Peg got in the driver's side and followed the cop in her car as he walked toward his vehicle – a blue Subaru with the words 'Manshire

Sheriff" painted in white. Then she followed him back to the Federal.

They both pulled into the driveway. Out of his car window, Officer Call said, 'Need help getting him inside?'

Peg said, 'You've done enough. Thank you.'

'Tell Linus that Artemis says hello.'

Peg nodded. 'Tell me the truth,' she said. 'You were giving me that trumped-up ticket just because I'm from New York.'

Sheriff Call said, 'New York? I thought you were from New Jersey.' Then he drove off into the night.

New Jersey?

Peg had never been so insulted in all her life.

24

Peg opened all the car windows. She'd have to leave Ray in the car for now. As she adjusted the seat down for his comfort, she examined him. Great body. But, in sleep, his slackened face lost its allure. Without the gooey toffee eyes, and the mischievous curve of his lips, Ray looked blank, almost unrecognizable.

It was just seven o'clock. The drugs would wear off in a few hours. She'd come back at ten and get him out of the car. She went inside, glad that ordeal was over. Peg was curious, too, about what was going on with Linus and Wilma. She would love to catch a few snippets of their conversation. Spying would be wrong, of course. And Peg so wanted to be right. She made her presence known upon entry by yelling a big hello to the house.

No hello back.

In the living room, Peg found Linus dead asleep on the couch. Wilma wasn't in sight.

Linus drank the Xanax cider, which explained his condition. But where was Wilma? Peg called out again. No response. Her hostess had either gone out, or was sequestered in her room.

Peg looked down at Linus on the couch. Even knocked flat by Xanax, he smiled in his sleep. Peg could imagine waking up to a smile every day. That would be a pleasant start to the morning.

The sight of a sleeping man had always made Peg's heart tight. Linus's face in slumber took on a beautiful softness. She adored the upturned corners of his mouth. She leaned down and, with two fingers, pulled his lips into a frown. As soon as she let go, the happy tilt bounced back. Peg tried again. Linus dopily brushing her hand away. The contact of his fingers gave Peg an illicit jolt.

She wanted to touch him, she realized. She was burning to. How bizarre, she thought. Usually, Peg's desire was reactive. Her boyfriend (at the time) would look at her in a certain way, whisper how much he wanted her, and her passion was stoked to full blast. Case in point: Ray.

And yet here she stood, over Linus's vulnerable, prostrate body, reacting to nothing, and her pulse was skipping through her veins. This was active desire. She liked the clarity of it. The purity.

There was just enough room for Peg to sit next to Linus's sprawled body on the couch, so she did. She put her hand flat on his chest, feeling his lungs inflate and deflate. She touched the pulse point on his neck, his skin toasty. Peg quickly glanced around the room. What she was doing? With Linus in his state of defenselessness, it was a violation, a crime, probably. She had no right.

Did she see herself as someone who'd molest an unconscious man? she wondered.

Strongly disagree. Vehemently disagree. With all her moral fiber, she disagreed.

Peg next tickled Linus's bare arms. They weren't as muscular as she usually liked. Hardly anything about Linus was what she usually liked. She edged her knuckles against his rough cheeks. In his sleep, he smiled wider and sighed. Peg placed her hand over his heart, registering the clip-clomp under her palm.

She didn't dare touch him below the belt. This foray had already ventured as far into the perv realm as she ever wanted to go. But she might as well get an eyeful or him, if not a handful. Scanning the length of Linus's torso, Peg remembered Wilma complaining (complaining!) that his cock was too large. Peg assessed the area. Was it her imagination, or did she see movement under his shorts? Linus mumbled unintelligibly. Was he waking up? Fearing the worse, Peg started to rise off the couch.

She didn't move fast enough. Suddenly, Linus grabbed her, pulling her on top of him, grappling her across his chest. He nuzzled her neck and bit gently on her shoulder.

One of his knees got between her legs, one hand on the small of her back, pushing her hard against him. His other hand was around her neck, holding her tightly in place. The nibbles on her neck, the leg between hers, Linus's chest squashing her tits. And, *blammo*, Peg came, gasping, with a lightning rod to the groin.

Peg had never come like that before. Not fully dressed, in five seconds, with a man who was sound asleep.

She scrambled to free herself and ran across the room. Her head swung to the left and right, searching for Wilma, Ray, any witnesses. Finding none, she loped upstairs to her room and locked the door. She set her alarm for ten, when she'd check on Ray, and turned off the lights. Hours before she fell asleep, Peg lay on her back in bed, staring at the ceiling, shaking from the inside, Linus's hand- and lip-prints burning against her skin.

*

'There's something wrong with my alarm clock,' said Peg the next morning. 'I meant to check on you, but it never went off.'

At the breakfast table, Ray said, 'Look at my face!'

'I'm so sorry,' said Peg.

'The swelling should go down,' said Ben. 'In a few days.'

Ray had spent the night in Peg's car, the windows down. He'd become a feasting ground for every mosquito in the Upper Valley. Big red welts covered his neck, collarbone and hairline. Little bumps ran up and down his arms and legs. A whopper had caused his eyelid to swell.

'What can I do?' asked Peg.

'You've done enough,' Ray barked. 'I wish I knew why I passed out.'

'It was the bloomin' onion,' said Tracy. 'That much grease will flatten anyone.' That made Ben laugh. Tracy joined him.

Ray said, 'I don't think this is funny.'

'It's just a few mosquito bites,' said Gloria, munching Grape Nuts.

'I'd say over two hundred,' said Luke, breaking his vow of silence.

That made Tracy and Ben giggle again. Peg said, 'You two must have had a good time last night.'

Tracy nodded. 'We rode the Tilt-A-Wheel ten times. And the Pirate Pendulum. And the Hurl-A-Coaster.'

The two new chums proceeded to relive their thrill rides. Linus and Wilma came out of their bedroom. Peg hadn't realized they were still in there. Wilma looked bright, fresh, rested and alert. Linus seemed okay. The sight of him made Peg blush furiously.

Linus sat down at the table. 'Everyone had fun last night?' he asked.

Grumbles from Ray, silence from Peg and hearty agreement from Tracy and Ben. Gloria and Luke merely nodded.

Linus asked Ray, 'What's wrong with your face?'

'Mosquitoes.'

Leaning in for a closer look at Ray's eye, Linus said, 'Two pincer marks. That's the work of an earwig.'

'I was bit on the eye by an earwig?'

Tracy and Ben laughed again.

Ray said to Ben, 'If you'd passed out on the Hurl-A-Coaster, I doubt you'd be yukking it up this morning.'

Linus said, 'There's a tube of Cortizone cream in the men's bathroom.' To the group, he announced, 'We have a couple of special guests coming to talk to you this afternoon. We'll meet on the back porch at two.'

'Anything scheduled before then?' asked Peg.

'Nope,' said Linus.

'Shouldn't we be Inward Bounding?' she said. 'I propose that you conduct individual evaluation sessions. I volunteer to go first.'

Linus said, 'At the end of week two, once we've finished the interpersonal exercises, we typically plan for a free day or two to catch your breath and reflect on your experiences.'

'Don't worry, Peg,' said Wilma. 'Next week is packed with activities. You'll find out exactly what you're made of.'

'How about a morning run? Linus? A quickie to the lake road? I don't mean a quickie. A longie? A long, punishing run?'

'Can't,' he said. 'Sorry.' Then Wilma and Linus left the kitchen together, holding hands. Watching them, a rock landed in Peg's stomach. Had they reconciled sometime between Peg's orgasm and breakfast?

The group resumed eating, and then cleaned up. Standing at the sink, Tracy whispered to Peg, 'If I didn't know better, I'd think you were trying to get Linus alone.'

Peg whispered back, 'That's absurd.' And then to the group, 'Well, I'm going for a run. My farm is about five miles away. Anyone want to join me?'

Demures from the group, especially Ray, who announced he was too stiff from sleeping in the car to run five inches. Tracy said, 'Take your cell. Call me, and I'll come pick you up at your farm. I'd love to see the place.'

'Don't expect much,' said Peg, afraid herself of what she would find. It'd been almost two weeks since she'd been out there.

Peg suited up, stretched and hit the road. Running was a strain. It always was for the first mile. She'd loosen up and then get into cruising mode. She made it to the mile mark. Trudging along, she wondered why her legs weren't falling into a rhythm. After two miles, her body still not kicking into automatic pilot, she slowed to a walk, put her hands on her hips and breathed laboriously.

She was pathetically out of shape. She shouldn't have expected to go five miles in this condition, but now she was two miles out, exhausted, the sun high and hot. No way was she going to run back.

Peg turned on her cell. Amazingly, she got reception. She checked voice mail. She had forty-three messages. Finding a rock in the shade, Peg sat to listen to them.

Twenty-one were from Nina, increasingly agitated. Her last one, recorded yesterday at midnight, said, 'Where are you? Peg, please, please call me. I'm frantic here. So is Jack. A few notes do not ease my mind. Are you okay? Why aren't you checking in? You must call me immediately.'

Fifteen were from her mom, including this one: 'Peg, sweetie. No pressure. I don't want to put pressure on you. You've moved, and have the right to privacy. I just want to make sure you're okay. Am I a horrible mother? Are you intentionally trying to hurt me?'

Three were from Jack. From yesterday: 'I'm sure you're fine. But I'm the only one who is. Nina is calling me fifty times a day. Mom and Dad are freaking out. I can't stand to be near them. If you don't call soon, I may be forced to move out and pay rent in some shithole.'

Three from the real estate broker who'd sold her the farm, asking how the extermination was going.

One from the exterminator, placed an hour ago. 'Ms. Silver. Chuck Plenet here. I'm over at your place. The cats are doing a great job with the mice. There has been a small unforeseeable complication. Give me a call.'

Peg pushed the buttons to return the call. Got Chuck Plenet's voice mail. She called Nina. Got hers. Same with her parents and Jack. She called the Federal. Thankfully, Tracy answered. Peg asked her to come get her, and they'd go out to the farm.

In ten minutes, Peg was sitting next to Tracy in her Camry, cruising toward Old Dirty Goat Road.

'Can you really run this far?' asked Tracy.

'Once upon a time. I'll have to work up to it again.'

'Why?' asked Tracy. 'I mean, just because you can do something doesn't mean you should.'

Which made Peg think of Linus on the couch. 'Here it is,' she said.

The Camry pulled into the driveway. Tracy made all the right noises. 'My God, Peg. The view! The pasture! The pond! It's beautiful. And this house is so cute. This is all yours? How did you find it?'

Peg said, 'Hold those thoughts. You're not allergic to cats, are you?'

'No.'

'Good,' said Peg. They got out and walked to the front door. 'Stand back. I'm going to open it.'

Peg opened the farmhouse door. She and Tracy slipped inside.

The stench engulfed them like a green fog. A mix of decay, cat litter, shit and ammonia. Peg covered her mouth and nose with the bottom of her shirt and forged farther into the house. Tracy followed.

When they walked into the kitchen, five cats jumped off the countertop. One sat in the sink, content as the day was hot, with the freshly killed body of a mouse in its mouth, little drops of blood on its white snout.

Tracy said, 'That mouse has no head.'

The women looked down at the floor by the sink. The freshly severed mouse head lay there, dead eyes open. The tiny puddle of blood made Peg think of crime scene photos on *Law & Order*. But in miniature.

As the women watched – as in, before their very eyes – the decapitated head was suddenly surrounded by a cascading wave of ants that had flowed from under the kitchen counter. Had to be hundreds of them. They surrounded the mouse head, feasting, making it shrink, and then lifting it and carrying it away, back under the counter. All that remained of the crime scene was the puddle, smeared and tracked by an army of crawling insects.

Peg tore through the whole house. Everywhere, scenes of carnage, trails of entrails, thousands of scavenger ants on the move, carting away dinner, or just indulging on the spot. The overflowing cat litter boxes, which Peg doubted had been cleaned in weeks, were also festooned with insects.

It was enough to make a girl sick. She had to get air. Peg ran outside, onto the deck. Dialing furiously, Peg tried to reach Chuck Plenet. No signal. She dialed again. Nothing. The phone a hunk of useless plastic in her hand. She dialed again. No signal. She would have dialed again, but instead, she heaved her cell phone into the pond.

Tracy, seeing that Peg might be losing it, ushered her down the deck steps and into the Camry. She drove the hell out of there.

'An exterminator who bring bugs *in*?' said Tracy. 'You should sue the bastard.'

Peg said, 'Sue him? I can't even call him. I just threw away his number.'

25

When Peg and Tracy returned to the Federal, Linus was waiting in the front doorway.

'Perfect timing,' he said excitedly.

'I need the phone,' said Peg.

He said, 'Our guest speakers have just arrived. They're having a drink, and then we'll get started.'

Tracy headed inside, curious to see who the speakers were. Peg held her ground. 'I really need the phone.'

'Their subject matter is of particular relevance to you, Peg.'

'Unless they're experts ant killers, I don't care,' she said.

'Ant killers?' he asked.

'Just give me the phone,' she demanded.

Excitement dimming, Linus said, 'They can't stay long. And it wasn't easy for them to get here.'

He might as well have said, 'You are a rude, selfish, demanding New York Jew bitch who shows no consideration for the efforts others make on your behalf.' Or maybe she was overreacting.

She sighed. 'As soon as this is over, I madly, truly, deeply need the phone.'

Linus nodded and directed her to the back porch, where the Inward Bounders were seated in chairs and on the railing. Wilma sat cross-legged on the floor, and seemed eager to begin. Two rockers were left empty. Peg leaned against the door frame, and waited.

After a minute, Linus brought an elderly man and woman to the porch. The woman had a bright silver braid twisted into a bun. She wore corrective sneakers, a mid-calf-length denim skirt and a flannel shirt in ninety-degree heat. The man had a full head of white hair, and also wore denim and flannel. He had on bright red Nike sneakers, which clashed violently with his orange socks. Despite their advanced age, they walked solidly to the rockers. A learned shine in their watery eyes. A natural dignity in their manner. Peg assumed they were accomplished veteran psychologists. Maybe they invented Wilma's OCEAN model of personality traits. They were certainly old enough to have clacked clipboards with Carl Jung.

Linus stood behind them, and said, 'Donna, Stewart, I'll let you introduce yourselves.'

The ancient ones nodded. Donna went first. She said, 'My name is Donna Judd. I've lived in Manshire for eighty-six years. I have ten children, seventeen grandchildren and thirty-three great-grandchildren. I own the Manshire used bookstore. Right up the street, next to the post office.'

The woman nodded at the man. He said, 'I'm Stewart Connor. Eighty-nine years young. I've got nine sons, and each of them has three sons, and each of them has a couple kids. I used to run a bed-and-breakfast outside of Woodstock, but I've been living in Manshire for the last ten years, to be closer to the hospital.'

Linus said, 'Donna and Stewart have the distinction of being the most married Vermonters in state history.'

Tracy asked, 'Most married? They've been married for the longest time?'

The geezers laughed at that. 'We've never been married to each other. I'm not married at all right now,' said Donna.

'I am,' said Stewart. 'Wish I weren't, though.'

Donna brushed some silver strands out of her wrinkles and said, 'I've been married eleven times. My ten kids are from five different fathers.'

Stewart said, 'I've been married twelve times. But only three of them gave me children. The other marriages didn't last long enough, or the women were too old. My current wife, her name is Jane, was eighty-two when I met her at the hospital.'

'How old is she now?' asked Ben.

'Eighty-two,' said Stewart. 'We met just four months ago.'

'Between the two of you, you've been married twenty-three times,' said Ray, blinking his non-swollen eyelid in disbelief.

Stewart said, 'Sounds like a lot, but when you're going through it, getting married and divorced, makes sense each time. I was a widower twice.'

'I was a widow twice, too,' said Donna. 'All the rest divorces.'

'Vermont has an unusually high divorce rate,' said Linus. 'I think these two have distorted the averages.'

Donna and Stewart laughed with pride. 'It's the winters,' said Donna. 'Every November, you get so damn cold, you need a body to keep you warm. So you just latch on to someone, and then, after the April thaw, you realize you're knee-deep in mud.'

Stewart said, 'Yup.'

Tracy said, 'But why get married? Why not just live together?'

Stewart said, 'I started getting married sixty-five years ago. Back then, you had to buy the cow, because no one was giving milk away for free.'

Donna laughed and slapped Stewart on the knee. They loved their cow jokes in Vermont.

'He's comparing women to cows,' said Tracy.

'It's just a figure of speech,' said Donna. 'Lighten up.'

'As I was saying, the women wanted to get married, so I married them,' continued Stewart. 'Women always want to get married. Even to me, when they know my track record. I think my history makes them want me more, like they know I'll say yes to them, or that getting married is more important than staying married.'

Linus said, 'What about you, Donna?'

'I represented a challenge,' she said. 'At least five of my husbands told me when we first started dating that they'd be the one to last. I would just nod and tell them I thought they might be right. Even if they didn't like me much, or like being married to me, they'd fight like dogs to stop me from divorcing them. It was pride.'

'Was it ever love?' asked Peg, finally finding her voice after being stunned silent. 'For either of you?'

Donna said, 'The first few time, yes, it was about love. But after that, marriage was about food. I had kids. I needed money and the protection of a man. I don't expect you girls to understand that. You live in a different world. My last marriage was the closest to a love match I've ever had. No kids to feed, no pressure to undo the stigma of being a single woman. That one lasted seven years. My record.'

'He died?' asked Gloria.

'No, I divorced him, too. He had an affair with a younger woman, that cradle robber. She wasn't a day over seventy.'

Stewart said, 'I married for love. Every single time. I loved those women with all my heart. Until I didn't anymore. And each time I fell out of love, it took me by surprise. I never saw it coming, and I never believed it would happen. I fell asleep in love, and woke up the next morning in despair. Every married man alive knows what I'm talking about. The ones who stay married ignore the despair, or they work around it. I woke up in despair yesterday. After only three months this time. It's getting worse as I get older.'

Linus said, 'By the time you're ninety, you'll be filing for divorce on your wedding night.' The seniors laughed at that, heartily.

Peg could not believe her ears. How could Linus be joking about this? These people were unthinking, unfeeling heathens, to take their marriage vows so lightly, callously leaving a trail of broken families in their wake. And look at them! Clean-cut and preppy; not rednecks by any stretch. They appeared to be socially conservative Protestant members in good standing in their community. But, in truth, they were home wreckers and heart-breakers.

She had to speak. 'Marriage is serious, Linus. It's not a punch line.'

'You misunderstand me, Peg,' he said. 'I was using divorce as the punch line.'

Her jaw dropped. She stood there like that, mouth open, catching flies, while Donna and Stewart took questions for an hour, until Wilma drove them home.

*

After dinner, Peg tracked down Linus in his bedroom. He was alone; Wilma had gone food shopping. She entered his room and closed the door behind her. Linus, who'd been sitting at his computer typing what appeared to be a journal entry, turned toward her and said, 'You wish to speak to me privately?'

'I have nothing in common with those people,' she said. 'You said, "Their subject matter is of particular relevance to you."'

'Wasn't it? Look at your reaction,' said Linus.

Peg started to defend herself. Linus spoke first. 'Donna and Stewart are kind, loving people, and deserving of kindness and love in return. They're both devoted to their children and grandchildren. I went to school with a dozen of Donna's grandchildren, and I know firsthand that she's made huge sacrifices for her family, and that her life hasn't been easy. But she's still got a sense of humor, and wants to have a good time. I hope I do at eighty-six. Don't you?'

'Of course,' said Peg. 'That's not—'

'Yes, getting back to you,' said Linus. 'I didn't think you'd relate to Donna and Stewart directly. How did you feel about the way they described their spouses?'

'Desperate women and vain men. I felt sorry for them.'

'Anything else?' he asked.

'What else? Stewart's wives married for the sake of getting married, so they deserved what they got. Donna's husbands were driven by a knuckleheaded challenge with no ultimate reward.'

'Okay, then,' said Linus. 'Why don't you meditate on that, and I'll finish up my business here.'

'I'll meditate on what an obtuse asshole you are,' she

whispered under her breath. And that's the last time I molest you, she thought spitefully.

'One more thing,' said Linus. 'Something important happened last night.'

Peg froze. Was he talking about what happened on the couch? No, couldn't be.

She asked, 'Something good?'

'It sounds bad, but it's good,' Linus said, 'Telling you about it does violate my professional distance policy. But the information is relevant to how the program will be run for the next couple of weeks.'

'Are you going somewhere?' asked Peg, suddenly hating that idea.

'Wilma and I broke up last night,' he said. 'After all of you left for Sunbridge, we sat down to talk. She went over her key problems in our relationship. The same ones I've heard about for a year now. I tried to pay attention to her complaints. But I could not keep my eyes open. Usually, I never feel tired unless I'm lying down in my bed. I realized then that Wilma must not engage me. The sound of her voice has the soporific effect of, say, a powerful prescription sleeping pill.'

'It wasn't her voice,' said Peg. It *was* a powerful prescription sleeping pill. Should she tell him?

Linus shook his head. 'We've been having a hard time for a while. She's twelve years younger than I am. And we have other, crucial incompatibilities of a personal nature. Which was driven home even harder last night by the dream I had.'

'Listen to me, Linus. You crashed because—' Peg paused. 'What dream?'

'I can't tell you the details,' he said. Was he blushing? 'But this dream was very stimulating.'

'Stimulating in what way?' asked Peg. 'Just pretend I'm not a client for two minutes.'

Linus paused. 'I've had some doubts in the last year about my abilities to, uh, *help* Wilma in all the ways a woman needs to be helped. And in this dream, I helped a woman. I helped her very well. And fast. My head spun from how fast.'

His head spun. Peg's head had spun clean off her neck. She said, 'So the dream gave you confidence. Sexual confidence.'

'The confidence you enjoy every day,' said Linus. And then, as if he got a flash of insight, he said, 'Maybe that explains it.'

'Explains what?' asked Peg.

'Nothing.'

'Who was the woman in the dream?' she pressed. 'Anyone I know?'

Linus definitely blushed this time. He said. 'Here's how it's going to work. Wilma will stay on for the rest of the July session. I'll edit her dissertation as promised' – he patted the top of the computer – 'and in August we'll go our separate ways.'

Peg took a few deep breaths. She should tell him the truth, that he'd been drugged. That his dream had been real. That his decision to end a yearlong relationship was based on two separate misdemeanors, both perpetrated by Peg. Or she could say nothing and hope that fate would step in to reunite them – if Linus and Wilma were meant to be together. Or, she crossed her fingers, that it *wouldn't* happen and Linus would be available in August. Peg would be out of the program, new to the neighborhood. They were friends already. Last night proved they had sexual chemistry. They could transform a friendship into a relationship, and have three times the chance of . . . of him dumping her in one year and marrying someone else six months later.

Peg didn't want to be Linus's last girlfriend. She didn't want to be anyone's last girlfriend. No matter what the research said about people changing after thirty, Peg Silver feared her curse was permanent. That no amount of self-improvement or Inward Bounding would change it.

Linus was smiling at her now. Probably remembering his faux dream. She had to turn away. The idea of Linus breaking up with her and marrying someone else hit her as painfully in theory as it had been in reality with Paul, and Daniel, and Oleg. Peg might have high scores in openness. She might be a risk-taker by nature. But she didn't have the guts to take on Linus.

Peg yawned broadly, her mouth a gaping cavern, which she patted with her hand. 'I am suddenly so *sleepy*. I've never felt so *tired* in my entire life. My *God*, this conversation is like mainlining Demerol.'

Linus said, 'Talking to you has made me feel wide-awake. I couldn't possibly sleep for hours.'

'I'd get cracking on that dissertation edit,' suggested Peg.

'Hard at work already,' he said.

'I'll leave you to it, then,' she said. 'Good night.'

'You, too,' he said sweetly.

26

'We're moving a mountain,' said Tracy the next morning as the women gathered around their communal sink to brush their hair and teeth. 'That's all Wilma would give us last night. You were standing right there. You didn't hear her?'

Peg said, 'I was distracted.'

Gloria added, 'She also explained that the first week of Inward Bound was to delve into our individual psyches. The second week was to see how we acted in a couple. Week Three is about the group dynamic. I think we're being put into threesomes.'

'Week Four will be foursomes?' asked Peg.

'The last week is "Inward Bound in the Wild." '

'So they'll leave us lost in the forest with a matchbook, a bar of chocolate, a piece of fishing wire and a box of condoms?' asked Peg.

Gloria spit out her toothpaste. While dabbing her lips, she said, 'We go out in the world and attempt to talk to strangers.'

'Thereby violating our splendid isolation,' said Tracy. 'The smallest rejection, and I'll be right back to Day One.'

The women finished washing and dressing and met the others for a breakfast of yogurt, topped with raisins and cranberries. A quick side note: Peg had been appreciating the fine functioning of her digestion of late. She had Wilma's high-fiber fare to thank. Not that she would thank her, or dare speak to her. Peg was in on her secret. Peg had too many secrets of her own to keep. If she didn't, she'd be thrown out of the program, and possibly arrested by A. M. Call, upon whose shit list Peg was, no doubt, on top.

After breakfast, Peg used Linus's phone to get in touch with Chuck Plenet. He said, 'Ms Silver. I've been waiting to hear from you. The cats have done an excellent job on the mice.'

'Yes, I saw their fine work,' she said. 'Now kill the ants.'

'If I go in there and spray, the insecticide could harm the cats,' he said.

Peg held the phone back and stared at it, her jaw on hinges.

Chuck continued, 'I recommend dogs – five or six – to scare away the cats. For a small additional payment. Then I can bomb for ants.'

'How much?'

'Four hunnert,' he said.

Linus called from the front door. 'Peg! We're all waiting.'

She said into the phone, 'Send in the dogs,' and hung up.

She piled into Linus's truck with the rest of the group. They drove out to Billings Farm in Woodstock, half an hour away. Wilma and Linus sat in the cab together. Peg watched them through the little window between the cab and the flatbed. They were holding hands. Theirs could be the kindest, most understanding, affectionate breakup in history. Or, Peg wondered, maybe they hadn't really ended it. Maybe he'd lied about it. Linus could just be fucking with Peg's mind for some ultimate Inward Bounding purpose. While Peg tried to imagine what that purpose might be, Linus looked back through the window, right at her. She turned away, her hair whipping in the wind.

They pulled up at Billings, a working dairy and vegetable farm, as well as a farming museum. Tracy and Luke had come here for the cornhusking bee, so they'd seen it already. The main building had a gift shop (lots of toy cows and sheep), a photo gallery showing Vermont farm progress over the last two hundred years – and some modern rest-room facilities. Once Linus had spoken to the museum director, a Mr Fillet (an FOL, he was overjoyed to see him, and greeted Linus with a two-handed shake), the Inward Bounders were led out the side door, toward the dairy barn. Along the way, Mr Fillet pointed out the different types of cows (Holstein, Jersey, Swiss Brown). He showed them a pen with a newborn Holstein calf, just a week old.

Mr Fillet said, 'Every time a calf is born, we have a contest to name her. If you'd like, take a slip of paper and a pencil, right there in the bucket, and write a name. We'll announce the winner at the end of the day.'

Everyone took a slip and a pencil and looked into the deep brown eyes of the sweet little black-and-white calf. She was innocent and adorable, vulnerable and quivering, a helpless, sweet, dumb animal.

Tracy wrote, 'Spot.'

Gloria: 'Checkers.'

Ray: 'Moo.'

Ben: 'Babe.'

Luke: 'Luke.'

Peg wrote, 'Rare.'

'Rare?' said Mr Fillet. 'As in, "a rare specimen"?'

'Rare, as in "raw." '

Mr Fillet, stone-faced, said, 'This is a dairy cow.'

'So she won't be eaten?'

He said, 'You must be from New Jersey,' before he pushed the group along.

As they walked, Peg whispered to Tracy, 'I should have written "Unpasturized." '

They left the first barn, and were lead into another one. The first was for show, for tourists. The second – three times the size, with at least a hundred animals – was the working barn. It smelled like a shit factory. It *was* a shit factory. As they walked down the aisle, each cow in each stall raised tail and dropped a load, seemingly in greeting. Mr Fillet spoke softly to Linus, gestured toward some shovels and wheelbarrows and left.

Linus said, 'We're going to have a little competition today to see how well you work in a group. You'll be divided into two teams. Peg, Gloria and Ray are Team One. Tracy, Luke and Ben, Team Two.'

'What do we have to do?' asked Ray, suddenly at Peg's side, his arm around her shoulder. His eye looked better. He could open it now.

Linus said, 'You have to fertilize the vegetables.' He gestured toward the back barn doors to the rows of plants. 'The garden has been ribboned into two parts.'

'That garden?' asked Peg. 'It's at least two acres.'

'You'll need to fill the wheelbarrow a few dozen times, or more, spread it around, pat it down. How you divide the workload is up to you. Whichever team finishes first wins. You can spread the fertilizer thin, but it has to cover the entire acre.'

Gloria said, 'This is like an episode of *The Simple Life*.'

'But not simple as in "uncomplicated," ' said Tracy. 'Simple as in "mentally challenged." '

'What do we get if we win?' asked Ray.

'The satisfaction of a job well done,' said Linus. 'The losers have to explain over dinner where they went wrong.'

Gloria said, 'What do we use for fertilizer?'

Peg said, 'Shit, Gloria.'

'Shit what?'

'We use cow shit.'

Gloria looked into Peg's eyes, searching for the joke. Not finding it, she screamed, frightening the animals, who – en masse – dropped a fresh pie in protest.

Linus said, 'This silo' – he pointed at a shed with a trapdoor on the bottom – 'is where you'll get the aged fertilizer. For every wheelbarrow of aged fertilizer, you have to replenish a load of fresh into this silo.' He pointed at the shed next to the first, with a trap-door on top.

Tracy said, 'Aged fertilizer.'

'At least a year,' said Peg.

'Yes, it does have the fruity aroma of vintage 2004,' said Tracy.

Linus said, 'So, get to it. Wilma and I will be back in an hour or two.'

And then they left, hand in hand. Peg slapped her forehead to dislodge that image, and then gathered her team around. She said, 'We should have a loader, an unloader and a spreader. We can rotate jobs for equitable distribution of labor and—'

Ray said, 'Whoa, Peg. Before we agree to a game plan, we should nominate a team leader. I nominate myself. I have the most experience.'

'You have experience shoveling shit?' asked Peg, who herself had worked closely with manure many times.

'I do.'

'When?'

'Does it matter?'

Gloria said, 'I have bad allergies. If I touch any cow dung, I could go into cardiac arrest. I nominate myself to be leader and oversee the two of you doing the work.'

Peg said, 'I nominate myself. I have a plan, I'm organized, I've used the material before and I know how to spread. Gloria, you're lying about having allergies. Otherwise, you'd carry an EpiPen in your personal drugstore kit, which I know you don't. And Ray, just because you're a man doesn't automatically make you leader. It's very unattractive, this domineering side of you.'

Ray said, 'Gloria, if you choose me to be the team leader, I promise you don't have to touch any shit.'

'Done,' said Gloria.

'Peg,' said Ray, turning toward her, '*your* domineering side isn't very attractive either. In fact, it's a major turnoff.'

'Said the man with hamburger for a face.'

The cow by Peg stamped her hoof.

Gloria whispered, 'You shouldn't say "hamburger" in here.'

'It's your fault I look like this!' said Ray. 'Now grab a shovel and start digging.'

Team Two, meanwhile, had already filled three

wheelbarrows with the aged patties and were heading outside.

Gloria said, 'Let me get that for you,' and held open the barn door for them.

'What is that?' asked Peg, staring into the dish.

'Carrot and cheddar casserole,' said Wilma proudly. 'The cheddar was made right at Billings Farm!'

The casserole looked as appetizing as the manure. Even if Peg were hungry – which she wasn't – she wouldn't have been able to choke it down.

Linus clinked his spoon against his water glass. He said, 'Tracy, as leader of Team Two, I offer my heartiest congratulations. You should know that, in the history of Inward Bound, you fertilized your acre in less time than any previous team, setting a new record of four hours and seventeen minutes.'

Applause. Tracy stood up and bowed. She said, 'Was it that long? The time just flew, didn't it, guys?' Her teammates nodded, Ben more enthusiastically than Luke. 'Our strategy was to move the aged shit out of the barn first, using three wheel-barrows, and then spread side by side. We kept count, and then replenished the fresh shit shed when we'd finished spreading. I knew that if we could keep each other company, then it wouldn't feel so much like work. I considered splitting up duties – loading, unloading, spreading – but decided that an assembly-line strategy wouldn't be much fun, and if we didn't have fun, we'd bicker or get tired. I've learned a lot about teamwork in my years with the Red Sox organization. And let me just say, I'm not used to being on a winning team. It's much better than losing. I also want to add that Ben showed amazing strength. For a small man, he's got a big shovel. And Luke couldn't be a more efficient spreader, like he's been smacking down shit his entire life.'

'Excellent leadership,' said Linus. 'Tracy, you've shown yourself to be a gracious winner and team player. Now, Team One. You barely covered half your acre in the same time Team Two covered their whole area. Tell us what went wrong.'

Ray stood up. Tried to anyway. He had to slouch. The day of digging had destroyed Ray's back, which was already tender after spending a night on top of a stick shift. He said, 'Team One lost today due to vanity and ego.'

He got that right, thought Peg.

Ray said, 'A member of our team decided that things had to be a certain way, and if they weren't, this member would obstinately slack off and be a negative influence on the team effort.'

Amen to that, thought Peg, nodding.

'If this person had carried her weight, we would have won, under my leadership,' said Ray. 'I'm sure Peg has learned some valuable lessons today about being part of a team and working well with others.'

'I sure did,' said Peg, standing (which killed her back, too). 'I learned that Ray is power mad and insecure in his masculinity. I suspect he overcompensates for this Cayman Trench-deep insecurity with sexual aggression and *domineering* tendencies.'

Ray said, 'You bitch!'

Peg said, 'You see? He *is* a misogynist.'

Linus told them both to sit. 'Okay, calm down. It's all a learning experience. Now, Peg, as a florist—'

'I am NOT a florist,' she said.

'Have you ever worked as part of a group?' asked Linus.

'I've landscaped alongside other people,' she said, 'but I do my best work alone.'

'Your family. Did you do a lot of things together?'

'We have our own interests,' said Peg. Her family's recreational approach was parallel play. On their annual Caribbean family vacations, for example, Peg would go snorkeling, Jack would sail, Mom would sit by the pool and Dad would swim in the ocean.

'Have you ever played a team sport?' asked Linus.

'I run,' she said, shaking her head. 'Preferably alone.'

'Yes, I know,' he said. 'So you've never really had a team experience.'

Peg said, 'That is irrelevant. It doesn't change the fact that Ray is inept and impotent.'

'You of all people know that's not true!' Ray said, and stumbled out of the kitchen, as fast as his hobbled, mosquito-drained body could take him.

They all watched him go. Peg said, 'I didn't mean impotent in *that* way.'

Linus said, 'Peg, you owe Ray an apology.'

Peg said, 'What about Gloria? She didn't work well with others. She didn't work at all.'

'Flinging blame is a hallmark of egomania,' said Wilma.

'I'm not an egomaniac,' said Peg. 'Am I? Do I seem like an egomaniac? What does everyone think of me?'

No one spoke. Finally, Tracy said, 'Come on, Peg. Let's take a walk.'

Numbly, Peg followed Tracy out on the back porch and down to the river. The night was hot and dry, the water still and black. Peg said to Tracy, 'I came here on a whim. I should have thought it through before I signed up.'

'Me, too,' said Tracy, the A+ student. 'It's been good, though.'

'For you,' said Peg. 'You've learned that you can attract men. First Luke, now Ben. You're a great leader. You're conscientious, extroverted and agreeable. All I've learned is that I attract the wrong men for the wrong reasons. And I don't work or play well with others.'

'You play well with me,' said Tracy. 'And I was primed to dislike you at first.'

'Why?' asked Peg.

'You seemed haughty. It's the New York patina, the perfect hair and body. You're intimidating.'

'I don't have patina,' said Peg. 'Gloria's got the hair and body.'

'But she's a scared little bunny,' said Tracy. 'She's not threatening.'

In a small voice, Peg said, 'I'm a scared little bunny, too.'

Tracy burst out laughing. When she eventually gained control of herself, she said, 'Aren't you glad now you never slept with Ray?'

Peg said, 'God, yes. Can you imagine the horror if I had?'

'If you were back in New York, you'd have done it the first night,' said Tracy.

'Second,' said Peg.

'You have Linus to thank for preventing that disaster.'

'I'll add him to my reparations list.'

They walked along the river, listening to the mating call of frogs.

27

'I nominate myself *not* to be leader today,' said Peg to her teammates, Ben and Tracy.

'Good thinking,' said Tracy.

'I'll be leader,' said Ben, jumping at his chance. 'Although I have little experience operating medieval torture devices.'

The three Inward Bounders looked up, to the top of the stable. Hanging from a pulley, attached to a winch, was a six-feet-long, three-pronged metal clamp.

Linus was standing several feet away, talking to Dr Andy, the FOL who owned the horse farm with his wife, Katie. Team Two (Gloria, Luke and Ray) were clustered together, laying out their plan of action.

'Dr Andy has to leave,' said Linus.

'I've got office hours this morning,' said the genial doc in a suit (first suit Peg had seen in her weeks in Manshire). 'The bales of hay are in the pasture. Just roll them to the stable, use the fork and lift them into the hayloft. It's a snap.'

'You heard him,' said Linus. 'Get moving. First team to hoist a dozen bales wins.'

Gloria said, 'Do we have to?'

'Doctor's orders,' said Linus.

The country internist laughed lushly at that. Linus

joined him. Their mirth was pure, unadulterated neighborly affection. And why not? Dr Andy was getting a free pasture clean-up. Peg could only imagine how he would repay Linus for the favor. Perhaps once the Inward Bounders finished their hours of hard labor, they'd require medical attention.

Ben said, 'Okay, team. To the field!'

Patsylike, Peg followed her leader. She watched Ray out of the corner of her eye. He seemed particularly quiet and subdued, taking direction from Luke with the mindless acquiescence of a teenage Nazi. His eye was still puffy, his back crooked. Peg had yet to apologize to him. She was waiting for the right moment.

That came three hours later, after both teams had used the medieval stable fork to hoist their respective bales of hay into the loft. The score was tied. Team Two had been at a disadvantage, since Gloria appointed herself caretaker of the stable's five horses, who 'might be scared,' she said, 'by the hay, which I'm allergic to.'

Ben said, 'Horses eat hay. They aren't afraid of it. Are people afraid of French fries?'

Peg, for one, had never encountered a scary French fry, but Gloria insisted that she stay in the stable and soothe the horses, not one of which deviated from its hectic morning schedule of chewing, crapping, twitching and swatting flies with its tail.

Linus said, 'We'll have to break the tie. Any suggestions?'

Peg said, 'How about a race?'

'Excellent idea,' agreed Linus. 'Each team, appoint one runner. Twice around the training ring should do it.'

The training ring was about a quarter-mile long, by

Peg's estimate. She volunteered herself. Tracy and Ben agreed. Team Two chose Ray. Linus counted down from four, and they were off.

Ray took an early lead. Peg expected him to. She didn't have speed, but she had endurance. As she ran, mud splattering her legs, her old rhythm returned to her. She felt good. The movement seemed to ease her back pain, too.

After one lap, Ray slowed considerably. Peg knew he would. He had nice muscles, but he didn't have conditioning. Midway through lap two, Ray was just jogging, and panting. Peg, pacing evenly, ran up alongside him.

'I haven't had a chance to apologize for what I said last night,' she offered.

He could barely speak from breathing hard. 'Forget it,' he said.

'I'm sorry for embarrassing you in front of everyone.'

He had the wind only to wave.

'It was unconscionable of me to say that you are threatened by women. Or that you are insecure in your masculinity. Anyone can see how virile and potent you are.'

Ray wheezed.

'So you forgive me?'

He nodded.

'See you at the finish line,' she said, and then she blew him away, sprinting the last thirty yards.

Team One cheered. Peg walked over to Tracy and Ben and accepted their congratulations. Ray stopped jogging, and walked the last stretch. Peg noticed he was limping.

Linus did, too. 'Ray? You okay?'

He said, 'I think I sprained something.'

*

The bandage was wrapped tight around Ray's right calf. Peg noticed it immediately as he swung his lame leg out of the cab of Linus's pickup, and limped toward the mansion's front door.

'Are you okay?' she asked Ray. 'What can I do?'

Ray said, 'Stay away from me.' And then he limped past her, into the house.

Linus was close behind. He said, 'Dr Andy thought he might have pulled a muscle, but there was no swelling or redness.'

No sign of actual injury? Ray was faking? 'So what's with the bandage?' she asked Linus.

'He needs the support,' said Linus. 'And he's going to get it from me, and you, too, Peg.'

She studied Linus's face, his blue eyes, the encouraging grin. He was asking her to have a heart, to be kind and generous. To see that Ray's journey Inward was just as difficult as hers. Instead of being antipathetic, she should be sympathetic. Linus said all this without words, without making a sound. The swell of telepathic perception in her head made her feel lighter.

Peg said, 'I'll do whatever you say.'

Linus said, 'Anything?'

She smiled.

'Good,' said Linus. 'Go rake the compost.'

Peg raked the compost.

Much-married granny Donna Judd, said, 'I made cookies.'

The Inward Bounders each took a cookie.

Donna said, 'Come on in.'

The group walked into Donna's used bookstore. She said, 'I heard you rolled hay yesterday. That's hard work. You'll have a much easier time today.'

Peg exhaled. Maybe the day's assignment was to read. She wondered if Donna had any Chuck Palahniuk novels.

'Girls against the boys,' said Donna. 'You've got two hours. Whichever team alphabetizes the most shelves wins.'

'Fantastic,' said Ben. 'I was president of the Hartford Library Association in 2001. I can alphabetize blindfolded.'

Gloria said, 'I'm allergic to books.'

Donna laughed. 'Don't be ridiculous, dear.'

The old woman directed each Inward Bounder to a zone. Peg got the space by the window in back. Donna flitted around (she didn't get too many customers, Peg noticed), dishing out more cookies.

Eventually, Donna found her way to Peg's zone. 'So this is your payback from Linus for speaking to the group the other day,' said Peg. Vermont trade seemed to be redeemable favors in kind. It was socialism on a dollhouse scale. No wonder locals referred to their state as the People's Republic of Vermont.

The old woman smiled, her face crunching into a network of wrinkles. 'Linus is such a wonderful man,' she said. 'But I don't need to tell you that, do I, Peg?'

'You remember my name?'

'Of course,' said Donna. 'I don't meet many new people, so when I do, I make a study of it. Especially a girl like you – so pretty, so full of life. I asked Linus about you. He told me you've moved to Manshire.'

'What else did he say about me?' she couldn't help asking.

Donna grinned. 'What else?'

'Forget it,' she said.

'He did tell me one thing,' said Donna.

'What?' asked Peg, too eagerly. That he was attracted to her? That he was being tough on her for her own good? That, when the program was over, he'd ask her on a date?

Leaning close, Donna said, 'He told me that you would be an excellent alphabetizer. And I can already see that he was right!' Then she added, 'Linus is always right.'

'Yes, his name should be Mr Right,' said Peg. 'On second thought, scratch that.'

'Miss New Jersey!' said Manshire Sheriff A. M. Call, pumping Peg's hand in greeting. 'Good to see you. Dressed again, I see.'

The other Inward Bounders looked at her questioningly. She said, 'The pleasure is all mine, Sheriff.'

The Inward Bounders had arrived early on Thursday morning at a Manshire sheep farm for the day's team contest. Apparently, Artemis Call owned the place.

Linus said, 'Peg has been looking forward to repaying you for your help last week.' Peg had no idea Linus knew about her near-arrest at the Sunbridge Fair. So this was payback for Artemis's help. And the wheel of favor turned again.

Artemis cut to the chase. 'Okay, people. Today, you're going to live-wire a fence.'

Peg said, 'We're stealing a fence?'

Linus explained, 'Not *hot*-wire. *Live*-wire. We're putting up an electrically charged line to keep coyotes and wolves out, sheep in.'

'I'm definitely allergic to wolves,' said Gloria.

'Will you please shut up?' asked Tracy.

'She's the girl who cried allergic-to-wolf,' said Ben.

'Leave her alone,' snapped Ray, moving to Gloria's side.

Gloria smiled at him. He returned it, and looked rather handsome despite his still swollen features, bandaged leg and crooked back.

Artemis, who seemed much friendlier without a gun strapped to his belt, led the group behind his log cabin, to the sheep pasture. Peg was impressed with his lush flower bed around back with waning pink and white peonies and just popping poppies of red and orange. Artemis had a green thumb. Instead of his uniform, he wore a pair of khaki shorts that flattered his legs, and a chambray work shirt. Wisely, he'd slipped ankle-cut rubber wellies on his feet. Peg wished she hadn't worn sneakers for a trip into a sheep pasture with piles of round pellets everywhere.

'Ewwww,' said Peg, stepping in one. 'I mean, ewe.'

The sheep made up for the sloppy conditions. The flock was so fucking cute. They jumped and skipped and frolicked in the sun. Peg's heart leapt right along with them. She'd spent countless childhood weekend afternoons at the Central Park petting zoo, feeding the goats, sheep and cows. Seeing these neatly shorn sheep jumping around the pasture was like a hug from Mom and Dad. She missed them badly all of a sudden, and had to put sunglasses on quickly before anyone saw.

Too late. 'The sheep get to me, too,' said Wilma. 'They're innocent, like babies.'

'Especially those little lambs,' said Peg. The sheep seemed to be divided into adult and child pens. 'Why are they separated?'

'The lambs are weaned, and it's best to keep them

away from the mating adults,' said Wilma. 'They'll be slaughtered in a month anyway. Don't look so surprised. Those lamb chops you pay forty dollars for in New York have to come from somewhere.'

Artemis appeared at Peg's side. 'Don't you get sad?' she asked. 'Killing them?'

The sheriff said, 'These animals aren't pets. They're food. They cost a fortune to keep. I've got mortgage payments. If I don't eat them, they'll eat me.'

Although Peg got his point, after five minutes of watching these frisky cuties cavort and gambol, stupidly, without any clue that they'd soon be mass murdered for their meat, she vowed never to eat lamb again.

Artemis gathered the group around and explained the job. 'Coyote problem this year. They got a couple of lambs. I've got to take preventative measures, live-wire the fence. Forty volts should do it.'

'Will that kill?' asked Gloria.

'Nope,' said Artemis. 'It won't kill, but it'll hurt.'

'How painful is it?' asked Ben.

'Want to find out?'

None of them did. Artemis said, 'You won't be in any danger installing the fence. I won't connect it to the generator until you're done. Now, Linus tells me you've been put into teams all week. Today, it's going to be a bit different. I'm going to observe your individual work and decide who among you worked the best.'

Linus said, 'The winner gets five pounds of ground lamb.'

'What do the losers get?' asked Peg. 'Ten pounds?'

Wilma found a place in the sun to sit. She had a folder and a manuscript with her – her dissertation, had to be. Linus and Artemis gave the group a crash course on fence maintenance and conductivity. The wire itself, which they were to thread through plastic hooks along the posts, was a flat strip of plastic with a pink strand running in the middle. It was so flimsy and light, Peg found it hard to believe that brushing up against it would drop a coyote to its knees.

The first step was to nail the hooks into over two hundred posts. The Inward Bounders set off with individual buckets full of hooks and a hammer, each assigned a zone. Peg went deep into the pasture. She got into hammering. The resounding *thud*, the shudder of muscle up her arm. A couple of times, a curious sheep tip-hoofed toward her, and then dashed away when she turned to look.

She emptied her bucket and walked back toward the house, as did the rest of the crew. Next step: thread the wire into the hooks. They were each given a spool of wire and sent back to their zones. Artemis and Linus linked the wires, one section to the next, until all six wires were connected.

Peg noticed that some of the sheep had streaks of color on their backs and chests. She asked Artemis about it.

'I use color chalk to mark the rams' chests. Different color on each one,' he said.

'So you can tell them apart,' said Peg.

'I can tell them apart by looking at them,' said Artemis. 'I chalk the males so I know which of the ewes has been mounted, and by which ram.' Sure enough, many of the sheep had smears of color on their backs. He said, 'Look at that one,' pointing to a ewe whose back was a rainbow of chalk. 'She's been mounted by nearly every ram here.'

'That slut,' said Peg.

'She's got no choice,' said Artemis. 'If one ram mounts a female, then the others want to mount her, too.'

Peg was sure there was some evolutionary explanation for such gangbanging (a survival-of-the-fittest sperm battle was waged inside the female's womb?). Tracy and Gloria wandered over to Peg. She pointed out the sheep's chalk markings and said, 'If one male fucks a female, the other males want a piece of her action, too.'

'Men are so predictable,' said Tracy.

Peg thought of Donna, and her many husbands. She thought back on her own sexual history. Not that she was proud of it, but Peg had fucked a few sets of brothers and best friends. Never at the same time, though usually within a few months of each other. Peg had assumed that the decisions had always been hers to make. But now, watching the sheep, she had to wonder how many of those choices had been made for her. How often she'd been seduced for bragging rights.

Artemis broke her depressing train of thought by waving everyone in. The fence was wired and now he would hook up the end pieces to the generator, a metal box the size of a shipping trunk, parked outside the main gate. The group gathered to watch the thrilling finale. Peg wondered if sparks would fly, if she would hear a sizzle.

Artemis lifted the lid of the generator's casing, connected the wires to a battery, flipped a toggle switch, closed the lid and said, 'We're live.'

'That's it?' asked Gloria.

'No flying sparks?' asked Peg. 'No sizzle?'

'You want to test it?' asked Artemis. 'Go right ahead.'

The Inward Bounders picked up pebbles and leaves

and sticks and threw them at the wire. They'd bounced off and fell to the ground.

'Are you sure this is on?' asked Peg.

'I'm sure,' said Artemis. 'Linus and I are going inside to pick a winner. The rest of you: Have a beer.' He pointed out a cooler by the house. 'Long Trail Double Bag,' he said, naming one of Vermont's five million microbrews.

Artemis and Linus left. Gloria found a shady spot, protecting her delicate skin from the sun. Peg noticed that both Ray and Luke watched her go.

'I don't believe this wire is live,' said Ray suddenly.

Ben said, 'Why don't you touch it and find out?'

'You touch it.'

'No way,' said Ben. 'I'll give you twenty bucks if you do.'

'Are you men – or mental?' asked Tracy.

Ray said, 'I'm doing it.'

He reached out his hand, inches from the wire.

They all screamed. He pulled back, laughing.

'You don't have anything to prove, Ray,' said Peg. 'You're not going to be more of a man by electrocuting yourself. You'll just be more of an asshole.'

'If that's possible,' said Tracy into Peg's ear.

Ben said, 'I don't know, Peg. Electrocuting himself certainly takes balls.'

'Which will shrivel into walnuts,' said Peg.

'What do you care?' asked Ray. 'You'll never see them.'

'Go ahead, then.' Remembering that Linus had asked her to be sympathetic, Peg backpedaled. 'No, don't. Let's get a beer instead.'

Ray said, 'Aren't any of you curious what it would feel like?'

Ben said, 'What are you waiting for?'

'This is ridiculous,' said Tracy.

Ben said, 'It won't kill him.'

Ray reached forward with his index finger. A centimeter away from the wire. Closer, and closer. Tracy and Peg screaming. Ben and Ray laughed at their distress. Ray reached forward, pulled back, taunting them.

'Okay,' said Ray. 'I'm really going to do it this time.'

He moved within a hair-width of the wire, his mouth in a grimace, bracing himself, his swollen lid narrowing. Peg couldn't stand it. She lunged forward and swatted away Ray's hand. A valiant gesture. Inspired by continuing guilt about Ray's eye, his calf muscle, his emotional unraveling. But a misguided gesture. Surely, a misguided swat. And Peg would have been kicking herself for doing it at all, if she weren't lying on the ground, twitching.

In batting away Ray's finger, her own wrist grazed the wire, sending forty volts of electricity through her body. A hot, yellow-and-orange flash of fire rocketed from her wrist, down her arm to her toes and back up to the tip of each hair on her head. And then it stopped, leaving the brittle, smoking, tinny essence of pain in her teeth and spine, and smoke pouring out of her ears (that was how it felt anyway). She didn't remembered falling.

Tracy shrieked. Ben was on his knees at Peg's side, slapping her cheeks harder than was necessary. Ray stood motionless, until Luke dropped him to the ground, pressing a knee against his spine. Ray screamed for mercy. Luke's expression was stony, merciless.

Linus was behind Peg now, lifting her to her feet, telling her to walk. Her legs felt noodley. Linus put his arm tightly around her waist. He lugged her forward until she regained a micron of strength and could take a step. She looked at him, his mouth moving in slow motion. Linus seemed panicked, furious.

He said gently, 'You'll be fine. I've been shocked many times. You'll be okay.' He turned her around, making her walk, keeping the patter going.

Facing the group again, Peg watched Artemis pull Luke off Ray, then whisper something to both men. From Ray's ashen skin, Peg imagined Artemis had made some soft-spoken threats of country justice. Tracy and Ben were frantically retelling the story to Wilma and Gloria. Luke stood back, arms folded across his chest.

Peg said to Linus, 'As horrible as that was, I'm glad it happened.'

'You'll dine out on this story for months,' he said, still holding her tightly against him.

'The jolt did something strange to my brain,' she said.

Linus said, 'I think I'll take you to the hospital.'

'I had a blinding flash of insight,' she explained.

'The insight that you never want to touch a live wire again.'

'That, too,' she said.

'What else?'

'I'm falling in love with you,' she said.

Linus stopped mid-step. He said, 'I'm definitely taking you to the hospital.'

He scooped up Peg in his arms and deposited her on the bench of his pickup. He went back to tell the group where he was going. Through the window, Peg could hear their reactions. Wilma's attempt to settle down the group, Artemis offering a police escort. Tracy insisting she come, too. Linus agreeing. The two of them walked back to the pickup and climbed into the cab. Tracy held Peg's hand on the ride, and kept repeating that Peg would be fine.

Linus didn't say a word.

28

Dear Nina,

*I've gotten the shock of my life, literally. I was
electrocuted, and the jolt made me realize that I'm
in love with Linus, the program director. We had
an encounter on the couch a few nights ago, after a
drug experiment. He's an amazing man. And he's
attracted to me, too. I know he is, because of the
couch incident, but he thinks it was all a dream.
Not sure if he loves me, though. But maybe that's
good. I feel like I've made a conscious choice with
him, instead of letting circumstance and lust steer
me around the park.*

Much happier now,
Peg

'Lower,' said Peg. 'Now harder. Oh, YES. That's it. More,
don't stop. YES! YES!'

'Be quiet!' said Tracy. 'You're getting me excited, and
the last thing I need is a sexual identity crisis.'

Peg lay flat on her stomach, on her bed, in a flimsy
pair of shorts and a tank top, melting under the
ministrations of Tracy's magic fingers.

'Linus was sweet at the hospital, don't you think?' asked Peg. 'Very protective. Very . . . loving.'

Using her elbow, Tracy dug into Peg's knotty shoulder muscles. 'He was weird,' countered Tracy. 'Quiet. Like he didn't want to say something he'd regret later in court. You should sue the bastard.'

'That's what you said about the exterminator.'

'Him, too.'

'I'm not suing anyone,' said Peg. 'I feel great. Better than I have in years.'

'Recharged?' asked Tracy.

'I have to say, shock treatment might be getting a bad rap. Yesterday morning, I was confused, disheartened, anxiety floating like the mist. One jolt later, I'm energized-yet-relaxed, focused-yet-expansive, hopeful, stressless, as if the shock lit up words in my head, and I only had to speak them for relief.'

'The word "relief" makes me think of laxatives,' said Tracy.

'It was a cleaning, voiding experience,' said Peg.

'Your "relief" begins and ends with the fact that you've been in bed for an entire day, people waiting on you, bringing you food, rubbing your back. Linus has instructed everyone to make you as comfortable as possible. I'm telling you, the guy is terrified. You should see his face.'

Peg would dearly love an extreme close-up of Linus's face, and the rest of him, too, but she hadn't seen him since they got back from the hospital yesterday. Tracy said, 'You know, Ray feels terrible.'

'He should.'

'Your letter? The one you wrote to your friend Nina? Ray took it to the post office himself,' said Tracy. 'He paid to overnight it to New York.'

'He could overnight the collected works of Shakespeare and nothing would change between us.'

'If you hadn't been electrocuted, you wouldn't have had your precious "relief."'

Peg said, 'By that logic, I should thank Ray.'

'Maybe you should.'

'I'll put it on my list.'

'My fingers are tired,' said Tracy. She stopped massaging Peg's back and shook out her hands.

'If you ever want to give up on the Red Sox, you could have a real future at Madame Quong's massage parlor on Mott Street,' said Peg, sitting up, noticing suddenly that the Federal was awful quiet. 'Where is everyone?' she asked.

'How about a game of cards?' replied Tracy, reaching for the deck on the night table.

'I hit my gin limit after ten rounds,' said Peg, squinting suspiciously at her friend. 'What's going on? You're keeping something from me.'

'How about TV?' said Tracy. 'Or we could go online.'

Peg and Tracy snickered together at those absurd suggestions. Television was impossible. The Federal got terrible reception. Only one channel, a local NBC station, was watchable, but even that was as fuzzy as an angora sweater. Internet surfing was more like drowning. Linus's ancient IBM with the dial-up modem took forever to start up, and an eternity to load. This part of Vermont didn't have an electronic superhighway. It had a single lane dirt road.

'Can't we get out of here? Find the others?' asked Peg.

'You are just dying to see Linus, aren't you?' said Tracy. 'Don't look so surprised. I have eyes. My eyes can see. You clung to him at the hospital yesterday like a leech. You didn't need that much support, Peg. Dr Andy said you were in perfect physical condition.'

'I wanted the support of the man I . . . so profoundly respect and admire.'

'Two week ago, you profoundly respected and admired Ray.'

'That was a knee-jerk reflex. He was just like all the other jerks I once thought I needed,' said Peg.

'But why Linus?' asked Tracy. 'I'll grant you, he is tall. I was the first among us to notice his crunchy cuteness. He's smart. He's got this house.'

'He's the mayor. He's wise. He's funny. He's got a surprisingly muscular chest. He's a runner. He went to Harvard.' He gave her a spine-adjusting orgasm in five seconds flat. In his sleep.

Tracy countered, 'He lives with another woman. He desperately needs a haircut. He lives with another woman. He's eight years older than you. Have I mentioned that *he lives with another woman*? And his clothes?' Tracy crinkled her nose in disgust. 'How do you know he has a muscular chest?' she asked as an afterthought.

'Who gives a shit about clothes?' said Peg. 'I can't believe I just said that.'

'It must be love,' said Tracy.

'He may live with another woman, but not for long. Linus and Wilma broke up. The night of the fair. She's moving out when the session is over.'

'I don't believe it,' said Tracy. 'Linus and Wilma have been disgustingly cozy all week. Holding hands, their arms around each other.'

Peg had noticed the increase in affection since their breakup, too. Seller's remorse on Wilma's part? 'If

Wilma is leaving Manshire in a week, considering how Type A she is, I'll bet she's already started to pack. We could poke around their room.'

Tracy squinted at her. 'Snooping is vile and low. It's like peeping. It's sick.'

'It's not sick. It's healthy,' defended Peg. 'Healthy curiosity.'

'It's unethical,' announced Tracy.

'Said the woman who mixes a mean Xanax cocktail.'

Tracy let a sly grin creep up her cheeks. 'Well, we *are* alone.'

Within thirty seconds, they were down the stairs and in front of Linus and Wilma's bedroom door.

'Open it,' said Peg.

'You open it,' said Tracy.

Peg grasped the handle, and pushed the door inward. The room was neat, orderly, undisturbed by the ravages of packing. Wilma's clothes hung in the closet. Assuming Linus didn't wear Jockey For Her white bikini briefs, Wilma's intimates dresser drawer was full. Pop psyche books were stacked high on her night table – *A Case Against Monogamy; The Ten Rules of Romance; The Good Girl, Bad Boy Syndrome*. The books were marked up, pages dog-eared, paragraphs circled in red.

'They don't have much stuff,' said Tracy. 'Adhering to the Vermont belief that clutter is evil.'

'Let's turn on the computer,' said Peg.

'You'll leave a record of when files were last opened,' warned Tracy.

Peg sighed in disappointment. 'Snooping has never been less satisfying.'

'Imagine if someone went through my drawers,' said Tracy.

'And found your purple plastic penis,' said Peg.

'Now, that would be satisfying.'

They left the bedroom. Went to the living room. Flopped on the couch. Maybe Wilma wasn't moving out. Was it possible that Linus lied about their breakup? Peg wouldn't have told Linus she was falling for him – in any state of electrocution – had she not thought he was soon-to-be available. She considered a previous fear: Had he really been paying her special attention – asking her to go running, telling her she was irresistible, confiding to her about his alleged breakup – or was this his method of forcing Peg to venture deeper into Inward Bound?

The contentment of an hour ago was quickly replaced with a more familiar miasma of doubt and confusion. How could she have told Linus she was falling in love with him? Thank God she'd said 'falling.' She could always reel it back in, blame her blurt on the shock. Blame it on him.

Peg said to Tracy, 'Linus *was* weird at the hospital.'

'Maybe it was something you said.'

Peg jumped to her feet. 'I'm going for a run. A long, vicious, unforgiving ten-miler straight uphill.'

'Last time you set out to run five miles, you went less than two,' Tracy reminded her. 'Take a drive with me. We'll go into Manshire. See the sights.'

'What sights? The general store? The commemorative plaque?' asked Peg.

'The air might clear your head,' said Tracy.

Peg couldn't disagree. The women got into Tracy's Camry. They drove. Over hill and hill. It seemed like for every uphill in Manshire, there was an equal amount of more uphill. As they climbed and climbed, Peg closed her eyes, letting the sun shine on her lids, turning the underside yellow and orange.

Too soon, Tracy made a quick right and stopped the car.

'We're here,' she said, removing her keys from the ignition.

'We're at my farm,' said Peg, opening her eyes. 'You thought I needed another shock?'

Tracy ignored her and got out of the car. Peg groaned and followed Tracy toward the house. That was when Peg noticed Chuck Plenet's red exterminator truck parked on the lawn. The grass under the truck was destroyed.

Could he do anything right? Rage suddenly took control of Peg's limbs. She marched toward the house, ready to face off with Chuck Plenet. She might have left New York, but New York hadn't left her. She'd stuff his mouse hole with steel wool. She'd insecticide his walls.

She'd . . . As she got closer to the door, Peg spotted Linus's pickup parked on the other side of the house. Linus had also parked on the grass, creating another patch of demolished sod.

She'd demolish his sod. She'd Bound his Inward. Linus and Chuck Plenet were probably best-fucking-friends, she realized.

She punched open the screen door. In her sudden-onset female hysteria, Peg didn't wonder why the exterminator had shown up today. Or why Linus's truck was there, or how he'd gotten her address. She wasn't thinking rationally, or at all. Anger, if not blind like love, was dangerously nearsighted. As she entered her house – once a diorama of the food-chain-in-action – Peg didn't notice the desanguinated lemony-scented floors. She overlooked the sparkling clean countertops, the freshly spackled, formerly-mouse-gnawed base moldings on the walls. She did notice that the only creatures scurrying from room to room were people. And there were dozens of them.

Many of the people had unfamiliar faces, men in grimy overhauls and 'Plenet Killer' T-shirts. They were spraying powdery insecticide from tanks on their backs into the wall corners and along the cracks of the floor in the living room.

There was Gloria, sunny in an orange top, polishing the mantel. Upstairs, in the master bedroom, Ben and Luke were lifting the decimated mattress – the one that had been low-income housing for several families of mice – and then carrying it down the stairs and outside, where they heaved it into Chuck's truck. In the master bathroom, Ray was scrubbing her bathtub with Ajax.

Stunned by the kindness on display, Peg drifted back downstairs and onto her deck, no longer caring about the mangled sod, shamed by her anger, letting a few tears roll.

Tracy tapped Peg on the shoulder. 'This was Linus's idea, making your house the last group project of the week. Except we aren't divided into teams. We're working as a single, multi-armed organism. My job was to keep you occupied. Linus convinced your exterminator – he who should be sued – to come out here with a crew and finish the job *today*. Gloria said it took most of the morning to round up the cats and dogs.'

'How did Linus know what was going on out here?' asked Peg.

'I told him,' Tracy said. 'Yesterday, at the hospital, while Dr Andy was examining you.'

Chuck Plenet lumbered through the living room's French doors and joined Peg and Tracy on the deck.

He said, 'Ms. Silver, good to see you.' He smiled obsequiously. 'You should have told me you were friends with Linus Bester. We could have saved ourselves a lot of misunderstandings.'

'There were no misunderstandings between us,' said Peg. 'You took advantage of my desperation. I know it, you know it and now Linus knows it, too.'

Chuck growled, and said, 'I've got your bill here.' He pulled a long sheet of paper out of his pants pocket and handed it to her. On it, he'd listed a hundred itemized entries, each with a price. The grand total: $1,490.

Peg said, 'We agreed on a total of six hundred dollars.'

'Additional expenses,' he said. 'I had to hire ten men to get this done today.'

'I'll gladly pay you the six hundred we agreed upon.'

'And the balance?'

'Where is Linus? I'm sure he'd like to check the addition on this bill,' said Peg.

Chuck grabbed the bill back from Peg. He said, 'Give me seven hundred today, and we'll call it even.'

'Six.'

'Six fifty.'

'Maybe we should ask the mayor to decide.'

The fear of pain of death flashed behind Chuck's eyes at the mention of Linus's name (which Peg *loved* dropping). He grabbed the bill back and agreed to $600. She said she'd mail him a check.

Five minutes later, Chuck and his crew sped away in the truck (tearing up still more sod). After they left, Wilma's green hybrid pulled into *the driveway* (thank you, Wilma). Linus and Wilma stepped out, opened the car's trunk and removed bags and boxes. Ray, Luke, Ben and Gloria came out of the house and helped unload Wilma's trunk of groceries, a bag of charcoal briquettes, a pony keg of Long Trail, a radio/CD player, which Ray brought over to the deck, plugged into the outside socket and tuned to the DCR station. Suddenly, music rolled over Peg's hill.

Confused, she said, 'I don't have power yet.'

'Linus got it turned on this morning,' said Ray. He joined Peg and Tracy by the deck railing. Ray smiled nervously at Peg. She smiled back. He took the opening, and put his hands on her shoulders. He drew her in for a hug. A brotherly hug. Sexless, and not unpleasant.

He said, 'We got off to a bad start.'

'We had a great start,' she corrected. 'Bad middle.'

'We can have a good ending,' said Ray.

'Who says our friendship has to end?' she asked.

They let each other go. Ray turned to walk to the driveway. Peg's eyes followed him as he went down the deck steps to relieve Gloria of a twelve-pack of soda. The two of them went back into the house, holding hands.

As she watched that odd couple, Linus crossed into her line of vision. He stood in the driveway, staring at her.

Peg's heart stampeded in her chest. She broke eye contact and dashed inside. In the living room, Gloria was setting up a makeshift bar (plywood sheet on two sawhorses).

'Nice house,' said Gloria. 'It is *now* anyway. The dusting and polishing? That was me. I did it with a rag and a can of Pledge. In Connecticut, we have servants for that kind of thing.'

Peg curtsied and said, 'I am honored by your condescension.'

'You may rise,' said Gloria. 'Unless you haven't figured it out by now, we're throwing a party tonight. A coming-out party.'

'For whom?' asked Peg.

'For the whole group.'

'We're all gay?'

Gloria said, 'I don't think we are.'

'So this is a coming out, like a debut.'

'Exactly. Minus the elbow gloves,' said Gloria, who'd probably had a debutante ball when she was sixteen. 'Week Four begins tonight. We're to apply our new understanding of ourselves in social situations with strangers. Linus has invited the people on the road and some of his friends.'

'An Old Dirty Goat Road block party,' said Peg. 'I hope no one brings an actual goat.'

Gloria said, 'Linus thought it would be a nice way to introduce you to your new neighbors.'

Linus sure was doing a lot of thinking about Peg. Wilma walked into the room, carrying bags of ice.

'Look who's out of bed,' she said, handing Peg the bags. 'Bathtub?' she suggested.

Peg put the bags in the bathtub on the first floor. She joined Tracy stocking the fridge with hamburgers and hot dogs. She helped Luke set up the Weber charcoal grill. She wandered into her pasture and picked wildflowers, which Ben expertly arranged (he'd once been member of the Hartford Flower Arranging Club). The grill was hot as the sun dropped, in perfect timing for the arrival of Artemis Call, Albert DeWitt, Donna Judd, Dr Andy and his wife Katie, who brought a case of

Smoking Loon wine. They all greeted the Inward Bounders as if they were old, dear friends.

Other folks arrived in good time. A middle-aged woman and her much younger husband – two houses down – brought sour cream brownies. Albert DeWitt, who'd plastered himself to Peg's side (his wife was covering the restaurant tonight), whispered in her ear that the woman was once a poetry professor at Dartmouth and she'd met her husband when he was a master's candidate. This was five years ago. The poet had since quit teaching to write a sex guide about Tantric intercourse, featuring photos of her young husband in congress with several other women.

Another man, mid-thirties, who came with ten-year-old twin boys, had been a chief advisor to Howard Dean, and greeted Peg by saying, 'Don't you dare put a penny into the New Hampshire economy. Those fuckers buried us in the primaries. But don't worry. The Deaniacs have plans for them. First, we're going to Nashua! Then Portsmouth! Then Concord!' He ended his rant with a primal screech. Everyone giggled and told him to shut up.

Another man, mid-fifties, shaggy like a sheep dog, was a former Olympic downhill skier who'd made his money in fleece endorsements and had retired to a farm four houses down to breed llama. A sixtyish woman (three houses up) owned and operated a wooden-toy shop, and had supported herself for thirty years by selling hand-whittled dolls and miniature rocking horses at country fairs. Another neighbor – a fortyish, quiet man – was, as Albert described, 'the worldwide acknowledged go-to guy for antique musket restoration.' A young woman, her husband and three pre-school kids came with a basket of fried chicken. They ran an organic chicken ranch (five houses up), and had killed the birds in the basket only a couple of hours ago, 'just for the occasion,' said the pretty redheaded wife with blond lashes.

Even with Albert steering her through the maze of faces, names and histories, Peg couldn't keep the information straight. Her neighbors were, as a whole (except for the shy musket guy), friendly, talkative, receptive and, seemingly, glad to have her on their road.

Peg said to Albert, 'When they say they're glad to meet me, they seem to mean it.'

'If they said it, they mean it,' he said.

Peg said, 'Linus is in his element.' She'd been watching him glad-hand his way around the party. Wilma, meanwhile, was keeping herself busy, away from the social swirl, by replenishing drinks, removing empty cups, slapping patties on the grill.

Albert said, 'I'm not going to talk to you about Linus. I would, but I'm a loyal friend. You can't drag me into a conversation that reveals his state secrets.'

'State secrets? Such as?'

He shook his head. 'You won't get anything out of me.'

'What exactly does Linus *do*?' she asked. 'In his capacity as mayor, I mean.'

Albert said, 'It's a nominal position, really. His salary is one dollar a year. Manshire is under the official jurisdiction of the township of Norwich. So Linus doesn't have many legislative responsibilities. He just keeps the town wheels greased.'

'That's New York speak for bribery.'

'I wouldn't call what Linus does bribery. I'll bet

you've seen some of his mayoral influence in action already,' said Albert. 'I can't resist that smell for one more second. How would you like a big, juicy hamburger?'

'I'm not sure about eating beef,' said Peg. 'I don't want to turn into a mad cow.'

'The cows in Vermont aren't mad,' said Albert. 'They have been known to get irritated. Annoyed. We have some very vexed cattle. Some might be seriously pissed off. But not mad. Never that.'

'Okay,' she agreed. 'I'll take one seriously pissed off burger. With ketchup.'

He left, and Peg headed toward Linus, across the porch, near the keg, at the center of a circle of people. Of course he was the focus of attention. Except for the rabid Deaniac, who was getting worked up about the new property tax laws, Linus was the most animated in the crowd. Peg wanted to get him to herself. She needed to thank him for all he'd done. And to acknowledge what she'd said yesterday, the love confession. As awkward as it might be, they had to talk about it. Linus knew it, too. He saw her coming, and smiled.

Peg said to the group, 'Can I steal Linus for one second?'

They were only too happy to release him to her clutches. As Peg took Linus's arm, she could have sworn she heard the poetry professor whisper to the toy-maker, 'Bachlorette number twenty?' Peg remembered what Albert had said about the residents of Manshire being keen to marry off their highest-ranking bachelor. Peg could make herself very popular indeed in town by being Linus's Ultimate Girlfriend. She'd gain a place in town history. Only problem, besides yet another trip to the Dump: Peg wouldn't be able to enforce her no-contact policy after the breakup. It would be impossible to avoid Linus in Manshire. Linus *was* Manshire.

He and Peg walked down the deck steps and toward the pond. 'I can't thank you enough,' she started. 'The house. The party. Spanking Chuck Plenet for me. I have no idea what you said to him, but he acted like you were going to exterminate *him*.'

Linus said, 'I gave him the Hollywood treatment. Told him he'd never work in this town again.'

'You threatened him?' she asked coyly. 'For me?'

Linus said, 'For you and anyone else who might hire him.'

'It's very exciting,' she said, 'to watch you wield your power.'

'Peg, you're flirting again,' he said.

Old habits. 'I'm trying to thank you for your many acts of *friendship*. I hope we will continue to be *friends*, even after Inward Bound ends. Because, in all honesty, getting friendly with you has been the best part of the program for me.'

He looked down at her, smiling, eyes sparkling. With any other man, she would think a gaze of such tenderness was a sure bet. That no man would look at her like that unless he wanted her, bad. But with Linus, Peg wasn't sure about anything

She said, 'You know when I said I was falling in love with you?' He nodded slowly. 'That was the electricity talking.'

'It *was* the electricity talking,' agreed Linus.

'The electricity from the wire,' she said.

'What other electricity could I be referring to?'

Peg sighed. 'How many other Inward Bound women have you confused mercilessly in this way?'

He laughed. 'In what way?'

'You know exactly what I'm talking about,' said Peg. 'And I don't like it. It's unsettling. I prefer to know what's going to happen next. And yes, I realize that, right now, as I speak, I'm having a huge breakthrough about my broken-record relationship history. Okay? Are you happy now? Is that what your sexy looks and "irresistible" comments have been leading to? So now I know. I fear the unknown so deeply that I'd rather repeat the same heart-breaking pattern than face something or someone I can't predict. That's why falling in love with you is so scary.'

'You're not falling in love with me.'

'I'm not?'

Linus paused. 'You asked if I've ever confused other women at Inward Bound,' he said. 'I guess I have. You're not the first client who's said she had feelings for me. I understand why it happens: I listen, I'm honest. Apparently, I smile a lot.'

'How many?' she asked.

'I've done four sessions of Inward Bound. And, so far, four clients told me they loved me.'

'Four?'

'Three women – including you – and one man.'

'And you don't believe these declarations.'

'The program can be intense and emotional. I seem like a good alternative to their ex-boyfriends. But the love isn't real. The ski instructor from Killington who told Gloria about the program? Claudia? She thought she loved me, too. Two weeks after the program ended, she met the man she eventually married. If she really loved me, that wouldn't have been possible.'

'Did you love her?' asked Peg.

'No,' he said.

'Did you love either of the other women?'

'No.'

'How do you know?'

'I wasn't attracted to them.'

'But you're attracted to me,' said Peg.

Linus didn't respond.

She said, 'Did you have erotic dreams about any of the others?'

Linus's jaw dropped. He said, 'How did you . . .?'

'Aha!' she said.

He said, 'Look, I don't have illusions about Inward Bound. I know some people come for an inexpensive month in Vermont, to live in a big house on the river. They merely tolerate the meditation and mountain-climbing. But even if people sign up for the wrong reasons, I want them to get something positive out of the experience. That's what I get out of it. If I were to get involved with a client – no matter how much I might be enjoying the idea of it – I'd lose all credibility. It would be ethically despicable.'

Peg said, 'What about when the program ends in a week? Would it ruin your credibility if you got involved with a graduate?'

'Wilma!' said Linus loudly.

'I know Wilma was a graduate student when you met. I meant a graduate of the . . . Hello, Wilma!' said Peg. 'You're as light-footed as a cat.'

Wilma had appeared at Peg's side. She was holding a hamburger, which she gave to Peg, and a Not Dog (tofu in a tube) for Linus.

'Is it true you threw your cell phone into the pond?' asked Wilma, eyes moving from Linus to Peg and back again.

Peg said, 'It's somewhere down there, unless a frog ate it.'

'The keg is dry,' said Wilma to Linus. 'I need help tapping a new one.'

'I'm your man,' said Linus.

Wilma said, 'You sure are!'

The two of them walked together back to the porch, leaving Peg by herself at the pond. She watched as Wilma put her arm around Linus's waist. He put his arm over her shoulder.

Peg turned toward the pond. The wind rippled the surface. Peg could have sworn she heard ringing, distant and gurgley.

Peg woke up to the glorious smell of bacon.

She opened her eyes, and crawled out of her sleeping bag. Careful not to wake up the other Inward Bounders, also in sleeping bags on the floor of the living room at her place, Peg wandered toward the kitchen.

At the stove, Ben was turning over slabs of bacon. 'Great party last night. Linus left you the pan,' he said upon seeing Peg. 'And the bacon. It's turkey bacon, unfortunately.'

'Where is he?' she asked, having noticed that he and Wilma weren't among the bodies in the other room.

'No clue,' said Ben. 'Maybe he and Wilma sneaked away.' He raised his eyebrows at her. 'If you know what I mean.'

She knew only too well. 'I'm not going back to the mansion,' said Peg. 'My house is habitable now, thanks to you guys. I'm staying here.'

'You can't,' said Ben, his fork hovering over the sizzling pan. 'You're part of the group. If you leave, the whole dynamic will change. And it's just started to get fun. For me anyway.'

The group *had* formed a bond, and Peg's leaving would disrupt that. As much as Peg liked being part of something bigger than herself, that plus didn't make up for the minus of Linus. He may or may not be attracted to her. He and Wilma may or may not be over. Peg may or may not be falling in love with him. But even if Linus was attracted and available, it didn't matter, because hooking up with Peg would be 'ethically despicable' to him.

'I'll miss you, too,' she said. 'But I've already learned so much at Inward Bound. I've had tremendous emotional growth. Any more growth and I won't fit into my clothes.'

She was still wearing her shorts and tank top from yesterday. Just the mention of clothes made her desperate to shower and re-dress. But all her stuff was back at the mansion. And her car.

Tracy and Gloria wandered into the kitchen. Ben said, 'Peg wants to leave the program.'

'You're not leaving,' said Tracy. 'Do you see yourself as someone who would let down her friends? Is a quitter? Runs away from her fears?'

'Absolutely.'

Ben said, 'That's a strongly agree.'

Gloria said, 'If you quit, I'm quitting.'

'Me, too,' said Ben.

'I suppose that forces my hand as well,' said Tracy.

Peg looked at her friends, and felt proud to know them. Proud that they liked her. She said, 'Thanks, guys.'

Tracy smiled and said, 'So you'll go back?'

'No way!' said Peg. 'You can all stay here. With me. Fuck Linus.'

'Do you want to fuck him over, or just fuck him?' asked Tracy.

'Both,' said Peg. 'But I'll settle for one.'

'You want to fuck *Linus*?' asked Gloria.

Peg nodded gravely. 'I'm afraid so.'

'What about Wilma?' asked Ben.

'Not her. Just Linus.'

'If you want him, then you have to go back to get him,' said Gloria. 'Staying here won't do you any good.'

'If I refuse to go back, he could drive out here and get me,' she said.

Ben shook his head. 'He won't.'

'Why not?' asked Peg.

'He'd file it all under "manipulative behavior." That's a major red flag, according to him. If a woman requires what he calls a "gallant response," Linus told us to rethink our opinion of that woman, that she's trying to create a story-book romance that has little or nothing to do with true, honest emotion. That it's possible the entire love she claims to feel is in her imagination.'

Linus already thought Peg's feelings were faux. Shit. She'd have to go back now, or she'd only confirm Linus's theory.

'The bacon is burning,' said Peg.

'Forget the training of childhood,' said Linus, standing in the center of the mansion living room later that day. 'It's healthy and essential to talk to strangers. We're fast becoming a society of isolationists. We prefer ATMs to bank tellers. We prefer shopping online to browsing in a store.'

'We prefer sharp sticks in the eye to Luddite missives,' said Peg under her breath to Tracy.

'The agenda,' said Linus loudly, 'is to get used to minor stranger interactions. That way, you'll get comfortable initiating conversations. More comfort means less anxiety. When you're anxious, you can't be yourself. Isn't that true, Ben?'

'Very true,' said Ben promptly.

'Wilma and I are going to do a little scene here,' said Linus. 'Imagine us standing on line at the cash register at Dombit's.' The two of them stood as if on line. Wilma pretended to hold giant organic watermelons.

Ray said, 'Excuse me, ma'am. Can I hold your melons?'

Linus said, 'That might get a response, but not the one you're after. How about, "Can I help you with those?" or "First day under ninety in a week. I could use a sweater." '

Wilma turned, still in her role as 'woman on line,' smiled radiantly, and said, 'Thank you, sir,' as if the intrusion from this handsome stranger had filled the gaping hole of loneliness in her melon-eating life.

Linus dropped his act and addressed the group. 'You can offer help, compliment someone's clothes, make an observation about the weather.'

Gloria said, 'I couldn't compliment someone's clothes.'

'It's easy. "Nice that," you could say. "Nice dress," ' suggested Linus.

'I couldn't say that to anyone in this state,' said Gloria. 'It would be a lie.'

'We're going to Wal-Mart. *Now*,' said Linus, his endless patience starting to crack. 'I want each of you to talk to three people. You can speak to women, men, it doesn't matter. As long as you initiate, I don't care who you talk to or what you say.'

They piled in the pickup, and drove to the Wal-Mart store in West Lebanon, New Hampshire. Peg wondered if Linus took them out of state intentionally, so they wouldn't humiliate him on his home turf. In the store, Peg and Tracy wandered off together, and quickly found themselves in the guns and ammo department.

A bear-sized lumberjack in a denim shirt with the sleeves cut off at the shoulder was stroking a rifle on the rack. Peg said to Tracy, 'I dare you to go up to him and say, "Nice hat!" Or "I could use a sweater!"'

Tracy said, 'I dare you to say, "Do you know where I can find the feminine hygiene products?"'

The two women tittered their way into the entertainment and software department.

Linus lurked nearby. Peg could feel his presence. She scanned the customers, then smiled, finding a stranger to talk to and a good reason to start the conversation. She walked up to a teenage boy, around fifteen, skinny and jittery.

Peg said very loudly, 'Hey, kid, aren't you going to pay for that?'

The teen went white (or should she say, *whiter*). 'You talking to me?' he asked as tough as he could.

Peg had to laugh. He was as intimidating as a baby chick. She said, 'The DVD you put down the front of your pants. Are you going to pay for it, or just pad your package?'

'There's no DVD in my pants,' protested the kid.

Peg took a step toward him. The kid jumped back. His movement made the DVD slide down his oversized jeans' leg and land on the floor with a clatter.

The kid yelled, 'Eat me, bitch!' and ran for the exit.

Tracy, shaking her head, said, 'You initiate a conversation and he runs away screaming.'

Peg said, 'I think I'm getting the hang of it.'

Wal-Mart was a bust, in terms of social interaction with strangers. But Peg made a few major connections with the sales staff, and managed to buy kitchenware, outdoor furniture and a full entertainment system for her new home. She even arranged a delivery date. Peg had never been inside a Wal-Mart before, but from now on, it was her favorite store in the whole wide world. Tracy made a minor connection with an older woman at the magazine rack. And Gloria easily met her quota cruising the cosmetics aisle.

As they filed out of the store, Linus said, 'Tonight, you're going to pair off and go to different meeting places in the area. Same assignment. Initiate conversation with strangers. I'll go with Ben. Ray and Luke. Tracy and—'

Wilma said, 'I'll go with Peg.'

Linus said, 'I thought I'd pair you with Tracy.'

'But Peg and I have so much to talk about!'

'Such as?' asked Linus.

'You know, girl talk,' said Wilma.

Peg doubted Wilma had girl-talked, ever. The idea of an evening with her at a bar was as appealing as the carrot casserole. But Peg's curiosity was cheddar sharp.

She said, 'First round's on me.'

Wilma and Peg sat next to each other at the Norwich Tavern. The joint tried to carry off the style of English pubs with names like the Slaughtered Sheep or the Gutted Hen. Dartboard near the pool table, oak bar, wood panels, dark, windowless, hot, acrid, packed with Dartmouth students who'd ridden bikes across the border to get away from New Hampshire's draconian alcohol policies (as Wilma explained, if a bar was busted serving a minor, the establishment was closed for business immediately until further notice – no warnings).

At thirty-two, Peg felt like the oldest woman in the room (not to mention the only Jew). Wilma, in her twenties, fit in well, with her perky ponytail and tan. Wilma sipped a Coors Light. Peg gulped a Manhattan.

So it'd come to this, she thought. Three weeks of Inward Bounding had brought her full circle, to a stool in a bar with a cocktail in front of her. If she had a Chuck Palahniuk novel, she might as well be back in Soho. Except, in Soho or even the Lower East Side, one didn't ordinarily see men peeing out of the bar window or spitting chewing tobacco saliva into Dixie cups.

Peg smiled at Wilma, waiting for her to talk. But Wilma didn't speak, or look at her. She might as well be a complete stranger.

Peg said, 'Nice melons! I need a sweater!'

Wilma shook her head reproachfully. 'Accepting you into the program was the worst decision I've ever made.'

Which, to Peg, was an open invitation to get personal. 'Are you and Linus over or not?'

Wilma flinched. 'Regardless of what you think of me, Peg, I do have feelings.'

Shit. 'I'm sorry,' said Peg. 'This must be tough on you. Breaking up after a year. Having to start over. On such short notice. I've been there. Many, many times.'

'I'm going to tell you a secret, Peg. You should know the truth about Linus,' said Wilma.

'Go on,' said Peg, her attention rapt.

And then she felt a tap on the back. 'Peg Silver?' yelled a voice behind her. 'Peg Silver? From Grand Street in Soho? The interior landscape designer?'

Both women looked at the man who was squeezing

himself between their stools at the bar. He was in his early thirties or late twenties. He had short, inky black hair. His skin was impossibly pale. Even surrounded by ethnically pure Caucasian Wasp co-eds, he was the whitest guy in the room. His lips, in the dark of the bar, seemed black. On closer examination, Peg saw they were blood red and full. His eyes: icy blue. His body – in stiff jeans and a Ramones T-shirt – was tall and skinny, like most East Village guys. In fact, thought Peg, you could have plucked him right off of First Avenue.

Peg said, 'Do I know you?'

'We met at 2A. A few years ago.'

A possibility. She'd been at that seedy bar nearly every night when she was with Daniel. But Peg would have remembered this guy. No matter how many cocktails she'd had. That preternaturally white skin and luscious lips. He was otherworldly attractive.

He said, 'I'm Oliver Ashfield.'

Peg introduced Wilma. 'We're supposed to interact with strangers, strike up conversations, attempt to make a human connection,' she told Oliver.

He said, 'Oh-kay.'

'Nice hat!' said Peg. 'Wish I had a sweater!'

'I'm not wearing a hat,' said Oliver. 'I have one in my car, in the parking lot. Why don't we go outside and I'll show it to you?'

He was luring her outside? For what? A drunken make-out session? Peg said, 'We're talking here, actually.'

Oliver took the hint badly. 'Do you smoke? I've got a full pack of cigarettes out in my car.'

Peg shook her head. 'Have a nice stay in Vermont, Oliver. Use sunscreen.'

She turned her back on him rudely, and he sunk back

into the crowd. Peg said to Wilma, 'Now, you were saying? A secret about Linus? That he has an abnormally large penis?'

'I want to tell you about my dissertation.'

Peg groaned. Bring back Oliver. Peg said, 'I'm sure it's fascinating. But we were talking about Linus.'

'We are talking about him,' Wilma answered, signaling the bartender for another round. 'He's the subject of my dissertation.'

'What's the topic?'

'You fit the profile, too.'

'Your profile of *what*?' asked Peg impatiently.

'Low scores in conscientiousness, agreeableness, neuroticism and extroversion; high scores in openness. The tendency to overcompensate for social failure by flinging yourself into new relationships. Preferring to observe rather than participate, to be alone rather than in a group. Narcissism and superiority complex as defense mechanisms for limited social abilities. You crave control, but relinquish it readily.'

'I don't really see what any of this has to do with Linus's huge penis.'

Oliver poked his head between the women again. 'You know, you can see a lot of stars up here. You want to come outside, Peg? Gaze with me?'

'Get lost,' said Peg.

'I was wondering,' said Wilma. 'Considering how well you fit the profile, if you'd let me interview you this week. As a case study.'

'I'd like to help, Wilma,' said Peg. 'But I'm not sure that I—'

'Have anything to offer?' asked Wilma.

Peg nodded. 'I'm uncomfortable—'

'Talking about yourself?'

'Yes,' said Peg. 'And I have doubts about—'

'My abilities?'

'Stop *doing* that,' said Peg.

'All part of the profile,' said Wilma.

Oliver again. 'Peg, there's a fight in the parking lot!' he said excitedly. 'Two guys are tearing each other apart! You've got to check this out.'

Peg put her hand over his face, and pushed him away. She said, 'You know, Wilma, that personality test. I lied on half the answers. I didn't fill out a third of it.'

'Counting how many questions the respondent gets through before blanking the remainder is part of the test,' said Wilma. 'You got through fewer than most, by the way. Like I said, low conscientiousness.'

Peg signaled the bartender for another drink.

Wilma said, 'Just listen to the title of my paper. Then tell me if it sounds like you.'

'Unless it's called "Intelligent, Charming and Witty People We All Love and Admire," forget it.'

'It's called "The Outsider Syndrome: Romanticizing Chronic Isolation," ' said Wilma, holding up her hand to keep Peg quiet. 'Outsiders believe they'll never fit in and will always be alone. It's their greatest fear, and also the foundation of their sense of self. I noticed this about Linus as soon as we met. His string of girlfriends. How he knows everyone, but is close to hardly anyone. I got drawn into the challenge of him, believing I would be the one to break him out of his self-imposed isolation. But I couldn't. After a while, I stopped trying. Linus will never really love someone. He prefers to observe, to be alone, to stay on the outside of his most intimate relationship. He's the ultimate outsider.'

'Linus is the ultimate *insider*. Everyone in Manshire genuflects in his presence. He's the mayor.'

'Overcompensation,' said Wilma.

'Isn't it possible that Linus can love deeply, just not with you?'

'Linus agrees with my thesis,' said Wilma. 'He's proofreading my dissertation. He thinks it's brilliant.'

'That's the big secret about Linus? That he thinks your thesis is brilliant?'

Wilma leaned in close. 'The big secret about Linus is that he is using you to pump up his ego, just like he used all those other women in the program over the past year. He's a narcissist. He's an egomaniac. He's addicted to the pain and loneliness of denying himself. He craves love, but pushes it away because, in layman's terms, he's fucked up. And I'm an idiot for falling for him. Just like you are, Peg. But I have the good sense to leave. Not you. Even now, you're counting the days until I move out. You can't wait to hurl yourself in front of a speeding train. Go ahead,' she said. 'Hurl.'

Speechless, Peg watched Wilma finish her beer, and order another. Which she drank in one long gulp, and ordered another.

Peg said, 'You're the one who's going to hurl.'

Oliver, meanwhile, poked his head between them again. Peg said, 'I'm ready for that cigarette now, Oliver.' She threw a twenty on the bar, and stood up.

To Wilma, she said, 'Consider me unenrolled.' She'd had enough of Wilma and her theories. Of Linus's push-pull treatment. She'd been moving Inward long enough. She had to get outward.

Using her shoulder like a plow, Peg pushed her way through the crowd. Oliver struggled to keep up. They made it to the parking lot, and Oliver said, 'I'm right over here,' pointing at a blue Volvo with New York plates.

Peg walked toward the car. Through her anger, Peg realized that Wilma, the injured party, might be playing saboteur. She could be attempting to destroy Linus and Peg's chances pre-emptively. Even if that was true, the psychodrama was too much for Peg. She had come to Vermont for simplicity, not to get mixed up in a man's complex.

A cigarette might help calm her down. She and Oliver were ten paces from his Volvo. Five paces. Suddenly, arms grabbed Peg from behind. A strip of duct tape sealed her mouth shut. A black sack was put over her head. Her neck was forced down, a push from behind toppled her into the backseat. A car door slammed, someone sat on her to keep her still. Wheels were in motion. The sound of crunching gravel.

Peg fought. She struggled. Oliver lay on top of her in the backseat. He was stronger than he looked. And nice-smelling, too.

He said, 'Faster.'

A woman's voice came from up front. 'Are you buckled in?'

'Just go!' said Oliver.

'It's the law to wear a seat belt,' said the woman. 'I don't want to get pulled over.'

'If we get pulled over, it'll be for kidnapping, not for seat belt scoffing!'

'You don't have to yell,' said the woman softly. 'Politeness speaks louder than volume.' But the driver did pick up speed. They went straight. Then a right. Peg tried to remember the turns, how long they traveled before changing direction, but she lost her sense of time.

After what seemed like an hour, the car came to a stop. The front door slammed. The back door opened. The two kidnappers pulled Peg out of the Volvo, and rushed her through a door and into a room.

The lights went on. Peg was lowered into a chair and her arms and legs were tied to it. Once she was secured with rope, the sack was removed.

Oliver stood over her, looking worried and sympathetic.

She glanced around the room. Standard traditional Americana motel décor. They could be anywhere in New England. Two queen-sized beds, a couple dressers. Clean bedclothes, plush carpeting, floral wallpaper. The room's furniture was old, but well cared for. Peg smelled pine air freshener. The green chintz curtains were closed.

Oliver checked her mouth tape. She knew now that she'd never met him before, that he'd pretended to know her to gain her confidence. She was an idiot to go outside with him. Had she learned nothing in all her years in New York City? It was page one from the city handbook: DO NOT TRUST STRANGERS. She thought of Linus, his 'forget the training from childhood and talk to strangers' rap. She smiled under her tape – tried to – imagining Linus's reaction to the news that she'd been kidnapped. He'll be desperate with worry, she thought. He'd realize how much he needed her, and loved her. Maybe she could stay kidnapped for a couple of days. Scare the shit out of him. The bullshit anyway.

The woman's voice from behind Peg. 'How's she doing?'

'She looks happy,' said Oliver. 'I think she's smiling.'

'It's the brainwashing,' the woman said knowingly. She circled around Peg and stood next to Oliver.

'Stmm Tmmm?' mumbled Peg from under the mouth tape.

'She recognizes me,' said the woman.

How could Peg not? This woman had made an indelible impression the first time they'd met in Nina's office a few months ago. Flaming red hair, pink cheeks, bow lips. Bright orange halter top and a magenta miniskirt, kitten-heeled mules.

It was Stacy Temple, president for insearchof.com,

the woman Nina had hired to track down Peg's ex-boyfriends. The woman who'd first called her a square.

Stacy asked, 'Should we take the tape off?'

Oliver said, 'What if she screams?'

Stacy tapped a pink nail on her red lips. 'That would be bad.'

'MSMM,' said Peg. 'Mbbmsmsms.'

'I've got cold beer,' said Oliver to Peg. 'You can have some beer if you don't scream.'

Beer would be lovely. Peg nodded. Stacy leaned forward and tore off the tape.

'Ouch!' said Peg.

'Just think of it as a free mustache wax,' said Stacy.

Oliver produced a brown bottle and held it to her lips. Peg drank. He detached the bottle and Peg said, 'Nina is behind this.'

'Correct,' said Stacy. 'Before we get into that, let me introduce Oliver. He's my husband and business partner.'

'The hacker.'

'Intelligence technician,' corrected Oliver.

To Stacy, Peg said, 'He's so cute.'

'And younger,' said Stacy with a wink.

'Well done,' said Peg.

Stacy sat down on the edge of the bed, and crossed her long legs, periwinkle toenails catching the lamplight. 'We were hired by Nina and your brother, Jack. They're afraid you've joined a cult and have been brainwashed by a man named Linus Bester, a charismatic messianic leader who lures the vulnerable and weak with promises of fulfillment and happiness.'

'She does look happy,' pointed out Oliver.

'Then it's true,' whispered Stacy gravely.

Did Peg see herself as someone who'd join a cult? Strongly, with the strength of Arnold Schwarzenegger, disagree.

'I am so not a joiner,' said Peg.

'You were brainwashed into it,' said Stacy.

Did she see herself as someone who'd be brainwashed?

'I couldn't be brainwashed,' she said. 'My mind is way too dirty. Nina knows this.'

Stacy said, 'You've been reprogrammed.'

'You've got it all wrong. Inward Bound isn't a cult,' said Peg. 'And Linus isn't a messianic leader. He's an atheist. And he's not charismatic. He wears Birkenstocks. Once with socks.'

Stacy gasped.

Oliver leaned toward his wife. 'She's defending him,' he said. 'She's in denial.'

'We'll have to deprogram her,' whispered Stacy. 'Do you have the clamps?'

'I can hear you,' said Peg. 'Brainwashing hasn't make me deaf.'

'Then you admit it!' said Stacy.

'Admit what? That I look happy?'

Stacy walked across the motel room toward a pink plastic shoe box on top of the dresser. She pushed a black button on top, and the box hatched.

'Is that a purse?' asked Peg. 'I've never seen anything like it.'

'It's from the sixties,' said Stacy, nodding. 'I collect.' She reached inside and withdrew a few envelopes. The letters Peg had mailed to Nina over the past month.

'The evidence,' said Stacy. She read from Peg's letters. 'Postmarked July eighth. You wrote, "Forced to eat raw vegetables daily . . . I had to give them two thousand dollars, but what's more important than my emotional well-being? . . . He's already threatened to beat the sarcasm out of me with a stick . . . If I miss breakfast, they starve me for six hours . . . We can't use cell phones." Postmarked July thirteenth. You wrote, "Recently discovered that I'm obsessed with sex . . . I may be an alcoholic . . . Undo everything I've always done . . . Linus has the mad mojo. Everyone in town is slavishly devoted to him . . . I had a fantasy about him . . . Trying to repress sex thought is doing strange things to my brain . . . My turn to be sprayed with poison." Postmarked July twenty-third. You wrote, "I was electrocuted, and the jolt made me realize that I'm in love with Linus . . . We had an encounter . . . after a drug experiment . . . Much happier now." '

Stacy dropped the letters on the bed. She said, 'They control your diet, your sleep, your sexual activity. They don't let you use phones, disallow contact with the outside world. They demanded money. They used starvation, poison, drugs and sex to control your mind. Force you to perform manual labor and pointless physical exercise, all designed to weaken your resolve. These sick-ass bastards used electric shock treatment to wash your brain, Peg! Can't you see what's happened to you?'

'Taken out of context, I can understand why Nina would be worried,' said Peg. 'But I'm telling you, I have not been brainwashed. I'm the same person I was when I left New York.'

'Really?' asked Stacy. 'You seem different to me. But we just had one coffee break. Nina made a list of your favorite pastimes. Things you'd ordinarily do unless you were under the influence of a cult. Have you, for example, had casual sex since you came to Vermont?'

'No,' said Peg.

'Have you gone barhopping?'

'There's only one bar in the whole town,' said Peg.

'Have you done any landscaping?'

'No time. We've been so busy—'

'Have you read any Chuck Palahniuk novels?'

'You mispronounced that,' said Peg. 'It's Pal-ah-NEE—'

'*Have you?*' demanded Stacy.

'I'm too tired at night to read, but no one told me—'

'Have you been running?'

'Not really,' admitted Peg. 'But running is an escape, a crutch.'

'Have you obsessed about your ex-boyfriends?'

'No,' said Peg. And what a relief that had been.

'Have you fretted about where your life is going?'

'Not at all,' said Peg, realizing she hadn't.

'Look at her,' said Oliver. 'She's happy again.'

Stacy said, 'Scary.'

'So Nina and Jack are working together on the kidnapping plot,' said Peg. 'Are they just *working* together, or are they *together* together?'

Stacy said, 'Is this a new development? They act like an old married couple.'

'It's a new development built on the foundation of an old one. They're definitely a couple, not just friends?'

'Unless friends snog in taxicabs,' said Stacy.

This pleased Peg. Her best friend and her brother reunited. Fortunately, this round, Peg wouldn't be jealous. Nor did she feel left out. She'd left them, and was glad they'd refound each other.

'I've got to give you props,' said Peg to her kidnappers. 'You're doing a great job here. You found me. Abducted me. Oliver, you were like a pit bull in the bar. I admire your tenacity.'

He smiled bashfully. Stacy beamed at him. He was a vision in black and white, she in Technicolor. No one in their right mind would have looked at the two of them and thought, 'They'd make a great couple.' Yet here they stood, a perfect mix-matched pair.

None of Peg's exes fit her, even imperfectly. She tried to cram them on, like Cinderella's slipper – or OJ's glove. She should have told herself, 'If he does not fit, you can't commit.' Peg vowed that she would not cram anyone into her life again.

Peg said, 'Okay, you've convinced me. I was brainwashed, but my mind is dirty again. I can feel the filth.'

'We can't let you go,' said Stacy. 'Nina and Jack are on their way. We're supposed to keep you here.'

'Where are we anyway?'

Oliver said, 'Can't tell.'

Peg said, 'I'll scream.'

Stacy said, 'Quick! More beer!'

He came at her with the bottle, label up this time. Peg read it. Jasper. An ale made in only one place in the world – the brewery under the Manshire Inn. They must be in one of the motel rooms behind the main Inn building. Poule au Dent, Albert's restaurant, was across the street. Dombit's was right next door. On her hands and knees, she could crawl to the Federal. Not that she would.

A knock on the door. Stacy said, 'Nina and Jack must have missed the traffic in Connecticut.'

Stacy opened the door. The business end of a shotgun rifle entered the room, and found a comfortable resting spot on Stacy's pink button nose.

'Hands behind your head, drop to your knees, plant your face on the floor,' said Artemis Call to Stacy. 'You, too,' he added to Oliver.

Stacy said, 'The police! Good. We want to report a cult.'

Artemis cocked his gun, with a slide and click. 'I said drop,' he repeated. Stacy and Oliver scrambled to obey. Without taking his eyes off the kidnappers, Artemis said, 'Status report, Peg.'

'Still single.'

'Are you okay?' he asked.

'I'm fine,' she responded.

He unsnapped two pairs of handcuffs from his belt. While cuffing Stacy's and Oliver's hands behind their backs, he said, 'Five people witnessed a woman being kidnapped in the parking lot of the Norwich Tavern. The perps were described as a weirdly dressed couple from New Jersey.'

From the floor, Stacy said, 'We are *not* from New Jersey.'

Artemis winked at Peg. 'I reported the kidnapping on the police radio, and got four calls from the Inn inside of five minutes. You two are the worst kidnappers in Vermont history.'

'How many kidnappers have there been in Vermont?' asked Peg.

He said, 'We had one back in 1876. Cows get snatched every year. We don't call that cownapping, though, because it makes you think that the cows are taking a nap.'

Artemis untied Peg. Once she was free, he said, 'Okay, Bonnie and Clyde. I'm taking you in.'

Peg helped Stacy and Oliver to their feet. 'I'm not pressing charges,' she said. 'It's my fault they kidnapped me. I sent some misleading letters to my friend Nina and she thought it sounded like I'd joined a cult, so she hired Stacy and Oliver here to kidnap me and deprogram me from my brainwashing.'

'She *has* been brainwashed,' said Oliver.

'It's true. Just look at her,' said Stacy.

Artemis turned toward Peg, who smiled prettily.

Stacy said, 'You see? The healthy glow, the lighter-than-air demeanor? That's nothing like the way she was in New York. She's obviously been tampered with.'

'Tampered with by who?' asked the cop.

'Some shyster named Linus Bester. He preys on the vulnerable and weak, uses mind tricks and manipulation to force his victims to do his bidding. We're not sure what he's after, exactly. Probably money and sexual favors,' replied Stacy.

'I can tell you firsthand that he's not after sexual favors,' said Peg.

'Linus Bester is the mayor of Manshire,' said Artemis. 'If he's the leader of a cult, everyone in town is a follower.'

Oliver said, 'My God. They're all under his influence.'

'What have we stumbled into?' asked Stacy in horror. 'These lunatic country people will probably sacrifice us in some ritual bloodletting. Our bodies will be chopped into little pieces and fed to chickens.'

'Now you're being ridiculous,' said Artemis. 'Chickens won't eat human flesh. Coyotes, bears, yes. But not chickens.'

Stacy and Oliver's eyelids sprang wide open.

Artemis said, 'If Peg won't press charges, I won't take you in for kidnapping. But you have made verbal threats to a police officer, and slanderous accusations against the town mayor. I'm going to write you a ticket.'

Stacy said, 'What about the cuffs?'

'Thanks for reminding me. I'll have to include a rental fee for the cuffs, too.' Artemis released Stacy and Oliver, and then took out his ticket book and started to scribble.

Peg said, 'Go easy on them.'

'I am,' he said. 'Total comes to twenty-three hundred dollars. Payable by mail. If you want to contest the fine, you can schedule a hearing with the county clerk in White River Junction.'

'This is extortion!' said Stacy. 'You bet I'm going to contest this ticket. And I'm going to demand that the judge hands me your badge on a plate.'

Artemis said to Peg, 'Sound familiar?' Peg nodded. Stacy's outburst was practically word for word what Peg had said to him at the fair. The disrespect, the condescension, the snottiness. Peg was embarrassed now that she'd ever spoken to Artemis that way.

'Now you understand why I give heavy fines to people from New Jersey,' he said.

'We are NOT from fucking New Jersey,' said Stacy.

Artemis giggled – giggled! – and said to Peg, 'I love how riled they get.'

Another knock on the door. Peg threw it open, to find Nina and Jack standing outside. When Nina saw Peg, she gathered her in her arms. Peg sank into the familiar embrace. Jack patted her on the back. They weren't a particularly affectionate family.

Nina said, 'Let me look at you. I'll know in one second if you've been brainwashed.' Nina backed Peg up to arm's length. 'You look fantastic!' she shouted. 'That tan! I'm so jealous. I've never been tan a day in my life. You've put on a few much-needed pounds, too. No puffiness around the eyes. And your bangs! They've grown out perfectly.'

'No sign of starvation or sleep deprivation?' asked Peg.

Jack said, 'She does seem okay. Happy, in fact.'

'Brainwashed!' said Oliver.

'That's another hundred dollars,' said Artemis.

Jack said, 'You're a police officer? I'm Jack Silver. I'm relieved to see you're here and in control of the situation.'

For Stacy's benefit, Artemis said, 'And I'm pleased to meet a flatlander who knows how to show the proper respect.'

'Flatlander?'

'Don't ask,' said Peg.

Peg clasped her best friend's hand. 'It's excellent to see you, Nina,' she said. 'You look great, too, with a glow that radiates from the inside. I've seen that look before, whenever you've been in love.'

Nina gave Peg a warning glare. 'We don't like to throw that word around so early in a relationship, Peg.'

Jack and Artemis, meanwhile, were standing in the corner together, confabbing. Artemis seemed to like him. Peg felt a welling of pride for her baby brother.

Stacy approached the other two women. She asked Nina, 'Did we discuss reimbursement of expenses?'

Nina said, 'I'll pay your expenses, sure. How bad can they be? You left New York yesterday.'

Stacy handed Nina the ticket from Artemis. Which Peg plucked out of Nina's hand and put into her pocket. She would deal with that later.

Artemis and Jack were shaking hands, pumping hard, like drilling for oil in the space between them. Jack said, 'Sheriff Call has explained everything to me, including the electrocution incident. It's all been a terrible mis- understanding. He suggested we go to the restaurant across the street and have a drink together. He can get us the best table in the house – turns out, he knows the owner!' Jack seemed deeply impressed by that. Peg didn't bother telling him that everyone in town knew the owner.

The New Yorkers (plus Artemis) crossed Main Street to Poule au Dent. Peg lagged behind, yanking Artemis by his utility belt.

She said, 'About this ticket.'

'What about it?'

'Can you rip it up?'

'Once I write a ticket, there's a copy in my book. I have to account for it.'

Peg said, 'You threw out the ticket you wrote for me at the fair.'

'That was a one-time thing,' said Artemis. 'I wanted Linus to owe me.'

'If you don't rip it up, I'm going to pay the fine myself.'

'You're paying the fine for the people who kidnapped you and trussed you up like a hog?'

'It seems like the right thing to do.'

'Don't get righteous on me, Peg,' he said. 'You'll take the fun out of harassing flatlanders.' He paused. 'Give me the ticket.'

She handed it over. He tore it in half and put the ripped paper in the trash at Poule au Dent.

He said, 'Now *you* owe me.'

That made Peg smile. She felt like she'd made her first Vermont trade (God knows what she could do to repay Artemis – maybe cut back his peonies?). Contrary to Wilma's thesis, Peg wasn't an isolationist-by-choice. She wanted to fit in, and if Artemis and Albert (who greeted her like a bosom buddy) were any indication, she would do just fine in Manshire.

Peg first introduced Jack and Nina to Albert. 'And here we have Stacy and Oliver. My kidnappers,' she added.

Albert said, 'I heard about the kidnapping on the police scanner. Must have been quite an ordeal, wrestling Peg to the ground. I guess the two of you need a stiff drink. I've got fantastic Polish vodka on ice in the bar out back. Right this way.'

They did shots. Artemis, Albert and Jack lit cigars. Stacy and Oliver sat at a table on the porch, holding hands and assuring each other that they'd done a swell job. Peg and Nina sat at the bar.

Nina said, 'This is like old times.'

'Not that old,' said Peg. 'It's been only three weeks.'

Peg gave Nina a succinct description of her country life thus far, including the ups and downs of her quasi-romance with Linus.

Nina stopped her at the couch incident. 'God smite, you took advantage of him!' she said, outraged. 'Sounds very sexy. I should try that with Jack.'

By the time Peg finished recounting Wilma's speech at the Disemboweled Wolf, she was exhausted. She'd had a long day at the end of long month (at the end of a long decade). No way was she going back to the Federal – ever again. Not after the way Wilma spoke to her. Not after what she'd learned about Linus. It made Peg's dirty brain throb.

She said, 'I need sleep. Can I stay at the Inn with you tonight?'

Nina said, 'Of course.' To Jack, she said, 'We're going across the street.'

Jack said, 'Mind if I finish my cigar?'

'Not at all,' said Nina. To Peg, she said, 'I think Jack was as excited about the trip to Vermont as he was to rescue you.'

Stacy and Oliver stood up, too. From the way they leaned against each other, Peg could tell they were looking forward to getting back to their room at the Inn as well.

Oliver said, 'If it's okay with you, Nina, we'll stay tonight, and drive back in the morning.'

'The room's paid for,' said Nina. 'Might as well.'

That was when Linus's pickup sped into the restaurant driveway. He parked, jumped out and rushed toward them.

Nina said, 'Is that him?'

'Yup,' said Peg.

'He's hot,' said Stacy. 'I would've let him brainwash me, too.'

Nina said, 'Want Jack to beat him up?'

'Give me two minutes,' said Peg.

Peg walked toward Linus. She made sure she stayed out of hugging range.

Linus said, 'Albert just called me.'

'Nice hat,' she said. 'I need a sweater.'

'Who are these people?' he asked, looking over her shoulder at Nina, Stacy and Oliver.

She ignored the question. 'For the ten minutes I was kidnapped, I got the chance to do a lot of thinking,' said Peg.

'Me, too,' he said.

'I'm going to stay in Manshire. But I'm leaving the program.'

'But there's another week to go,' he said.

'Can you ask Tracy to pack my stuff and bring it to the farm tomorrow? Maybe Ben can drive my car out, too.'

He said, 'I'll do it myself.'

'Tracy and Ben can do it.'

'Let me.'

She said, 'No, Linus. I don't want you . . . to.'

He stared at her. She stared back. He said, 'I knew Wilma would try sabotage.'

'Sabotage *what*, exactly?' asked Peg.

'You know what,' he said.

'You mean our "ethically despicable" attraction?' she asked. 'Which may or may not exist?'

'Wilma is angry and hurt about the breakup,' he said. 'I don't know what she told you tonight, but you've got to give me a chance to defend myself.'

'Your name didn't come up.'

'I *am* attracted to you, Peg,' he said. 'I felt it the first time I saw you.'

'If I made such an impression,' she said, 'then what was I wearing that night?'

'I only saw your face,' he said, smiling. 'And your overly developed calf muscles.'

Nina appeared at her side. She nodded curtly at Linus and said, 'Let's go, Peg.'

'Please wait,' said Linus.

Nina linked arms with Peg, and led her away.

At the door of the Inn, Peg glanced back across the street at Linus, standing in the restaurant parking lot, next to his pickup, watching her, looking very much alone in the world, which was, according to Wilma, just how he liked it.

32

'I'm moving in,' said Jack, on the morning of his third day at Peg's farmhouse, nearly furnished now with an eclectic mix of Wal-Mart's finest, Vermont Salvage pieces and antique fixer-uppers. It had been a frantic, expensive three days for Peg. Good thing. She was too busy shopping to think about Linus.

'Moving in where?' asked Peg, bare feet up on the deck railing, sitting in her new teak patio chair, a mug of Green Mountain Coffee in her hands. '*Here?*'

'You're the one who's been telling me to get my own place,' he said.

'But this is *my* place,' said Peg. 'You want to leave Mom and Dad's to shack up with your sister?'

Jack sat down on the twin chair next to Peg. He said, 'This place, this town. It feels right. After wringing that chicken's neck at the Burnetts' yesterday, I knew I'd found my true home.' Peg had sent him down the road to her neighbor's organic chicken ranch to buy a dozen eggs. He'd returned covered in feathers, with a bag of fresh kill.

Peg said, 'You pay half of all expenses.'

Jack whooped. 'I'll call Mom today and have her ship my stuff.'

'She's not going to like this.'

'She'll love it,' he said.

He was right. Peg and Jack hadn't been close as kids – or as adults. Maybe this was their time to get to know each other. Besides, it wouldn't be a terrible thing to have a man around to chop wood and shovel snow. Jack had savings (all those years of not paying rent). He could quit his corporate job, help her with the perennials. Live cheaply.

Nina appeared in the deck threshold. She yawned and stretched sexily, and padded outside in a camisole and tap pants. 'I love the privacy up here,' she said. 'I can walk around – outside – in lingerie, and no one knows or cares.'

'I care,' said Peg.

'So do I,' said Jack, grinning. 'I'd care even more if you walked around naked.'

Peg said, 'Are you moving in, too?'

Nina stopped suddenly. 'Who else is moving in? Jack?'

Jack glared at his sister. 'You didn't tell her?' Peg asked.

He said, 'Nina, baby, look at those mountains! Listen to the birds! Smell that mint!'

Nina's lips quivered. She sniffled and ran back into the house. Jack said to Peg, 'I'm still moving in,' before he ran after his girlfriend.

Crunch of gravel in the driveway. Peg figured it was Tracy. She'd been stopping by every day to deliver the daily Inward Bound news. Yesterday morning, Tracy brought hot croissants and great gossip.

'Wilma left in the dark of night,' she'd reported. 'We just found out. Gloria and I slept late, and wandered into the kitchen looking for breakfast. But there wasn't anything to eat. And I mean, nothing. Wilma cleaned out the fridge and pantry. She stole the food. Every last morsel.'

Peg said, 'That is too bizarre.'

Tracy said, 'You hear about people sneaking off with the jewelry.'

'Not in Vermont.'

'Linus was dumbfounded,' said Tracy. 'He sent me to Dombit's to get breakfast, which is what I have here.' She patted the big bakery bag. 'Must rush back. But I had to tell you about Wilma first.'

'How is Linus?' asked Peg casually.

'Our cult leader?' asked Tracy. 'Very tense. He and Wilma have been snapping at each other, and now this thief-in-the-night business. It's been tough on him. He's not complaining, still trying to keep up with the program. But that's been a struggle. He gives us more and more free time.'

'And what are you doing with it?' Peg asked.

'Hanging with Ben, mainly. He's a pal. I can't get Luke's attention. To be honest, I don't really want it.'

'What about Gloria?'

'Gloria is otherwise occupied,' Tracy said, snickering. 'With Ray. He's been humbled. She's been emboldened. They've fallen and risen, respectively, to each other's level.'

'Gloria and Ray,' said Peg. 'The princess and the pea brain. That might be weirder than Wilma the food burglar.'

'After you left, the air went out of the program,' said Tracy. 'Out of Linus. He asks me about you. Wants to know if you're okay. I think he misses you. You know, Peg, now that Wilma's gone . . .'

Peg shook her head. 'I can't. Some information has come to light. Linus doesn't want a relationship. I'm not going to hurl myself in front of a train.'

'What information?'

'Things I've heard.'

Tracy paused. 'I've really got to go. Everyone is waiting for breakfast.'

'See you tomorrow?'

Tracy nodded. 'About those things you heard, Peg? You'd do yourself a favor to consider the source.'

Peg would rather not. It would be wiser, she thought, to block out thoughts of Linus, what might have been. The moment had passed. Peg had to move on. Maybe she'd get lucky. Like Claudia, the ski instructor. Shot down by Linus, only to hook up with a marrying man a couple of weeks later.

The car in the driveway came to a stop. With Jack and Nina fighting upstairs, Peg was grateful for a guest. She walked off the deck, toward the front of the house.

But her guest wasn't Tracy in her Camry. Peg nearly choked to see Wilma stepping out of her green hybrid. The backseat was packed to the roof with bags, boxes and, Peg noticed, mason jars with flour, rice and pasta.

Wilma waved. Peg approached, a bit nervously. 'Going somewhere?' she asked, pointing at the car.

'I'm driving to New York City,' said Wilma. 'A cousin of mine is letting me stay on her couch for a few weeks. Thought I'd try to find a publisher for my dissertation. It reads more like a pop psychology book than an academic paper anyway.'

'You'll love New York,' Peg lied. 'You should change your book title, though.'

'You don't like *The Outsider Syndrome*?'

'How about something grabby, like *The Allure of Alone: Symptoms and Solutions for the Chronically Single*.'

Wilma said, 'I love that! Can I use it?'

'My parting gift to you,' said Peg.

'I'd like to give you a parting gift,' said Wilma.

A slap on the kisser? A poison-pen letter? 'How about five pounds of brown rice?' asked Peg.

'You heard,' said Wilma, frowning. 'Want to know why I stole the food?'

'Because you're crazy?'

'It was the only thing I could take that would upset Linus,' she said. 'Although I got rid of something else that seemed to devastate him.'

'Don't bother,' said Peg. 'If Linus is sad that I'm gone, it's because I can't satisfy his hunger for self-denial.'

Wilma said, 'I'm not going to take back what I said about him. But I might be wrong about you.'

'I'm not an outsider?'

'You probably are,' she said. 'I mean that, with you, Linus may have met his match. Before, with those other women in the program, he talked about them every night. Linus wanted to assure me that he didn't reciprocate their feelings. This session, though, he never spoke about you. He barely mentioned your name to me. That's why I knew I was in trouble. And I acted badly. Unprofessionally.'

'You were hurt,' said Peg.

Wilma looked into Peg's eyes, and Peg saw how much. 'He tried to spare my feelings,' she said. 'Keeping you at a distance – which I'm sure was a struggle for him – was Linus's last kindness to me. You can take that information as a peace offering. Or an apology. Or a fond farewell.'

Peg said, 'Fond?'

'No,' said Wilma, smiling genuinely, beautifully.

'You should smile more often,' said Peg.

'Maybe I'll have reason to in New York,' said Wilma.

33

From the sound of it, Nina and Jack were making up. As comfortable as Peg was with their relationship, she wasn't interested in listening to their sex noises.

Peg quickly dressed in jogging shorts and a sports bra, and laced her New Balances tight. She hit Old Dirty Goat Road at a slower than usual pace, determined to enjoy this run. She would smell the flowers, inhale the exhaust-free air. Run for the pleasure of outdoor exercise, not as a way to distract or punish herself.

A mile later, jogging in peace and quiet (only one Subaru cruised by on the road), Peg's legs lifted easily. As she ran, she counted mailboxes, each painted a bright color with the homeowner's name stenciled in white. Peg recognized many of the names. She'd meet the rest of her neighbors soon enough. Wilma could take Manhattan. She could have the Bronx and Staten Island, too. In Manshire, Peg had never felt the ground so solidly beneath her feet.

She made it all the way to Main Street, five miles, in an hour. Slowing to a walk, Peg stopped into Dombit's for a Snapple. Waiting for the cashier, she felt a tap on her shoulder.

Turning, Peg beheld a devastatingly handsome

woodsman, as if he'd walked off the Alaskan hunks calendar, and onto the line behind her.

He said, 'Can I help you with that?'

'I think I can manage a Snapple.'

'You can't blame a guy for asking.' Indeed, she couldn't. She smiled at him, paid and left the store.

'Peg!' shouted a voice from across the parking lot. It was Donna, sitting on the steps in front of the used bookshop, waving. Peg walked over. Sat down. Opened her ice tea.

'First day under ninety all week,' said Donna.

'I could use a sweater,' said Peg.

The woodsman was walking toward them. It wasn't a long walk.

Donna said, 'Peg, let me introduce my grandson, Reed. He just moved back to Manshire. From Alaska. He was logging there, but came back to live with me. I told him I could take care of myself. But he insisted.'

Peg said, 'That's awful sweet of you.'

'It's the least I can do for my grandma,' he said.

Donna said, 'Peg just moved to Manshire from New York City. She doesn't know too many people. You should take her around, Reed.'

He nodded. Peg drank her Snapple.

Donna said, 'Have you heard about Trevor Martin yet?'

Trevor Martin? Gloria's father, the billionaire? 'What about him?' asked Peg.

'He's in Manshire. You know Bud? Over there, by the Dombit's gas tanks? The one with the tattoos?'

Donna was pointing. Bud saw her and waved. Peg waved back. Donna said, 'He told me that Trevor Martin pulled up at Dombit's about an hour ago in a limo the size of a school bus. The driver asked Bud to fill it up. He did, but not quick enough for Trevor Martin. He lowered the window and yelled at Bud to hurry up. Bud said, "I can't move any faster, but I can move a whole lot slower." Trevor Martin didn't like that. He threw a hundred at him, called Bud an "inbred mountain idiot," then had his driver speed off. Bud barely got the gas cap back on.'

'Where did Martin go?'

'Down Main Street, and up River Road. Why on earth do you think a man like that would come to Manshire?' asked Donna.

Peg knew only too well. Trevor Martin had somehow found Gloria, and he'd come to take her home. Peg gulped down her ice tea, told Donna she had to run, then did.

Reed trotted after her. When he caught up, he said, 'I hope Grandma didn't embarrass you. About my taking you around.'

'I don't embarrass easily,' she said.

'Can I call you?' he asked.

Peg stopped walking, took a gander at him. He was exactly what she'd come to Vermont to find. An honest, caring man who could swing an ax. His eyes hiked across her body as if she were the Appalachian Trail. The way he looked at her, Peg knew she could have him. The old Peg, the Square Peg, would have been all over that, parting her lips, brushing her bangs, flirting provocatively, letting her sexual confidence do the work of ensnaring him. But that instinct had been beaten out of her. With a stick.

'I'll call you,' she said. 'Or not.'

She didn't bother watching his reaction. She ran to

the Federal at a fast clip. It was only half a mile, and she made it in under five minutes.

She could hear the shouting from the driveway.

Bursting through the front door, Peg followed the voices to the living room. Gloria sat on the couch, crying. Her father, Trevor Martin, billionaire, world-renowned for his savage business practices, was seated on the couch across from his fragile, weeping only child. He was wearing, by Peg's guess, the in-need-of-a-trim wig, along with a navy suit and wingtips. He had to be roasting in all those clothes, but his forehead was dry, the kind of man who'd never let anyone see him sweat.

Behind Trevor, Luke stood rigidly with his arms crossed against his chest. He was wearing a navy suit like Trevor's, and dark glasses. He looked like a G-man. Linus, standing behind Gloria, looked like a hippie freak in comparison. He seemed ruffled, too, unprepared for the verbal violence of the pharmacy titan.

'I'm going to take you apart, Bester, piece by piece, until there's nothing left but spare atoms,' said Trevor. 'Sending my daughter to backwater bars to pick up some country maniac who probably fucks his sheep? You call this therapy?'

'I did not send your daughter to bars to pick up men,' defended Linus.

Luke said, 'I stand by my report, sir. Linus Bester has trained your daughter to make suggestive comments to men in bars. He's an overeducated pimp, sir.'

'Luke, you bastard scum-sucking traitor!' said Tracy, entering the room with Ben on her heels. 'I can't believe we kissed, and that I liked it! I spit on you.' And she spit. On the carpet.

Linus said, 'I'll thank you to spit outdoors, Tracy.'

Peg, not yet noticed by the others, went over to Gloria on the couch. She put her arms around the weepy blonde.

'Who the hell is this now? Get your hands off my daughter!' shouted Trevor.

Peg ignored him. 'Gloria, stop crying. You're not a little girl.'

Gloria said, 'I can't help it!'

'Take a deep breath,' said Peg. 'Contemplate your navel. Do you see yourself as someone who crumbles under pressure?'

Weakly, Gloria said, 'Strongly agree.'

Luke said, 'For the record, sir, I only kissed that spitting woman as part of my deep cover.'

'Was your hard-on phony, too?' asked Tracy.

Luke said, 'This man' – he pointed at Ray, who was sitting on the bottom step of the staircase – 'as I wrote in my report, has been pushing marijuana on your daughter. He's seduced her several times. I have one of their trysts on videotape, sir.'

'I need a pill,' whimpered Gloria.

Peg said, 'Did Luke report that he got so drunk he passed out on the kitchen floor?'

Luke said, 'That incident was also part of my deep cover.'

Trevor said to him, 'You've done an exemplary job, Kardash. Wait for me in the limo.'

Like a trained dog, Luke jumped at his master's command. He picked up his suitcase – already packed – and headed for the front door.

Tracy said, 'Come on, Ben. Let's help Luke with his bag.'

Ben said, 'Yes, let's.'

They wrenched Luke's suitcase from his hands, and chased him outside, slamming the door behind them.

Trevor said, 'Bester, you will hear from my lawyers. Consider your life over. Gloria, we're leaving.' He stood up. Man, he was short, thought Peg. Gloria must have gotten her height from her mother, the Swedish ex-supermodel. And what an enormous head Trevor had. Peg was amazed that such a puny neck could support that bulbous cranium.

From outside, Peg heard Luke yell, 'Get away. Leave me alone!' followed by a crash.

Peg whispered to Gloria, 'Say something.'

'What?'

'What one word comes foremost to your mind?'

Gloria turned to Peg. Her silken hair was tangled, her cheeks wet. Her eyes locked on Peg's, Gloria said, 'No.'

'Tell him,' said Peg.

Gloria turned toward her father. She repeated, 'No. I'm not leaving. No, you're not going to do anything to Linus Bester.'

That's when the loud *thwomp-thwomp* of helicopters cut rudely into Gloria's triumphant moment.

Tracy ran back inside. She said, 'This is incredible. There are three news helicopters circling the house.'

From the open front door, Peg heard Luke scream, 'Help! Someone help me!'

Tracy said, 'I think Ben needs me,' and ran back outside.

'How the hell did those jackals find me?' ranted Trevor.

'Only one thing moves quickly in Vermont,' said Linus, smiling. 'Gossip.'

Gloria, seizing rare opportunity, said, 'Unless you do exactly what I say, I'm going to run outside. Naked.'

Trevor fumed, 'You do not threaten me!'

Gloria stood up, and took off her top.

Trevor said, 'Stop right there!'

She slipped off her shorts.

'I'm warning you,' barked Daddy Dearest.

Gloria hooked a thumb under her bra strap.

'Okay,' relented Trevor. 'What do you want? I've given you everything a girl could desire. Clothes, jewelry, well-screened boyfriends, trips around the world, the best education money can buy. And still you're not happy.'

'There's one thing you've never offered me, Daddy,' said Gloria, sitting again, in her bra and panties.

Trevor sat down, too, clearly exasperated. 'I'd love to know what that is.'

She took a deep breath, and said, 'I want a job.'

'A job.'

'A good job.'

'Like what?' he asked.

'The cosmetics buyer for Martin Pharmacies,' she said.

'What about the person who does that now?'

Gloria answered, 'He can work for me.'

Trevor actually laughed. 'Although it disgusts me to say this, Bester, you may have helped my daughter grow balls.'

'Balls,' Linus said, nodding. 'And a bat, too.'

Trevor said, 'Okay, Gloria. If you put your clothes on and agree to leave this pitiful state immediately, I'll give you a job.'

Gloria dressed herself, and walked over to Ray. He stood up and took her hand. She said, 'Ray is coming with us.'

'The pothead?' asked Trevor. 'Absolutely not.'

'We're engaged,' said Gloria.

Peg slapped her forehead. 'I don't even have to date them anymore to be their Last Girlfriend,' she moaned. 'One or two makeout sessions, and I turn men into prime marriage material.'

Gloria and Ray kissed tenderly. Trevor turned puce from the sight. When they broke their embrace, Gloria said, 'Ray would like a job, too.'

The three of them, father, daughter and future son-in-law, left the Federal, Gloria pleading Ray's case. Peg and Linus followed them out.

Luke's clothes were scattered all over the lawn. His screams drew everyone to the back of the house. Tracy and Ben were carrying Luke (she had him under the armpits; Ben had him around the knees) down the mansion's boat dock. Like a fish on a hook, Luke struggled and squirmed.

Tracy said, 'Count of three.'

Ben counted. On three, they heaved Luke into the river. He made a satisfying splash. Peg, Gloria, Ray and Linus applauded. So did the jackals in the news helicopter above.

Peg said, 'Excellent form.'

'I give him an eight,' said Linus.

Trevor yelled, 'Kardash!'

Luke, splashing and groping toward the riverbank, sputtered, 'Yes, sir?'

'I told you to wait in the limo!'

'Yes, sir.'

His suit dripping, river weeds clinging to his collar, Luke sloshed back to the car.

Gloria and Ray stepped into the massive automobile

(big enough to be visible from space). Trevor got in last. Before he closed the door, he barked, 'Bester!'

'Right here, Mr Martin,' answered Linus.

'One leak about anything that went on here, you will spend the rest of your life with five lawyers up your ass.' He slammed the limo door, and away they zoomed, news helicopters following in the air like balloons on a string.

Linus and Peg stood in the driveway, waving as the car disappeared down River Road.

He said, 'Luke had me fooled.'

Peg nodded. 'He must have gotten low scores in conscientiousness.'

The two went back inside, stepping over the detritus of Luke's luggage along the way. Peg flopped down on the couch where Gloria had been weeping. Linus sat next to her.

He said, 'It's official. This has been the worst session in Inward Bound history.'

'But probably the most exciting,' Peg said.

'I'm in love with you,' said Linus abruptly, reaching toward her, cupping her face with his hands. 'Even if you don't love me back, I want you to know.'

Peg removed his hands from her face. She leaned away from him on the couch, and stood up.

He said, 'You're leaving.'

'I'm not leaving,' she said, laughing. 'I've been thinking about this moment for weeks. I have to stand up to take off my clothes.'

'So do it,' said Linus, smiling. 'I'll watch.'

'One warning, having just seen Gloria nearly naked. I might disappoint in comparison.' She took off her shorts.

'I have no idea what Gloria's body looks like,' he said.

'She undressed two minutes ago, right in this spot. Didn't you notice?' asked Peg.

He shook his head. 'I was looking at you.'

Peg said, 'You're still testing my gullibility.'

'I might have peeked a little.'

'One other warning,' said Peg. 'I've been running.' She removed her sports bra.

He said, 'So you'll taste like a salt lick.' Linus pulled her toward him. She straddled him on the couch.

'A salt lick?' she asked.

'Candy for horses,' he said. 'But I can think of a salt lick that would be like candy for you.'

They kissed. For all the heat that generated, Peg appreciated the warmth, too. Their kiss had a backstory, it'd been delayed by circumstance. And since they already had a past, it stood to reason that she and Linus would have a future. She pressed herself into him, melting all the way inward. He groaned and shifted under her.

He said, 'As your therapist, I recommend that we do this once quickly, and then slowly for the rest of the week.'

She unzipped his shorts, gripped him tightly, then pushed her panties aside to slip him in.

And then, *blammo*. It happened again.

He came fast after her. Both breathing hard, they stayed just as they were, holding on tight.

Peg said, 'Now that we're a couple ... we are a couple, yes?'

He kissed her on the neck, along the collarbone. 'A couple of what?'

'That's my line,' she said. 'Now that we're a couple – of what, we don't know – be aware that within eighteen months, you will be married. Not to me. To someone else. The entire town of Manshire will rejoice. In their gratitude, they may elect me to replace you.'

Linus said, 'Why should I buy some other cow when I get milk for free from you?'

'If I'm going to be your cow, you should give me a name. Like the newborn calves at Billings Farm.'

He said, 'How about Rare?'

'As in, "raw"?' she asked.

'As in, "a unique specimen," ' he said, and carried her to his bedroom.

34

'Taste,' said Peg Silver, thirty-three, as she filled a ladle with rhubarb brandy and poured the liquid into a cup.

Linus Bester, her boyfriend and co-director of Couples Inward Bound, a month-long adult education program in Manshire, Vermont, for romantic partners who wished to deepen their relationship, said, 'You followed my recipe?'

She handed him the cup, the brandy steaming and thick, hot on the tongue, yet somehow cooling, even in July. 'I tweaked it,' she said.

'It's a thirty-year-old recipe,' he said.

'If people can change after thirty, so can recipes.'

Linus blew on his brandy, and sipped. 'Different,' he said. 'And better.'

He could have said the same about her, but he wouldn't dare. Nor would she about him. But everyone knew, especially Peg and Linus, that their relationship of one year had been evolutionary for both.

'Tracy and Ben are doing great,' said Peg about one of the couples attending the program this month. 'Just like Wilma always said, "You can convince a friend to marry you three times as easily as a boyfriend."'

'Is that what she said?' asked Linus.

310

'Not in those words.'

He said, 'Jack and Nina present an interesting problem.'

'How to live three hundred miles apart, and still have a committed relationship. Although, Nina told me yesterday on the dock that she's going to ask Gloria if she can relocate to Vermont. Martin Pharmacies has gotten the best PR in its history this year, thanks to Nina. I don't think Gloria would dare fire her.'

Linus said, 'One more drink?'

'You need to ask?' Peg ladled one more for him, and one for herself. 'We have to conduct a meditation session this afternoon. We can't get too drunk.'

'I canceled it,' he said. 'I told everyone to contemplate their partner's navel instead.'

Peg raised her eyebrows suggestively. 'So we're alone? Want milk? I'm giving it away.'

Linus smiled (the sight of which continued to thrill Peg, even after waking up to that face for three hundred and sixty-four mornings in a row). He said, 'It's our anniversary.'

She said, 'Is it really?'

'I'm supposed to break up with you today. You told me, one year ago, that I'd buckle under your marriage pressure, dump you, and call it an act of sacrificial love.'

'I haven't pressured you,' she said. 'I haven't made demands. I've been happy with how things are. Ecstatically happy, as you fucking well know. I haven't even thought about marriage.'

'Well, I have,' he said. 'I want to buy the cow.'

Peg inhaled deeply. 'Are you saying what I think you're saying?'

'I am,' he said. 'But if you're ecstatic with the way

things are, then maybe I shouldn't put that kind of pressure on you.

'Not so fast,' she said. 'You can't unring a cow bell.'

Linus said, 'So how about it? Want to be the First Lady of Manshire?' He grabbed her around the waist.

'Love to,' said Peg. 'Do I get business cards?' She put her arms around his neck.

'Nah,' he said. 'You do get to be loved and cherished for the rest of your life.'

'Finally,' said Peg. 'The cows have come home.'

You can buy any of these other
Little Black Dress titles from your
bookshop or *direct from the publisher*.

FREE P&P AND UK DELIVERY
(Overseas and Ireland £3.50 per book)

The Rules of Gentility	Janet Mullany	£4.99
Handbags and Homicide	Dorothy Howell	£4.99
Trashed	Alison Gaylin	£4.99
A Romantic Getaway	Sarah Monk	£4.99
Drama Queen	Susan Conley	£4.99
Not Another Bad Date	Rachel Gibson	£4.99
Just Say Yes	Phillipa Ashley	£4.99
Everything Nice	Ellen Shanman	£4.99
Hysterical Blondeness	Suzanne Macpherson	£4.99
Blue Remembered Heels	Nell Dixon	£4.99
Honey Trap	Julie Cohen	£4.99
What's Love Got to do With It?	Lucy Broadbent	£4.99
The Not-So-Perfect Man	Valerie Frankel	£4.99
Lola Carlyle Reveals All	Rachel Gibson	£4.99
The Movie Girl	Kate Lace	£4.99
The Accidental Virgin	Valerie Frankel	£4.99
Reality Check	A.M. Goldsher	£4.99
True Confessions	Rachel Gibson	£4.99
She Woke Up Married	Suzanne Macpherson	£4.99
This Is How It Happened	Jo Barrett	£4.99

TO ORDER SIMPLY CALL THIS NUMBER

01235 400 414

or visit our website: www.headline.co.uk

Prices and availability subject to change without notice.